No Honor Amongst Thieves:

A Hit Man's Tale

No Honor Amongst Thieves:

A Hit Man's Tale

Brick & Storm

www.urbanbooks.net

Urban Books, LLC
300 Farmingdale Road, NY-Route 109
Farmingdale, NY 11735

No Honor Amongst Thieves: A Hit Man's Tale

ISBN 13: 978-1-60162-086-6
ISBN 10: 1-60162-086-1

First Trade Paperback Printing March 2019
Printed in the United States of America

10 9 8 7 6 5 4 3 2 1

Distributed by Kensington Publishing Corp.
Submit Orders to:
Customer Service
400 Hahn Road
Westminster, MD 21157-4627
Phone: 1-800-733-3000
Fax: 1-800-659-2436

Intro

Sabrina

My husband was not a good man. He had never been a good man. The day I met him, I knew he was evil personified. I wouldn't make excuses for his behavior because I'd never been one to coddle any person in their wrongdoing. I did know that, by day, we ran a very popular deli. Everybody who was anybody—and even the nobodies—dined with us. On the outside, we were the normal but young, Cliff and Clair Huxtable.

"Mommy," our 3-year-old daughter cried out.

She was scared to the point I think she had pissed herself as I felt the wet heat pooling on my lap.

My tears matched hers, and as she held on to me for dear life, I held her just the same. I cradled her head to my chest to keep her from seeing what was happening before us. My husband's Karma had returned to him tenfold. He was reaping the harvest he had sown. Men in black suits had our car surrounded and more than once within the last five minutes, I prayed we'd just packed and left like originally planned.

"Yes, baby," I whispered.

"I'm scared, Mommy. I want Daddy," she whined hysterically.

"Shhhh, please be quiet, baby. Please," I cried while still shielding her face from what was going on in front of us.

My husband was down on his knees, bloodied, battered, and beaten. He'd always been a warrior. My warrior. They would kill him; I knew that. I felt it with everything within me. I couldn't hear everything that was being said because he had turned on the classical music so it would drown out the sounds of the melee. My husband was going to die, and it was all my fault.

Chapter One

Sabrina

August 2009 . . .

I heard the man walking behind me before I saw him. . . .

Being alone in my neighborhood was never a good thing. Especially when you were 19, taller than most girls your age, no hips, no ass, and had dark skin. I had breasts, but nothing to go with them. My clothes fit awkwardly, and my hair was a natural 'fro, which wasn't all that popular then. It was like I was a walking advertisement for something fucked up to happen to me.

Daddy had left Mama for something younger and more willing to be in the traditional housewife role that he wanted. That meant we had to move back to Georgia where Mama was from originally. A house full of dark-skinned women in the South. While my older sisters looked like they had been crafted by God herself, I was the ugly duckling. Mama tried her best to get me to see my beauty back then, but it never worked. I was still the proverbial, awkward, and ugly dark-skinned girl.

My older twin sisters could be assholes when they wanted to be. I'd just gotten out of study hall on campus at Clayton State and was expecting them to wait for me the day I met him. But they were in their second year of law school and had other important things to do. I ended up having to walk home. We lived on the Southside of Jonesboro, Georgia, in a neighborhood that had been built to resemble Harlem with brownstone-type houses. When it was first built, it had been the talk of the town, but as always, with anything government funded and advertised for black people, shit went downhill fast.

Walking in that neighborhood no matter what time of day it was, was *never* a good thing, especially for a girl. Rain poured down on me, and I was thankful for the plastic book bag I had. My hair had been in a short 'fro, so I didn't too much care about my hairstyle. All I wanted was to get home out of the rain. A white man in a coat passed by me quickly. It wasn't unusual to see the scarce white face in my hood, although he did look a bit out of place. It wasn't them who often made me hate walking to the store around the corner or to the bus stop.

I'd heard tell of the shadows that sometimes stalked the streets. There had been people who came up missing who no one thought to ever look for again: men, women, and children. That time was scary around our hood. I glanced behind me to see the man again. I couldn't see his face, but I knew it was him. Broad shoulders, built like he worked out for fun. He wasn't a bodybuilder type, but more like a basketball player's build or a track runner.

The hood of the black leather coat he had on hid his face. His hands were gloved, and combat boots were on his feet. Which was odd. . . . He had on combat boots, but there was a sound, almost like taps on the bottom of his shoes. He had followed me for at least two miles by then, and I had another four to go. I was scared. Didn't want to come up missing like those who people didn't speak about around the way.

I sped up to put some distance between us. I'd never been raised to be a pussy of a woman. I'd learned to fight early on. Growing up in Flatbush dictated that I throw hands like the hardest of niggas if I wanted to survive. Still, I was new to the area and didn't know the man following me from Adam. I felt goose pimples rise on my arms. My breathing became erratic.

At that moment, I knew I wouldn't make it home if I didn't get the upper hand. I slid my hand in the pocket of my raincoat and gripped the pocketknife there. I flicked it open, then spun with swiftness to catch my "would-be" attacker off guard. But to my surprise, he wasn't there. I turned back and forth quickly, trying to see if he had somehow gotten in front of me, and I didn't know about it. There was nothing; just a few cars passing in the distance, rain, and wind.

Normally, people would be out, but I guessed the weather had everyone inside. I turned back around and found myself face-to-face with a maniac. His breath was tart, eyes cold. Face pale and scaly. He smiled coolly at me when I tried to punch him with my hand holding the knife. He blocked the hit, and the weapon fell. Looking at the man, I knew he was a different kind of evil. Instinct told me to run, and before I could scream, he clasped a hand over my nose and mouth. I couldn't breathe, so I panicked. I clawed at his face, trying to do anything to make him let go of me. He had a strong arm around my waist as he dragged me into an alley, then into an abandoned storefront.

"Nooooo," I screamed. "Let me go," I yelled.

He grabbed a fistful of my 'fro and threw me headfirst into a wall. I crumbled to the floor like a sack of potatoes. My world tilted, then spun as I moaned. I slowly rolled onto my stomach so I could crawl away. My vision was blurred as I watched his booted feet thud against the concrete floor. I hadn't crawled an inch when the man straddled my back and cut my shirt from my upper body.

The cool brisk of wind I felt chilled me even more. I tried to turn and fight back, but another yank of my hair and my head beating the floor put an end to that. As the man yanked my pants and underwear down my thighs and legs, tears burned my eyelids. The man stood, then pulled me by my arms across the room. Debris cut into me. I could feel my skin ripping and tearing against the broken glass, wood, and whatever else was on the floor. I had floated in and out of consciousness by the time he handcuffed me to the wrought iron bedrail.

At that moment, I blamed my father for what was about to happen to me. If he hadn't run off and left us, no man would be able to do what was about to happen to me. I think it was at that moment, I knew what animosity was as I began to hate the man who had donated sperm for my creation. It was the budding disdain for my father that created a burn within me. I kicked one of my long legs out, striking the man in the face. I kept at it until he grabbed my ankles.

I had no idea what he was about to do when he pulled a blade from his pocket, but my heart stopped at the thought. I was going to die. I knew at that moment, he was going to kill me.

"Damn shame that a man has everything and still wants more," a voice spoke out.

I didn't know where the other man's voice was in the room. The voice was deep and settled over me like a warm blanket. If there were only men in a room, you'd be able to tell who this man was as his voice was that distinctive, a honeyed-type voice. There was that sound again. The distinct sound of taps on the bottom of a shoe. It was then that I realized the man who had been following me hadn't been the one who snatched me.

The man who had been about to kill me jumped back, fell on the ground, then rolled around until he was up on his feet. He took a defensive stance, the knife out in front of him as he looked around, panicked because of the voice he'd heard.

"This ain't none of your business, boy," the man with the knife shouted. "Who sent you, nigger? Who sent you after me?"

The man with the knife was spooked, just as I had been moments before. I sniffled and tried yanking my hands from the cuffs on the bedrail, to no avail.

"Antonio Sepriani, your father wants you to know he can no longer afford to have you out here snatching young girls up in this community and killing them. You're causing too much heat around this way, making it hard for him to do business with the blacks," the other voice spoke, closer now than it had been before.

The man who I now knew as Antonio frowned. "My father?" he asked, confusion on his tanned face. "My father sent you to kill me, boy?"

"Would you like to say any last words, Antonio Sepriani?"

Antonio laughed maniacally and hopped on the mattress. "You ain't smart enough to take me out, boy," he spat with a scowl.

He yanked my head up by my 'fro and placed the blade against my neck, forcing me to kneel in an awkward position in front of him. I could feel the blade piercing my neck. I held my breath, believing that if I breathed too hard or swallowed the wrong way, the blade would cut deeper.

"Tell my father," Antonio yelled and spittle rained down on me, "tell that fucking old-ass bastard that his time is coming. The Family will have him dead, and when I take over, I'll run shit the way it should be run! Won't have no nigger doing my dirty work for me because I'm a man! And a man always handles his own affairs. Ain't that right, bitch?" he asked me, dragging his tongue across my head. "When I handle this here boy, you and me gonna have us some good old fun. Gonna teach you how to fuck—"

Before the words left his mouth, a loud sound came whizzing through the air. Antonio's voice creaked, then stopped. His hold loosened on me, and the blade fell from his hand. Something wet and red trickled down my face and chest. I glanced around the room quickly, then looked up. My scream got caught in my throat. A dead man was behind me, slumped over, arrow between his eyes. I panicked, started screaming, and yanking at the rails on the bed. I'd never seen a dead body before. Piss stains had saturated the front of the white man's jeans and the muscles in his hands jerked every so often.

"It's never about smarts in my line of work, Antonio. It's about skill," the other man said coolly, his voice calm and even like he hadn't just killed a man.

It was safe to say that I had probably pissed myself too. That tapping sound kept coming closer and closer. The nearer it got to me, the more I screamed. I moved, angled my body to semi-face the rail. Terrified, I glanced over my shoulders, then back to the wrought iron headboard. I'd yanked and pulled so hard my wrists were burning and bleeding.

I kept my head turned when I felt him behind me. I stopped screaming as shivers and shakes had overtaken my ability to do so.

"I didn't see nothing," I spoke up quickly. "I didn't see nothing. I swear."

"How old are you?"

"Ni-nineteen. I didn't see anything. I swear to God. I won't say nothing," I pleaded. Slobber and snot rolled down my lips while sweat covered me.

The man walked around to where my hands were. I turned my head so I wouldn't see him. I heard keys jingling in his hands.

"Where do you live?" he asked me.

"Golden Gates."

"The pseudo Harlem?"

I nodded slowly. He yanked the cuffs, unlocked them. I fell back on the bed, keeping my face down, eyes closed.

"Address?" he wanted to know.

"1964 Brushwick Lane. Door 6111." I was so terrified, I told him whatever he wanted to know with the hopes that it would spare me.

"Name?"

"Sa-Sabrina."

"Sabrina what?"

"Sabrina Lanfair."

I felt when he tossed my clothes at me. I grabbed them close to my chest and covered up.

"Do you know why I'm asking you all these questions, Sabrina Lanfair?"

I shook my head. "No."

"Now I know where you live. I know where your family lives. If you tell anybody about me being here, I'll make my presence felt in *your* life. Understand?"

That was a threat. I was smart enough to know that. So I nodded.

"Count to one hundred, then leave. You do not leave this room until you reach a hundred. If you do, I will know. Start counting, Sabrina."

I did what he said, started to count silently. He must have known that.

"Out loud so I can hear you."

"One. Two. Three. Four. Five. Six. Seven," I went on counting slowly and at the top of my lungs until my voice was ready to give out. Finally, I reached a hundred.

I had no idea if the man was still there or not as I didn't hear that tapping sound. As I counted, I stood and pulled my jeans back on, then my shoes that the man had snatched off. Grabbing the ripped shirt, I slid my arms through the sleeves, then tied the shreds in the back. It would do until I could make it home. I pulled my raincoat back on and grabbed my book bag. He must have brought them along so no one would find them. I would have been truly one of those who just "disappeared." When I made it to one hundred, I ran out of that abandoned store like a bat out of hell.

As the days followed, I was a paranoid mess. I jumped at every sound. Couldn't tell anyone about what had happened to me as I truly believed the man in the room would find me and kill me. I wrapped my own wrists and wore long sleeves. My mama rarely paid attention to me as she was working two jobs, one day and one night. My older twin sisters were focused on doing their own things. None of them paid attention to me. I was left to deal with the demons of what happened to me alone.

It would be two years later when I ran into that man again who had been in the room, the killer who had saved me. Two years before I would hear that voice again and know I was in his presence. Funny thing was, he would know me too.

Chapter Two

Marcel

People are shaped by either their environment or by specific situations that happen in their lives, or I should say, can be shaped. My life, shit, it was good. I had both parents in my life, grew up valuing education, sports, and making a man of myself in the DC area. Yeah, around me wasn't that squeaky clean. I mean, back in the day, like any kid, I tried to fit in every day, but I also soaked up the street life because I could and was bored with the perfection of my home. My family taught me about love and support, but the streets taught me about survival and loyalty. However, after all those lessons, what I did learn from scrapping in whatever hood I found myself in never was very deep. Not until I graduated from college and found myself homeless in the streets of Atlanta, Georgia.

A brotha was hungry, sleeping in my ride, and looking for work in an environment that wasn't seeking to hire my ass. Shit, it was tough. But when I found a job in a small restaurant, I never thought that it would lead me to becoming a killer, but it did, via my boss. I was reluctant at first, but due to the upgrade in pay and the opportunity to get out of the backseat of my car, I accepted the job on the spot. Hell, I never thought I'd enjoy it, but I did, and it all started back in that small room. I was 21 then, and that's when I unintentionally met Sabrina for the first time.

That was two years ago, and it seemed that Karma had a hand in crossing our paths again because she walked into the same crowded room I was in. I stood amongst a diverse set of snobby-ass people who were supporting several city officials running for government positions in Atlanta. Two years was all it took for me to move up in the game. My boss's son, which also made him my boss by proxy, was one of the running officials, and I was his aide. My degree in communications helped me get that position.

Keeping my eyes on the woman I recalled being an awkward-looking female with a wild thicket of hair on her head and justifiable fear in her eyes, I tried my best to keep my distance from her. I wasn't sure if she saw my face back then. I mean, yeah, I spoke to her, but through it all, I tried to keep my appearance as incognito as possible. As I was trying to do now.

I was a six-foot-tall, dark-skinned brotha, the tone of espresso. The well-trimmed beard that lined my defined jaw was there to keep my identity low-key. It ran right up into my, what I liked to call, a fuck-boy fade. You know the one, low-cut fade with the S-curl and curved part in it. That's how my mane was. I was on what my pops would call, my Billy Dee Williams tip. Casket sharp in my hand stitched Italian suit, thanks to my boss's tailor, and Italian leather shoes that were polished so nice that I could see myself in them.

My size was not that big at all. I was a muscular, lean type. Not so skinny that you'd have to worry about a brotha, but big enough where I still looked as if I could handle my own in a brawl fight. I wasn't ugly, but I wasn't a pretty boy. For tonight, I had a distinguished, rugged, hipster look, and I had plenty of women trying to get in my face. But I wasn't paying them any attention. First off, I was at this event to learn more about my latest mark, and second, since Sabrina walked in, she drew my attention elsewhere.

Baby girl had grown up. People chattered and chuckled around me while I studied her. When I saved her life back then, I had decided to do my homework on her. I had to just make sure she never talked about me. I learned her people were nobodies, who had just moved to the A. Once that was made clear, I didn't think that I had anything to worry about. Now, I was questioning that.

Sabrina moved around the room with a bright smile upon her face. Where there once was nothing but a boyish frame, meaning flat all around, except for her chest, which was different, was now framed by some mini-curves. She had a body like Rihanna, just with bigger breasts. Petite and cute. Her small 'fro had grown and was now straight hair that fell down her back. From how lush it was, I knew it wasn't permed. Blame that on me having a sister and mother who stayed in the salon and had my father and me stressing about it.

"Marcel," I heard a soft-spoken but deep baritone voice call my name. It was the son of my boss, and I had to comply. Turning my attention to the tall, handsome, swarthy Italian dude dressed just as casket fresh as me, I stepped his way.

"I'd like to introduce you to some very important people," my coboss said with an outstretched arm.

My co-boss, Leo Giulio, was one of the popular political candidates running for alderman in my area. What made him popular wasn't just his charisma, it was that his mother was a well-known South African opera singer, and his father ran the best Italian bistro in the Metro-Atlanta perimeter. It also was because he could persuade anyone to do what he wanted, and because he was a young, 30-year-old, good-looking dude. That part was what made him extremely dangerous in the world I was coming from, but no one knew the brotha's dark side, and it was my duty to keep it that way.

Keeping a warm but expressionless manner to me, I stepped forward. "I'm honored, Mr. Giulio."

It was an effort for me not to fall into my relaxed state of slang, but as Senior Giulio always said, if I want to move up in this world and make the money I needed, I must be a man of many faces. Therefore, I made sure to follow that model and embrace my role. I stood back watching as an older brother, around my height with wispy grays in his hair, beard, and temples, came my way. I knew who it was immediately as my mind hit me with an old memory.

"Marcel Raymond, meet future Commissioner Othello Lanfair. He just settled into Atlanta from New York," Leo explained.

Grasping Mr. Lanfair's hand, I gave him a welcoming smile and shook it in a way that let him know I had respect for him, but also was a player in the political world. "Mr. Lanfair, it is an honor to meet you."

"And it is good to meet you too, young man. Leo has been speaking very highly of you. Top of your class at Georgia State. Communications major with a duel degree in political science. Very interesting," Othello said in a controlled and pleasant voice.

"Yes, sir," I said back, still shaking his hand before letting it go. The old head had a grip like a pit bull, but I held my own.

"Came here from DC to soak in the environment of Atlanta and add my piece to the puzzle," I said in a lighthearted manner.

"From what I heard, you are already on a good start, son. I'm sure your parents are exceedingly proud of you," he said with a wide smile studying me with interest.

"They and my younger sister passed on, but I'm sure they are." I kept my stance wide and pressed a hand against my heart.

This old man seemed to be the type who liked to take in all the information about a person by one glance and one quick conversation. I wasn't tripping about it at all.

"Is that so? I'm sorry to hear that. What happened?" he asked.

I guess he was seeking out a flicker of emotion from me. I could feel Leo observing me. I knew that he was seeing how I'd move on this board with the future commissioner, and I found myself enjoying the dance going on between us.

"On the day of my graduation, they were sideswiped in their car by a semitruck. Died on Peachtree," I explained.

"Damn it! These drivers are horrendous on the roads. See, these are some of the many issues we must address if we are going to change Atlanta for the better," Mr. Lanfair said. "I'm sorry for your loss. One should never lose family in such a way."

I nodded. "Of course. Thank you. They are what led me to be an aide for Mr. Giulio."

"Then they are a welcomed guiding light, son," Mr. Lanfair continued watching me, then clapped a hand on my shoulder, squeezing gently. "My wife and daughter are here. Let me introduce you all."

An uncertain concern dropped in my spirit when Mr. Lanfair's wife and daughter approached me. Both were locked in their general "be nice for the people who Mr. Lanfair needs on his side" smile. At first, there was no issue. Both women glanced at me quickly as Mr. Lanfair introduced me.

But when I was asked to speak on my dreams for change in Atlanta, that's where things became tricky. I didn't want to speak. Didn't want to trigger shit being that I knew my voice was the only thing Sabrina could possibly remember, but I was locked in a stalemate and had to handle my shit. Never let anyone break your cool. I learned that from Senior Giulio as well.

Holding my champagne glass, I took a drink, then licked my lips. "Atlanta is not only known as Hotlanta, due to its seedy entertainment scene, but Atlanta is also known as a welcoming state for young, up-and-coming businessmen and -women. We need to focus on making Atlanta about family, about bringing in stable job markets for the young people, so that they will stay here."

Sliding a hand in my pocket, I kept a cool demeanor as I spoke, making eye contact with every bigwig in front of me. "We need to grow the entertainment part, meaning our growing film industry so that we can keep a lucrative hand in becoming the second Hollywood, Hollywood of the South. In doing so, this ensures substantial money and constant tourist allure. Atlanta will grow, and money will stay lining our government's pockets."

Once my attention went back to Sabrina, I knew trouble was brewing. From how she intently watched me, I knew from the slight change in her breathing, the way her eyes slightly widened, and a subtle fear changed her whole body language, that she knew who I was. Real recognizes real, and past traumas can brand the truth in one's mind for a lifetime.

I wasn't sure how I was going to get out of this, but when laughter broke my concentration while watching her, I knew I had wiggled my way into Othello's circle.

"Young man, it seems as if you are perfect for Leo's party," he said in a booming voice.

Sabrina continued staring.

I laughed, and as I drank from my glass, I allowed my index finger to appear to brush my nose, but in reality, I was signaling to Sabrina to keep her mouth closed. It didn't take anything for me to see that she understood my small hand gesture. She turned toward her father's wife, whispered, then tried to excuse herself.

As she did so, Othello reached behind him to bring her forward. "My daughter, Sabrina, has said the same to me. Protect the culture here, the family life, the entertainment life, the food industry here. . . . Everything Atlanta builds brings attention to, and we must keep it that way, isn't that right, baby girl?"

"Of course, Daddy," she said, tucking her hair behind her diamond-earring-dressed ear.

I saw that her hair was still very much natural, just flat ironed. She hadn't changed that much, ran in my mind.

"How can Atlanta survive if we do not emphasize family first? We are a hospitable people. We have to let the nation see that we aren't just some seedy or shady crime-laden city," she said locking eyes on me.

I was amused. So, shorty wanted to fence words with a brotha? I was down, but Leo's hand on my shoulder as he stepped forward kept me silent.

"Exactly, which is why we must start at a grassroots level in tandem with us government officials, don't you think? If we get our hands dirty with our fellow, everyday man, trust can be reformed in the government, and positive change in our way could occur," Leo added moving in front of me.

An amused chuckle had me smirking as I turned to see the man of the day, the mayor of Atlanta, walking in. Immediately, my killer instinct turned on. Leo's move was not simply a dick move, but it was done to signal me on the low that my mark was in the room. As he ran his mouth, I excused myself and disappeared through the crowd. My agenda was in front of me, and, since we were in his house, I could start on taking what I was told to: his life and several documents of plans for a new building in College Park.

Moving through excited people, mostly women flocking to our mayor, I made my way to the study he just came out of. By using the bathroom next to it, I slipped on my mask and gloves, then proceeded to climb out the window. Behind me were the quiet, lit-up gardens encasing the mansion. I knew there was nothing to trip on in being caught because security was currently distracted by the mayor's presence and all the people trying to get next to him. That's why I took the time to do some spy shit.

Fiddling with the window, I broke in, then hopped in the massive, old-world designed library with a spiraling staircase and impressive study. Books were around me, the scent of fresh lit, cheap cigar smoke fucked with my senses, but I kept my cool. I knew that there was a vault in there, and I knew that a camera was recording my movements. It was on Leo's tech team to cloud the channels. When I was working the window, a chirp outside was my signal that everything was good. I had ten minutes to handle business, so I did.

I worked my way through the office, found the vault hidden behind the stairway, then I used the code given to me to open it. Inside was everything I needed. I made quick copies, and I swapped out expensive jewelry with replicas. I looked over his desk, fucking with things, then made my exit. Taking several strides to the window, I whistled loudly, dropped the bag I had put everything in, and watched it fall into the bush below. After that, I moved to several of his glasses, lined them with a clear dissolvable poison, and added the same to his rum decanter, then returned from where I came.

This move was on some old-school shit as a request by my main boss. He wanted to test me and see if I could cut it as a hit man in the classic sense. When I told him that I could, that he could trust me in this, he laid out this plan, and the rest was history. I knew that I would not be able to return from the outside; that would be suspect enough, so I dropped back into the gardens, whistled to my crew again, then entered back into the house and party from the bathroom.

Too many people around this dude to even care to check the rest of the mansion. I easily was able to fall back into the groove of things with the party. I glanced at Leo; he gave a wide smile, and we both moved on to campaigning for his cause.

"I remember you," I heard to the right of me while I took a sample of some stuffy and bougie food off a server tray.

Chewing slowly, I kept my eyes on the mayor, watching him intently. "That's good to know Leo's pull has people recalling me."

"You know that's not what I'm talking about," I heard again.

Stepping backward, then to the side, I ended up directly behind Sabrina and kept watching the mayor.

"See, no, I don't, and I believe that's a good thing, do you? Besides, shouldn't you be by your old man's shoulder?"

Her silence amused me, but what made my day even more was when the mayor clutched his heart, tumbled around, then fell to the floor, dead. See, my movements were purposeful, and I'll hit the rewind for ya. When I was parting through the crowd to the bathroom, I had made one sneaky move. I knew that the mayor would be focused on giving handshakes, kissing babies, and signing crap, that he would not have noticed the smear of poison against the palm of his hand amongst the many hands in his way.

It was easy for me to get close enough where I could hit him with that dose. No CSI could detect what I hit him with, and no camera could tell that I was really anywhere near him. So my rouse in his office was nothing but a setup to make his officials look faulty once an investigation started. As I spoke quietly with Sabrina and enjoyed how her petite frame seemed to fit me, I also was getting off from watching my mark die right before me.

Drinking my liquor, I kept my cool and looked concerned when Sabrina shouted, "Oh my God, what's happened to the mayor?"

I enjoyed the feel of guns, but this poison shit was on some OG level, and I dug it.

"Damn, that is insane. We need to check that out," I said following behind Sabrina while she rushed forward.

My mark was down, and I had many more to tackle. The mayor was a problem for Senior Giulio and son, and a problem in the streets of Atlanta. By taking him out, I had just upheld what Sabrina had said to me in retort. If we clean up the criminals of Atlanta, then Atlanta could be great again. I wasn't a good man, but sometimes, my kills were for the greater good, and I dug that. I knew one thing, though. I was able to run into Sabrina again, and I was now way more interested in her than I should have been. I mean, I helped her out in ridding the world of evil, fair exchange is no robbery, right? Even though there was no honor amongst thieves, as the saying goes. I had no honor when it came to my kills, and I always took what I wanted if that was what's required of me. I wanted Sabrina now that I saw her again. She didn't need to know my secret life, and I wanted to keep it that way. Pushing through the crowd appearing concerned, I kept my gaze on Sabrina. That was the day I planned to make her mine.

One body drop at a time.

Chapter Three

Sabrina

August 2011 . . .

"Oh my God," the mayor's wife cried out.

"Somebody get help," my father yelled.

Which made me turn to look at him. He was kneeling next to the mayor's limp body like he actually cared. It was well known that my father and the mayor were basically archnemeses. My father turned back up in our lives a year and a half ago. I didn't know what brought on the change at first, but it wasn't a happy family reunion. He hadn't come to make amends with my mother. He came to tell her that he had remarried and would be moving to Atlanta to run for office.

When we lived in New York, Pops always hung out with the movers and shakers, politicians and other elected officials, but as the years passed on, he cared more and more about his image than our home. My pops' news that he had remarried and would be living in Atlanta to run for city office sent my mother into an emotional downward spiral. My older sisters wanted nothing to do with my father as they found what he had done to be disgusting.

I couldn't really explain why my hate dissolved for him as soon as I laid eyes on him again. For the longest, I had been mad at him for leaving us. I'd blamed him for me almost being killed in that abandoned building. I was so set to lash out at him and give him a piece of my mind. But when I saw him on that day a year and a half ago, I rushed into his open arms. I cried so hard and, while my mom and sisters thought it was because I'd missed him more because I was the baby in the family, it had way more to do with the fact that I, once again, felt protected.

He had always protected me. No man could harm me with my daddy, Othello, around. That was . . . until I heard that voice. Marcel was the name he had been introduced as. That man's voice chilled me to the bone. I quickly glanced behind me to find he was no longer there. Just like the day he had disappeared the same way he'd come after killing Antonio, without a trace, until now. After being attacked by Antonio, I watched the news to see if anyone would ever find the body. No one ever did.

While everyone crowded around the mayor as a doctor in the room administered CPR, I kept back.

"Danny, take my daughter and my wife home," my father told one of his guards.

Danny was the only one of them I remotely liked. My only disdain for him was that there was something weird between him and my father. His loyalty was quite unnerving at times when it came to my father.

"Baby, I'd like to stay with you," Kat said to my father.

I didn't particularly like my father's wife, but I didn't hate her either. She was okay when she wasn't trying to force a relationship with me. For as much as I welcomed my father back into my life, that didn't mean I had to be friends with the woman who had come between my mother and father.

My father frowned as he looked at Kat. "Can't you see I'm handling business, woman? Let Danny take you home, and I'll be there later."

My father was a man who didn't like to repeat himself. Kat had been with him long enough to know that. My father had that look in his eyes that said his word wasn't up for discussion. Kat knew not to test him in public, so she huffed, spun on her heels, and stormed out.

"Sabrina, are you ready?" Danny asked me, holding a hand out in front of me.

"Yeah, I guess."

I hugged and kissed my father's cheek, then made my way out as well. The ride home was a quiet one. I was grateful for that. I didn't need Kat trying to talk to me when I really didn't feel like speaking. Between the mayor having a possible heart attack and confronting the man from my past, my mind wasn't up for the task.

Danny parked in front of the high-rise where the penthouse I owned, courtesy of my father, was. While two men guarded the car Kat was in, Danny escorted me inside. The lobby of the place was exquisite. Italian marble flooring shone beneath our feet. Lush greenery decorated the bottom of gold columns. The floor-to-ceiling windows had their golden drapes pulled close, creating an intimate-like atmosphere. I smelled food cooking, which reminded me that all I'd eaten were the small hors d'oeuvres at the function. The bar was lined with other tenants who owned penthouses in the exclusive building.

The bottom of my heels clacked against the floor. The attendants at the concierge desk smiled at me politely. I returned a tired smile and nodded a greeting back to them. Flat screens in each corner of the room showed that the media was already reporting what happened at the mayor's mansion.

"An insider has told us that they believe the heart attack to be fatal," the reporter spoke.

"Oh my goodness," I mumbled as Danny and I stepped on the elevator.

I'd just thought the man had suffered a simple heart attack. The fact that he was dead had my gears turning. Once Danny had led me to my home, I patiently waited as he checked my home from top to bottom. No matter how many times I fussed and told him he didn't have to do it, my father had trained him well enough to know better. He knew if anything happened to me because he failed to make sure I was safe, Daddy would kill him.

"Thank you, Danny," I told him as I closed and locked my door.

"Rest well, Ms. Lanfair," he said.

I knew he would stand at that door for another ten minutes to make sure all was well. Sometimes he stood there for longer as he said he never wanted to have a set pattern, just in case someone was watching. There was a panic button on the outside of my door that dubbed as a doorbell. If I pressed on the similar buttons in my home, Danny would see the red light flashing. I popped on the dimmers as I didn't want too much light. Since I lived on the top floor, which was the most expensive, I had the best view in the place. A panoramic view of the Atlanta skyline greeted me. My home was clean, for the most part. A few pairs of shoes lay about here and there. Some files I'd been working on for my job were strewn about on the mocha-colored microfiber sofa in my front room.

Having my MBA with a concentration in finance management afforded me the luxury of working for a top financial analyst firm. It amazed me how much my life had changed over the course of two years. So much I had learned from being Daddy's "favorite," as my sisters often called me. His little puppet, they would say. While their words hurt, they had no idea the mental trauma I'd dealt with since that day I was abducted, then essentially rescued. So, I never told them the real reasons I stuck close to Daddy.

An hour passed. It was nine o'clock when I took a quick shower, dressed in a thin, spaghetti strap shirt and boy shorts, then sat up in bed. I kept a watch on the news as I tried to get some work done, to no avail. I was tired, and my brain reflected that.

"Monica, have your sources told you anything else on the mayor's condition?" another anchor asked the reporter from Fox 5 Atlanta who was on the scene.

I'd seen her throughout the night. She still had on the gown she was in when I left the party. Her black hair blew in the wind as she spoke.

"So far, all we know right now is that his immediate family has been told to get to the hospital as the mayor was rushed to Emory an hour or so ago," Monica answered.

"Now, if the mayor has indeed suffered a fatal heart attack, what does this mean for the city of Atlanta? Will the vice mayor, that many people don't even know we have, step in?"

"That's a good question, Richard. As we know, Alderman Leo Giulio is running against Sheila McIntire in the upcoming election in a few months. She is after his seat as alderman. But as of right now, he is still alderman for Atlanta, and he is also vice mayor. So, if Mayor Kasim has died, more than likely, Alderman Leo Giulio will step in as special interim mayor until a special election is held . . ."

As I was watching the news, my mind was in a fog. None of what had been said clicked for me. As I drifted off to sleep, the commotion of the night escaped me. I hated the nights when my nightmares would force me to toss and turn. Sometimes, I would hear Antonio's voice in my head as I slept. Would relive the moments of that day over and over in my dreams. The fact that I had come so close to being a victim of the serial killer ate away at me.

Then there were times when the clicking noises, that taplike sound of the other man's boots in the room, would also torment me. The sound of that arrow whizzing through the air, the way Antonio's body had slumped over me, his blood trickling down my face and chest, seeing the arrow between his eyes—it all haunted me. There was that tapping sound again. It was far away, yet so close, that I jumped up from my sleep, frantically looking around the room.

I slammed my hand against the lamp beside my bed, trying to turn on the light. The shades in my room were open, so moonlight shone through casting shadows around my room. I was sweating I realized as I ran my hands down my face. I looked at the time to find it was three in the morning. My TV was on mute, but breaking news was flashing at the bottom of my screen. It had been confirmed that Mayor Kasim had indeed died.

I was just about to call my father when I heard it again. There was that tapping sound. It startled me so badly that when I tried to get out of bed, I fell to the floor, hard. I'd knocked my lamp off the nightstand beside the bed causing the light I did have to black out. My phone went crashing to the floor as I realized I wasn't alone.

"Who's there?" I called out, already having a sense of who it was.

I got no response which annoyed me.

"What do you want?" I yelled out into the room. "I didn't say anything. I never have. What do you want?" I screamed out again.

Panic burdened my voice as I desperately snatched open the drawer to the nightstand and pulled out my gun.

It was already loaded. I took the safety off and slowly stood.

"You can't kill what you can't see," he said to me.

"I know who you are. I have cameras in my home," I said in hopes it would make the man I knew as Marcel leave me be.

That tapping sounded again before he said, "That's going to be a problem, now, isn't it?"

I'd started crying and didn't even know it. Ever since that day two years ago, I'd been afraid of dying. Had a healthy fear of being sexually assaulted. I still had the scars on my wrist and body to attest to my trauma.

"Just leave me alone, please. I've kept my word."

"Your word was fine until I saw how easy it was for you to know who I was by my voice alone."

He was closer now. I stayed in the glow of the moonlight as I knew he was in the shadows of my room somewhere. The only area where light existed was my bed and the small space next to it because of the moonlight. I heard a click. My shades started to close. He'd activated the sensor for the shades to close on their own. Now darkness engulfed the room. I was still sane enough to know I shouldn't shoot blindly in the room, but fearful enough to jump on my bed and try to run for my closet which had a secret escape route behind the wall of my shoes.

I never made it to the closet. As soon as my feet touched the floor on the other side of the bed, he snatched the gun away from me. A strong set of hands lifted me from the floor. One arm around my waist and another hand over my mouth.

"Shhhh," Marcel said to me. "I want you to see and feel how easy it is for me to get close to you. Your security detail is good, but I'm better. Your cameras have been disabled."

"Please, please, don't kill me," I mumbled behind his hand.

A tiny pinch against my neck made me think he had injected me with something. I still bucked and kicked. *Not again,* was all my mind kept screaming. Still, no matter how much I kicked and tried to get away, nothing worked. My adrenaline made my heart beat loudly in my ears. My eyes fluttered, and I was breathing so intensely, my chest hurt. I fell limp against his hold. I remembered little after that as life seeped left my body.

My eyelids felt heavy as I slowly lifted them. Where was I? Was I dead? Had he killed me? I moaned out as I turned over. Took me a minute to get my bearings.

"Finally awake, sweetheart?"

I jumped and fell forward to the floor. I heard heels run toward me. They sounded too much like that tapping sound Marcel's shoes made anytime he was near. When hands reached for me, I swung out.

"Oh, holy fuck," I heard Kat gasp. "She hit me, Othello."

"Sabrina Lanfair, what in the hell is wrong with you?" my father barked.

I looked around frantically, finally realizing I wasn't dead and my father was in my home. I was groggy like I had been drinking. I tried to get to my feet and stumbled around a bit, knocking wineglasses and an empty wine bottle from the table.

"I-I," I stuttered my words. "What happened?"

"You drank too much is what happened. I know work is getting to you, baby girl, but getting sloppy drunk ain't ever been the answer," Daddy told me.

Drunk? I didn't even remember taking a drink the night before. As the events of the night before came back to me, I knew alcohol hadn't been what knocked me out. I looked up at him from the floor. He was dressed bespoke in a tan suit that had been tailored to fit his frame.

I frowned, still a bit confused. "What?"

"Get up and get dressed, Sabrina. Pop some aspirin and get moving. We have lunch scheduled with Leo and a few others today. Have you paid attention to the news? Mayor Kasim has died."

Lunch? Mayor Kasim? Didn't he know I'd been attacked in my home last night, or did he not care? I was about to speak my mind when I remembered Marcel's words. Why didn't he kill me? Why didn't he just put me out of my misery? Did he leave me alive to assert some kind of power over me? Why did he let me live?

Daddy helped me from the floor while Kat stomped around in my kitchen grabbing ice from the freezer for her eye. She had a light complexion, so I was praying I hadn't bruised her too badly. My head was still foggy, and a headache was imminent, but I got myself together as my father had instructed. I kept it simple. . . . Black, wide-leg slacks, sleek red pumps to match my red blouse, and I pulled my hair back in a bun at the nape of my neck.

As I looked in the mirror while doing my makeup, I studied my neck. I'd felt a small prick or something last night when that man had accosted me but didn't see a mark or point of entry. While my hands were up, I took notice of the faint scarring around my wrists. I often took care of what I wore. When I wasn't wearing long sleeves, I kept bangles and bracelets on to cover the reminder of what had happened to me.

I didn't have time to dwell on that at the moment as my father was knocking on the door asking me to hurry.

"Now, Leo gave you some files on his companies the other day. Have you had time to look them over?" Daddy asked me once we were nestled safely in the back of his Navigator.

Danny was the driver, and Kat rolled her eyes at me anytime we made eye contact.

I nodded once. "I have."

"So, what are the numbers on his father's deli and such?"

"The financials look well, but there is too much money here and not enough business. Don't get me wrong; the deli is very popular, but there are some figures here from Thursday through Sunday that make very little sense. This goes for the Laundromats and car washes as well."

Daddy looked a bit nervous and chuckled. "Well, that's why he wants to hire you. He wants you to fix the numbers; make them make sense."

I sighed softly, then looked at my father. "So, he wants me to cook the books? Be honest with me, Daddy."

He used his thumb and pointing finger to rub his eyes. I could tell he didn't want to say too much in front of Kat.

He patted my hands in that fatherly way and said, "Why don't we wait to talk about this once we get to the deli, baby?"

I had so many questions but nodded my head in understanding. Daddy had always run with the Italians, Jews, Hispanics, Arabs, and Asians. He was well-known in the underworld, very respected as well. That had never been kept a secret from us.

We made it to the deli and were escorted in by one of Leo's men. I couldn't help but wonder if Marcel would be in attendance. The deli was never opened on Mondays, so we were alone with the rest of the attendees. The place smelled heavenly. Whatever was cooking in the back, my stomach told me I needed to have some. I searched the room thoroughly and breathed a sigh of relief when I didn't see Marcel.

Leo spotted us, smiled, then stood. He was a handsome man. No way could that be denied. His mixed race brought out the best of both worlds in him. Dressed in black slacks, a silver button-down, and nifty loafers, he smiled.

He wiped his mouth quickly with a cloth napkin. "Othello, good to see you, my man," he greeted, taking my father's hand and kissing his cheek.

That was the Italian in him. The sheik, Mustafa, stood with a smile as well. He nodded at Daddy. Same with Feinstein, Iglesias, and Sook Ahn. The elder Giulio was also in attendance. He greeted my father same as Leo had.

"Sorry we started eating without you, but we were starving," Leo told my father, then walked over to Kat. He kissed her cheek. "Kat, the wives are waiting in the back for you."

He was looking at her eye when he told her that. That didn't sit well with her, but she smiled, greeted the other men, and made her way to the back.

"Sabrina, good to see you," he finally greeted me.

"Same here, Leo," I said.

Daddy pulled out my chair for me, and I sat at the table with the big boys, literally. Once pleasantries were out of the way, and my father and I had ordered food and drinks, I got down to business.

"Leo, I've gone over the files and—"

"Damn, right down to business, huh?" Leo cut in. "You don't want to eat first?"

"I work best on an empty stomach as it reminds me never to get too comfortable. If I'm hungry, then I work harder toward my goal. It reminds me that if I don't work, then I shouldn't eat," I told him pleasantly.

To be honest, all I wanted to do was get back home and crawl into the comfort of my bed. Marcel being in my home the night before still unsettled me. But, for my father, I'd do anything. So, I put my game face on and my best foot forward.

Laughter echoed around the table as Mr. Giulio spoke up. "I like your girl, Othello. Always have. She doesn't mince words." His voice croaky and filled with unsaid wisdom.

"Got that from her mama. Trust me, it's only cute at this age," he said, then laughed.

All the other men laughed as well at a joke I didn't readily get. But I continued.

"As I was saying, looking over the files you gave me shows way too much revenue for the deli. If I'm to understand what my father explained to me, you want me to fix this."

Leo and his father nodded. He got ready to speak, but I held up a finger to cut him off.

"First thing first, if I'm to fix this, I need honesty up front. Is this money laundering? I ask because if there is a possibility I can go down in a RICO case, I want to be well aware of that."

There was a hushed silence in the room.

Sook Ahn said smiling, "Othello, you said she was a financial analyst, not a lawyer."

"Please, Mr. Sook Ahn, address me as I'm the one with whom you will be doing business. I understand in your customs and tradition, it may not be common for a woman to speak as such, but if anyone is going to gamble with my ass, it will be me. My sisters are lawyers. It helps if I'm up to par with certain terms and phrases in the business I'm in."

I looked at each man around the table, square in the eyes. Most people would have assumed I was some badass chick who could hold her own in a room full of men, and that was true on some fronts, but to be honest, after last night, I wasn't sure of what I was. That would make the second time I'd begged one man for my life. And it was eating away at me.

All the men looked at my father with curious expressions.

He proudly smiled, then said, "You heard the woman."

The rest of the meeting went off without a hitch. The talk eventually turned to Leo taking over as interim mayor.

With a smile on his face, my father asked, "When is the city council meeting to vote on when to swear you in?" he asked Leo.

"We'll talk about that later when the lady isn't around," Leo answered.

For some reason, this made all the men at the table very happy. Didn't take a genius to figure out why. With the kind of business they were in when no one was looking, Leo being in office was a good thing. If Leo did a good enough job while in interim, he would be a sure win for mayor if he decided to run in the special election.

I was all faux smiles until my food was brought out. I frowned. My heart leapt to my throat. Palms started to sweat at the sight of the man holding my food. Marcel. He was dressed in all black, hair net on his head, white marinara sauce-stained apron tied around his waist. I stared at him so long that if any of the men had been paying attention and not looking at the proposals I'd given them, they would have known we knew each other.

"Steak and potatoes for you, Mr. Lanfair, and chicken Parmesan for you, miss," he said to me like he hadn't been in my home, uninvited, the night before.

He was a cook. A measly cook in the back of a deli. A cook had come into my home and made me beg for my life. I didn't know why that bothered me so much at the moment.

"You cooked this?" my father asked Marcel, having already cut into his steak.

Marcel nodded once. "I did, sir."

Daddy looked to Leo. "You make your aide cook?"

Leo chuckled. "Cel started out as a cook. I think I remember him telling you that last night, but I understand because of last night's events how it may have slipped your mind."

Daddy nodded as he chewed. He closed his eyes like he was in his heaven. "Best goddamned piece of steak I've ever had."

"Thank you, sir," Marcel replied.

"I don't want this," I spoke up looking at my food. "I didn't ask for this."

"Baby girl, I could have sworn I heard you ask for chicken Parmesan," Daddy said to me.

He thought I was talking about the food, but I wasn't. I caught myself as I was about to have a nervous breakdown.

I knocked the plate on the floor. "I didn't fucking ask for this," I snapped as I stood.

I looked Marcel in his eyes. He knew what I was referencing but kept a stoic look on his face.

"I'm sorry, Ms. Lanfair. Maybe I misunderstood what the server told me. Would you like something else perhaps?" he asked me.

My eyes watered.

Daddy asked, "You okay, Sabrina?"

I didn't want to come off as the typical, emotional woman. "I'm fine. Just hungry, and this one got my food wrong. Excuse me," I said, then turned to head downstairs to the bathroom.

Once I was inside the small bathroom with only two stalls, I threw water on my face. I snatched a fistful of brown paper towels to dry it.

A cook . . . A *fucking cook* had me bent out of shape. He was not the boogeyman . . . was he? He was just a fucking lackey for the Giulio family and a cook.

It was safe to say that seeing Marcel in this way did nothing to take away from the fact I knew he was a killer; at least, he had killed Antonio. Still, in my mind, it helped to humanize him. I was so lost in my thoughts that I almost jumped out of my skin when the bathroom door opened.

I expected another woman to walk in, perhaps one of the wives, but when Marcel walked in, I whipped around from the mirror and backed against the wall. We played the staring game for a long while. His eyes had an uncanny glare in them. They were pitiless. I wondered if the man even had a soul with the way his eyes cut into me.

"I'm not afraid of you," I told him.

"Good. I don't want you to be. Fear makes people do stupid things. . . . Like, I don't know . . . talk."

His voice, anytime I heard it, always settled over me. It was penetrating, nice even, but it also meant I couldn't trust him. Any other time, if I had been paying attention, his looks would have appealed to me. He was an exotic shade of chocolate. Tall, mysterious eyes that held a sadness about them; one you wouldn't see if you weren't paying close attention. He walked with purpose, yet took slow strides like he had all the time in the world.

"I told you I wouldn't say anything, so why don't you leave me alone?"

"You have to stop."

"Stop what?"

"Stop reacting a certain way around me as my boss picks up on every little thing, and we can't have that," he said moving closer to me.

I had nowhere to run as I had already backed into the wall. *He's a cook, Sabrina. Merely a cook. You don't have to be afraid of him,* I told myself.

The closer he got to me, the more my adrenaline spiked. My fight-or-flight instinct kicked in, and I decided flight was no longer an option. Before he could reach me, I lurched forward and smacked him. I hit him so hard I scared myself. I gasped in shock, then realized that I was fighting back. In my own little way, I was fighting back. I didn't have to be afraid of him. I didn't have to become powerless anytime he was around.

"I'm not scared of you," I said again.

"If you say that enough, it'll eventually become true, even to you."

For some reason, it seemed as if he got a kick out of seeing me ruffled. I felt that he was sarcastic, so I lashed out at him again. I smacked him again. At least I tried to. He caught my wrist and forced me back against the wall.

Hands above my head, in a firm, nonthreatening manner, he spoke. "Think about this; if I truly wanted you dead, I could have done it twice now. All I'm asking is that you relax around me. I don't want to have to pay you another visit, because if I do, this time, I will kill you," he said.

I swallowed. His lips were so close to mine, I thought I was breathing for him. I was confused for a few seconds. Wasn't sure if I should have been attracted to him or repulsed. I noticed crazy things about him at that moment, like the way his eyes had darkened, the piquant woodsy-like scent in his smell, the perfect line of his goatee, his breath. It smelled like spearmint. Was I crazy? Had I lost it? I guess my mind wanted to take notice of anything other than the fact he had again gained the upper hand.

My chest heaved up and down.

"Will you leave me alone then?" I asked him in a shaky voice.

"Maybe" was his simple answer.

Chapter Four

Marcel

I kept my distance, watching her because girlie was on edge as is, and a brotha knew when one kept shaking a bottle, that shit would explode. I had already tested her by showing up in her place. I needed to determine whether I had made a mistake in letting her live. When she showed up in the restaurant, I knew that she was coming.

I needed to be clear about something. When I was told to take someone out, I never asked the justification or reason behind it. Yeah, in the case of the mayor, I put two and two together while I was at the party, but it wasn't something I cared about because it wasn't my place. I learned well from Senior Giulio, and I had a protocol to follow. Don't ask and don't care.

My joy came in after everything went down, and the news confirmed the mayor's death. That was all I cared about, that clean kill. But back to Sabrina. I wasn't sure what type of chick I was dealing with, which was why I followed her in the bathroom after she wigged out. I stood back from her, blocking the exit, studying her.

When I got too close to her, she had messed a brotha up. I wasn't mad about it, but it had me feeling some type of way like I couldn't understand why she was so afraid of me. I wasn't the nigga who had kidnapped her or tried to rape her. If anything, she should be standing there singing my praises and thanking me. But I mean, not everyone thought like me.

But yeah, pressing her against the wall, I then let her go after she swung on me too many times for my liking, I kept my distance. I had peeped that she was on some hit-a-nigga shit because she was reliving her ghost. Again, I wasn't offended by it. Kind of enjoyed the fireworks, just as long as she kept her mouth shut and didn't slip out and say the wrong thing.

Which was why I said, "Maybe," when she asked if I would leave her alone.

Pushing off the wall, I shrugged my shoulders and moved to walk out the door.

"That's not an answer, though," she said while keeping her distance.

"I thought you were smart," I responded looking over my shoulder.

"Don't insult me," she whispered harshly, anger mixed with fear caused her dark skin to flush a slight red.

"Ditto," was all I said walking out and heading to the kitchen, saying over my shoulder, "Try the Parmesan. It's not poisoned, I promise. I'll bring you out a fresh plate."

Her expression amused me, but her body language let me know that she was still on edge. While heading to the kitchen, I found myself walking up to Leo, who stood around tasting the food and dictating to several of the cooks in the kitchen.

"Cel, come holla at me for a minute," he said holding out a hand as he usually did when throwing an arm on the shoulder of the one he addressed.

Feeling the weight of the arm on my right shoulder, I kept my cool. I wasn't fond of being touched, but debating that with my boss's son wasn't going to be on my agenda for the day.

"We appreciate the delicious food you laid out for us," he stated as we walked out of the kitchen.

"Thank you," I said.

Cooking became a talent that I had no idea that I would get good at doing. Whenever I got my hands on anything food-wise, all of my attention turned into creating something not only tasty but, also, visually appealing to the eye. I never thought a simple deli that eventually turned into a bistro deli café would give me the avenue to flex my artistic skills, but it did. Murder and cooking both gave me a simple pleasure, and both were an outlet for my artistic side.

I could hear Leo talking about nothing until we stepped into Senior Giulio's office, and he closed the door.

"We need your services again," he said, rounding the desk where his father normally sat.

He flipped through papers and then reached under the desk to pull out a yellow writing pad.

Ripping off a sheet and folding it with his finger, he handed it to me, then sat down to watch me read it. "You did well, and we'd like that same clean-cut precision used again."

Several names were listed, as well as addresses, descriptions, ages, locations, and then some were written in Senior Giulio's script. Leo was speaking in codes because he knew that if anyone had bugged the restaurant as a whole, then we all would be caught up. But back to the paper, I knew that it was the latest hit list.

A few of the names were familiar to me, high-name businessmen associated with specific politicians who had been blocking the rise in the game of Leo and several of the men in the dining room. For me to devote my time to take these people out in ways that were not obvious and that were timed right was an important task that I happily accepted. Memorizing everything on the paper,

I ripped it up and handed it back to Leo, who burned it immediately.

"A'igh . . ." Before I could finish my response, I quickly cleared up my lingo. "Of course. I'll take care of it as soon as I'm able."

"Good. Now with the unfortunate death of the mayor, there is a high possibility that my schedule will change. That means the same for you." Leo stretched his legs, then dropped his hands on the arms of the chair he sat in. "You'll have to prioritize your work here as our senior chef and your work for me as an aide. Is that going to be too much for you?"

Shaking my head, I continued standing where I was. "No, it's not. It's an honor to be given this chance. All I wish to do is to continue making this restaurant into something lasting in respect to your father and your family. Taking on this job will allow me that."

"I like those words. You know your pay grade just went up, so go celebrate that. We won't need you in the kitchen as much, which I was hinting at, but if you find the time, and you have that itch to cook, you're always welcomed to do you," Leo said with a smile on his face.

"Thanks, I'll keep that in mind." Stepping back, I moved toward the door.

Leo shifted in his position and stood. "I have to get back to the dining room. . . . Oh yes. Along with your change in position, the restaurant will be going through some changes as well. That is why Mr. Lanfair's daughter is here today. You'll be handing out the financial itinerary sheets to her now."

"That strange chick?" I laughed, then nodded. "All right."

"She did strangely flip the fuck out, didn't she?" Leo said with a grating laugh. "Kind of pretty, but shaky. She might not be a fit for us, but we'll see. Pops is adamant about her employment."

"I heard you all say she came highly recommended due to how well she is with finances," I added as a sly reminder. "You all said that she's about loyalty and isn't for everybody, right?"

Having Sabrina here was of interest to me now as well. Not because of the help she would be able to provide for the bistro, but because I'd be able to see if she could keep that trap shut.

"That's what Dad said, but we'll see. If that shaky shit happens again, we might have to disassociate ourselves from her," he replied, walking my way.

That was all the information I needed to know. If little momma could get her mental in check and keep her head above the water, then there would be no problem for the Giulio family, or for me. We walked out of the office speaking about the affairs of the restaurant. In my mind, I was repeating the names and info attached to those names and not truly paying Leo any attention.

When we ended up back in the dining room, I saw the men all enjoying their meals. It seemed that they all had seconds, and I slyly watched Sabrina without anyone noticing. She was timidly eating and discussing what she needed if she was going to be working as a financial assistant to the family.

As Leo took his seat, his father clapped a hand on his shoulder, squeezing gently in fatherly respect, then looked my way. "Marcel! The food . . . I know Leo told you. *Grazie di tutto!*"

Giving a respectable nod to him, saying, "Thank you for everything," I smiled. "*Prego,* Senior Giulio."

For anyone watching, they would assume that I was being respectful, and I was, but I was also signaling that it was time for me to leave to handle business.

My boss returned his smile and said, "Good kid," as I quietly backed out of the room.

While I headed to the back of the restaurant, I removed
the white smock around my waist, then headed to the
lockers where I kept my duffle bag. Snatching it, I exited,
scoped my area, then hopped in my simple black Infinity,
an upgrade from my busted 1992 Impala that I was
sleeping in when I was homeless. Heading away from the
bistro, I cut through traffic and wrapped my way around
Atlanta to make it to my unassuming high-rise condo.
After arriving at my place, I undressed, showered, and
changed my clothes, then headed back out.

The life of a hit man wasn't glamorous for me. Yes,
the money I made gave me certain perks, but, overall,
a brotha didn't live in a mansion somewhere in the cut.
Nope. I had my simple two-bed condo that overlooked
Atlanta. I paid my HOA fees like everyone else, and I kept
a low-key lifestyle as not to stick out. I liked my life that
way, and I wasn't trying to shake it up for anyone.

After getting Sabrina out of my head, thinking about
how easy it was for me to break into her penthouse, I
pulled up into an unassuming brick building that was
attached to one of the meat package joints that Senior
Giulio owned. Across the street from it was my second
spot, where I handled all my work. I pulled up into the
brick building's garage, got out, and then took the hidden
tunnel way down that led across the street to my spot.

Once upon a time, this place was used during the
Prohibition to transport illegal booze and other wares.
Now it was my place of business. Clicking lights on,
hip-hop started to play once I made it into my building.
Several strides in had me walking past two huge boards.
One a whiteboard with my awesome penmanship on
it, and another board with various names linked to
pictures. Some of the images had red crosses through
them. Others had bull's-eyes on them. Each picture was
connected through a string pinned near them.

All around me was my simple world, and I felt more at home than I ever felt since living in Atlanta. Going through my routine of undressing, I dropped my things and headed to the open concept chef kitchen I had in my loft. Pulling out a beer from my refrigerator, I walked to my computer, pulled out a notepad, sat, and began clicking and writing.

I liked to jot down everything given to me by the Giulios, which is what I did as I looked up every person on the list. My head tilted in curiosity about one specific name. This guy was a football player for our local team, the Nightwings. As I looked up information, I laughed as it dawned on me. Just like Antonio, who I'd killed two years before, this guy, Paul Watts, was rumored to disappear in the hood from time to time. Strangely, every time, as if on cue, the streets would begin talking about street runners coming up dead and missing kilos of dope.

Printing out Paul's picture, I chuckled while studying the dude's face. Brotha was a clean-laced-looking cat. About the same height as me. Stocky, a crisp, lined haircut, wide jaw, the color of dark ochre brown, and known for his aggressive personality on the field. Dude was preppy tough and only 22 years old. I remembered that the city was hyped to get his ass straight out of the college draft. Nigga was killer, but he was also known for his hate of kids in the streets scraping by and banging just to make a life outta nothing.

I'd never forget hearing him label every young black man that might live near, or in the hood, or who visited the hood, "weak thugs." Shit pissed me off for days, but I was thankful to our local news for outing his ass for self-hatred, considering he came from the hoods of Boston. His only saving grace was that back when he was 10, he was picked to voucher into a private, Irish-based school.

From how he acted, spoke, and how he always kept a
blonde on his side with an interesting set of tits and fabri-
cated ass, I understood that this fool wasn't operating on
a normal level. He was about some self-hate and trying
all he can to be what nonminority society wanted him to
be. *Go! Bojangles!* That's what I thought about him, but
shit, that disrespected half of the good Bojangles did in
his life, so I didn't want to disrespect that.

But anyway, now, I had him on my list.

Taking the printed pictures of my marks, I made notes
on my map of Georgia and then pinned them to the zone.
Stepping back, I made me a cup of coffee from one of
those pod machines, then went back to thinking about
what would be the best course on taking down an athlete
who might have a drug problem. I also thought about
several shit starters around Atlanta, two more political
marks, and would need to keep an eye on an aide who
happened to work for Mr. Lanfair.

From the marks on the original notes shown to me, I
knew that these people on the lists were not just Senior
Giulio's; they were also people every man at the table
today had issues with, which amused me. Adjusting
my hardening dick, I grinned. I had some people to
take down, and a nice amount of money to make in the
process. I needed to time this all just right and keep it all
clean, but I knew that I could do it; I just needed to pick a
day and time to get it going.

Stepping back, I rubbed the back of my neck while
drinking my coffee. I was barefoot, chilling in black,
low-riding, drawstring pants with no top on. On my bare,
deep brown skin were marks from where I had either
been shot, burned, or cut due to taking down a mark.
Each indictor chilling on my back or arms. Now, how
they were situated, I wasn't embarrassed or nothing for
anyone to see them. When they did, I calmly explained

that I once was training for the military, but I couldn't hack it, so I backed off that career path. I also explained that I once was homeless, and being on the streets of Atlanta can be hard.

That usually shut the person up and had them thinking about other things to ask me. Each mark was my trophy, and each one I inked up just because I wanted to dress up my reminder. Holding my hot coffee, I kept my eyes locked on Paul's picture while thinking. If he was into killing and drugs, going after him could be something fun for me. Torturing him could be a prime choice for him, but cleanly taking him out would be the best thing.

I couldn't afford anyone checking his body and seeing any indication of foul play, which had me thinking yet again. I could give him a lethal cocktail of drugs, but after poisoning the mayor, that now felt boring. I needed something different.

Tapping my cup in thought, I moved back to my computer, sat down, and continued reading up on my marks. Whatever I did next, I knew that it would be good. Now, the next thing on my list was trying to figure out why I was so attracted to a woman who attempted to beat my ass because she was scared of me.

"Because you're fucked up, nigga," I said aloud to myself in laughter.

On some real shit, I really was. I wasn't sure when that switch in my brain clicked on to being into killing no-named people usually, but I was into that there thing. To me, there was no logical reason why I'd bring someone up into this insanity, but I was heavily thinking about it and thinking about Sabrina.

I guess I was on some hero shit with her. I saved her life, which was a first for me who takes out people. The power in that fueled me, but anyway, on to other things. A flashing notice popped up on my computer alerting me that one of my marks, who I had been working hard in tracking down, was on the move.

This dude was a Dutch South African diplomatic. I didn't know why Senior Giulio wanted him out, but as I said, it wasn't my job to ask; just do, and that's what I had to do. I felt like being showy with this one because he had many enemies I had learned from my research on him. Putting on my clothes and yanking down my black skull cap, I moved around to grab my weapons. This one was going to be good for me.

I learned that this guy had ties to apartheid and with taking land from the people there and keeping it from black hands. Now, shit, I wasn't about having agendas or whatnot, but after I learned that, I could see why the nigga had so many enemies. This shit made it more fun for me, and part of the reason why I moved out quickly to get him.

Homie was known for moving from place to place quickly as to not be easily threatened. Luckily for me, where he was going, there would be a large crowd, and I could move through it easily without detection. However, as I said, I wanted to be showy, so that's what I planned on doing. I hopped in an unmarked white van and headed out. I ended up near the Cobb Energy Centre, a couple of blocks over, where, interesting enough, Senior Giulio's wife was performing an operatic quartet representing South Africa, which I knew as supposedly buzzworthy around Atlanta.

Finding a spot where I could not be seen, I used high-powered, long-distance viewing binoculars to scope out the scene as cars upon cars pulled up to the red carpet that was outside the massive asymmetrical building. The wind and the weather were good to me. No wind, which meant I didn't have to worry about my shots shifting in the wind. Earplugs in my ears as I listened to music, I continued waiting and watching. Limo after limo paused to let out stars, several political faces including Senior Giulio and son, and everyday wannabes. What had my attention and had me chuckling to myself was the sight of Sabrina with her father and stepmother around her.

Shorty was just a beacon for death, wasn't she? This would be the second time that I had to take someone out close to her. I found it hilarious and ironic, all at the same time. But fuck it, she would get over it and get used to it, was my thought. She'd have to with working around undercover criminals.

As everyone snapped pictures and gloated, I noticed the South African flags attached to a stretch limo pulling up. It only took the man a few seconds to get out, grinning and lifting up a pasty hand as he waved. Which was good for me, because it helped me out where I was standing.

Whistling to the music, I aimed my Remington 700 5R with .300 Winchester Magnum ammo, made sure my target was in my direct line of vision, then pulled the trigger. What I could only assume were screams and shouts as women looked around frantically and men instinctively fell to the ground for cover satisfied the beast within me. I watched my mark's head jerk back when the bullet met its mark. His guards scrambled and tried to shield him, to no avail. It was too late. The damage was done.

One . . . two . . . three . . . four . . . then five for good measure, I took out his driver and four of his guards. They all fell tumbling down.

"Ashes to ashes," I muttered, then went back to whistling.

Busta Rhymes began to spit some rhymes, and I bobbed to the music as my gloved hands smoothly broke down my rifle, packed it up, and I then walked away. See, I was blocks away from where the center was, but having the grade-A weapons I had, I was able to be showy and clean with my kills; besides, I made sure to plant several German patsies as my fall guys in this game. Each one of those faces on my board back home would now get an "X" crossed through them.

My night was good, though I kind of felt bad that Sabrina's now wasn't.

Chapter Five

Sabrina

August 2011 . . .

For a brief moment, my world had shattered again. I didn't readily know what was going on. I heard a woman scream, blood splattered on my dress, and my father pulled me to the ground. Chaos ensued. Danny covered me with his body. Someone's heeled foot almost drilled a hole through my hand. I yelled out in pain. My father yelled for Danny to get us out of there while Leo and his father rushed inside of the center. Everything after that went by in one huge blur.

"Jesus Christ," my father murmured. "You okay, baby girl?"

I nodded. He asked the same thing of Kat. She was visibly shaken.

I looked at the speckles of blood on the cream silk gown I had on while cradling my hand against my chest. I'd been looking forward to a night out. After tangoing with the devil in the bathroom, I needed the reprieve.

"What just happened?" Kat asked my father.

She had tears in her eyes. The swelling and bruising of her eye were still visible under the makeup she had on, but not as much as before. She was trembling as she held on to my father's hand. Danny and his security had ushered us into the back of the stretch Hummer limo so quickly that we barely saw what happened. Oddly, though, my father seemed calm.

"I-I don't know," he responded.

Knowing my father the way I did, I could tell there was something he wasn't saying, just like I could tell he was lying about not knowing what happened.

Kat was panicking. "I heard a gunshot."

"Be quiet," Daddy snapped at her.

"Be quiet?" she repeated incredulously. "Be quiet? How dare you tell me to be quiet when I just saw a man dead at my feet! First, the mayor falls dead, and now a South African diplomat? Be quiet?"

My father backhanded her so quickly that even I gasped at the intensity of the hit. Kat screeched out, then grabbed her mouth where my father had struck her. Blood pooled through her fingers.

"Daddy," I called out to him, appalled at his behavior.

His pensive look before had now turned to one of anger.

"I asked you to shut the fuck up. I asked you nicely the first time," he said acidly to Kat as he frowned down at her. "You won't let me be nice to you lately, Kat. Why is that, huh? Now, again, be quiet."

For as long as I'd known Kat, she'd been a spitfire. She had always been feisty, and to see this side of things between her and my father made me extremely uncomfortable. Daddy handed her his handkerchief so she could put it to her mouth, then pulled out his ringing cell to take a call. Tears rained down Kat's high cheekbones. She sniffled, glanced up to see me watching her, then looked back down at her shoes as she wiped her mouth. Reason number one Daddy left my mama: she fought back.

"Everything okay over there, Leo?" Daddy asked into his cell. He nodded as if listening to instructions. "Okay. Let me get my wife and daughter tucked away safely, and I'll meet you all down at the station . . . Right . . . Yes . . . Absolutely . . . See you then."

Once Daddy finished his call, he tapped the partition. It rolled down slowly.

"Danny, take Kat to Sabrina's home. Stay with them until I get back. You make sure that nobody comes to that top floor without security clearance, you hear me?"

Danny nodded like the robot he was. "Yes, sir."

Daddy gave a curt nod, then gazed at me. "Good."

I glanced back at Kat who sat stoically now. I wanted to tell Daddy that the night before, his security detail wasn't worth shit since Marcel had so effortlessly gotten into my home, but I didn't.

"Sorry about that," I heard Daddy say.

For a moment, I thought he was talking to Kat, but when I looked up, his eyes were on me. Was he seriously apologizing to *me* and *not* his wife whose mouth he had almost caved in?

I nodded my response.

"Didn't want you to have to see that," he said to me as if he was discomfited I'd finally seen that part of him up close.

As kids, we'd heard the fights between him and Mama but had never seen them. All we had seen were the bruises Mama had tried, unsuccessfully most times, to hide. Daddy had the occasional battle scars as well. Mama never laid down to take an ass kicking. I felt bad for Kat.

"It won't happen again will it, Katrina?" Daddy asked his wife.

His eyes were cool while he looked upon his wife. He was blaming her for him having to pimp smack her in front of me.

"No. No, it won't happen again," her voice soft and emotionless when she replied.

A few minutes later, Danny pulled up in front of the valet of my high-rise. Other members of the security team were already there. Daddy exited the limo first, took my hand and helped me out, then did the same for Kat. He kissed my cheek, then made Danny take me inside. I looked over my shoulder to see Daddy speaking to Kat. His right hand cupped the back of her neck as he kissed her forehead.

She was nodding and crying again. I had no idea what he was saying to her, but her spine was stiff, and she was beet red. I wanted to ask Danny if Daddy hit Kat a lot, but I knew he wouldn't utter a bad word against my father. We waited by the elevator until Kat walked up. The ride up to my home was the most awkward and tense filled it had ever been between Kat and me. Once Danny had made sure the inside of my home was secure, he left Kat and me to our own devices and made his post just outside the door.

While I wanted to talk to Kat, it was clear she had no intentions of speaking to me. She made a mad dash for my guest room as soon as we were alone. After undressing and showering, I bagged my dress in plastic since it was splattered with blood and cooked dinner as it was obvious we wouldn't be making our reservations for dinner later. I turned the news on to see what had happened.

" . . . Yes, Richard, that is correct. Nieuwe Haarlem, who is a major political player in South Africa, has been shot. We're not sure of his condition yet, but there is speculation that this may have been an assassination attempt as several of his guards and his driver have all been killed," reporter Monica Hayes stated.

My eyes widened. "What the fuck?" I asked no one.

"This is not a good time for us. As you know, Mayor Kasim suffered a fatal heart attack just last evening, and, now, it is possible that Nieuwe Haarlem, a top South African diplomat, has been killed. That is purely speculation on my end, Richard, as far as his death, but I can say for certain, he has been shot."

Richard looked perplexed on my TV as he frowned. "And several of his guards have been killed?"

Monica nodded. "Yes, that has been confirmed."

"Our sister stations are reporting that sources have told them, this is being looked at as an assassination attempt, so your earlier assessment may be right. Please stay with us here at Fox 5 Atlanta as we keep you updated on this sudden turn of events."

As the hours passed, the city of Atlanta was on lockdown. No flights were permitted in or out of the state. Major highways had been shut down. Police and military presence were strong. The president was said to be behind closed doors with top brass officials. And I felt as if I were in a John Grisham or James Patterson novel.

"Would you like something to eat?" I asked Kat once she emerged from the room.

"No," she replied softly.

She had changed into a short pajama set that formed to her petite curves. There were always extra clothes in my guest room as sometimes Kat had to bunk here when Daddy was on the move. Kat was the complete opposite of my mother. My mother was a rich, dark shade of brown. Kat was so light people assumed she was of mixed race. My mother was tall and voluptuous. Kat was average height and petite. My mother had a mouth that could slice God Himself. I thought Kat was a hellcat in her own right, but I guess I had been wrong.

She gingerly sat on the love seat next to me. "Do you mind if I unmute this?" she asked me nodding toward the TV.

"Sure, go ahead."

I wasn't surprised she was interested in the news as I was sure everyone was. However, to keep peace of mind, I went back to going over the books for Mr. Giulio's businesses.

"He's dead, you know?" Kat said out of the blue.

"Who?" I asked.

"Nieuwe Haarlem." She shook her head as she spoke.

"I figured as much. The leaders of the free world are just going through the motion with formalities now."

"First Mayor Kasim is killed, now this."

"Well, Mayor Kasim died of a heart attack. He was too young for that and seemed to be in great shape. You just never know when your heart will give out these days."

Kat turned to look at me. She blinked once. The look she gave me was one that borderline suggested I had another head growing on my shoulder.

"You really believe he died of a heart attack, huh?" she asked.

"I mean . . . yeah, he—"

She tsked, then grunted. "Stop looking at the trees and see the forest, Sabrina."

"I'm not sure I follow."

And I didn't. I had no idea what Kat was talking about, and since she didn't elaborate any further, I doubted I ever would.

"I'm sorry about punching you," I said after an awkward moment of silence.

Kat had her arms folded tightly across her chest, left leg crossed over the right one, and she leaned away from me like she was afraid I had a deadly disease or something.

She gave a fake smile. "Don't worry about it. You Lanfairs have been kicking my ass since I've known you."

I figured that was sarcasm since it was clear that wasn't the first time Daddy had hit her. Now her lip matched her eye, and for some reason, that bothered me. I didn't attempt to make any more conversation with her after that. She kept her eyes on the news, and I kept working. A few hours later, Daddy showed up to get Kat, and I was alone again.

For the next two weeks, things in Metro Atlanta and around the world remained on high alert. A dignitary had been assassinated on American soil. The terror level was on orange. While the rest of the world was focused on what had happened to the diplomat, I was stuck in the back office of the deli with Marcel. I had a feeling that he liked the idea more than me.

As always, he was dressed in all black. The way his shirt fit him made me take notice of his physique. The black boots, a black belt buckle that held some kind of dream catcher on it, and the jeans, plain in nature, but he made them look good. His lips were plush, and I couldn't help but always pay special attention to his eyes. They always called out to me.

"Is this it?" I asked once he had set the box of receipts in front of me, trying to keep my voice neutral so he wouldn't be able to pick up on what I was thinking.

He nodded once. "Yup."

I sighed heavily. "You guys kept a tally of things, important receipts, by keeping them in a box?"

"No. They keep receipts in a box. I keep track of my spending and incoming in this," he said, then dropped a leather-bound book with the word "Receipts" in gold lettering on top. "Everything you find in the box I've kept track of it in there as well."

"Have you guys ever heard of the digital age?"

"Senior Giulio isn't too fond of change, and he likes to keep this as authentic as his old place back in Sicily.

So, all this digital and tech stuff you're used to won't be found here. We do everything by hand."

I shook my head. I'd run into the same problems at the carwash and the Laundromat, only neither of the managers there had thought to be as organized as Marcel was with the book.

"Thank you," I said.

"Welcome."

I was still kind of timid and jumpy around him. He had exerted that much control over me. But I realized he was right about the fact that I was always freaking out around him. I did need to stop that. Especially since I assumed I would be working around him from time to time because we were both employed by the Giulios. Daddy always told me that a person only had as much power over you as you allowed them to have. I believed that and respected it; still, Daddy didn't know what I had seen this man do to another human being, and Daddy didn't know how easy it had been for Marcel to break into my home.

I opened the book to get down to business when I noticed he was still in the room with me.

"You can leave now," I said, blandly.

His black eyes bored into me. "I'm waiting to see how long it takes you to freak out on me again," he said.

"I know you get some kind of kick out of that, but don't worry; it's not happening today."

I knew it. I knew he got some kind of nauseating pleasure from the reaction I had to him. If I was to be honest with myself, after that day in the bathroom, I couldn't explain the feeling I got after our exchange then either. I was actually embarrassed by it. To know the man I'd been so afraid of mere moments before could make me feel anything other than disgust for him was mind-numbing.

"I saved your life, you know. Yet, you're afraid of me. Why?" he asked pensively.

In return, I looked at him as if he was remedial. "You threatened to kill me. I saw you kill a man."

"Did you really?"

"Did I really what?"

"See me kill a man?"

I was a smart woman, and I'd figured out that the man sitting in front of me was just as smart. He was testing me or something, I was sure. When I didn't answer right away, he smirked.

"I'd like you to leave now. I have work to do," I said.

I didn't know what I was expecting, but it wasn't for him to lean forward and say, "We started off on the wrong foot, wouldn't you say? Allow me to make it up to you, as it was never my intention to frighten you in any way."

"Is this some kind of joke? Is this your way of what? Trying to keep tabs on me?"

"Nah. If I wanted to keep tabs on you, it would be easy. What I'm asking for is a chance to show you Marcel the man and not Marcel the 'alleged' killer."

I paid close attention to him. Noticed how sometimes he spoke proper English, then noticed how at other times slang snuck in here and there.

I frowned because I didn't know what to say.

"You broke into my home."

"To make sure you were okay."

"You're a liar."

He shrugged and turned his lips down. "Among other things."

"Are you asking me on a date?"

He chuckled, and then it turned into an outright laugh. "Do you want to go on a date with me, Sabrina?"

"I want you to go to hell in gasoline drawers."

"Will you be meeting me there at eight?"

I sucked in a breath to keep from spitting on him. He smiled. Dimples that I hadn't paid much attention to before suddenly appealed to me.

I stood abruptly. "Get out. Get the hell out."

He stood. "Is that a no?"

"You can't be serious."

"Say yes, and let me show you just how serious I am."

"You're—you're a—"

"A what? A cook? Is a cook not good enough for you, Ms. Lanfair?"

My chest heaved up and down slowly as I watched him. He was calm. I was unnerved. He looked at me like he knew something I didn't.

"Text this number with your answer no later than eight tonight. If you say yes, I'll pick you up tomorrow at six," he said, then turned to leave as smoothly as he came.

I was done for the day. Marcel had me rattled again, but this unnerving was of a different manner. I didn't know if it was curiosity or what, but I picked the card up from the desk he had left. Why I was entertaining the notion of calling him was beyond me.

I was all set to walk out until I heard voices coming from Leo's other office.

"What we've got to do is get a secured seat on the police commission as well. Everything else is falling into place," I heard my daddy saying as I walked from the back office.

"What about those shipments coming in from the Port of Miami?" Senior Giulio's gravelly voice asked.

Leo spoke up. "All is well on that end, Pop. They're also going to swear me in sooner, especially with Nieuwe Haarlem dying like that."

"Best damn news we've heard all day," Daddy chimed in. "Sepriani still flying in tonight?"

"Yeah, the son of a bitch is," Leo answered.

Daddy said, "We have to do something about him."

"True, we do."

"Is he on the list?"

"He is."

Senior Giulio finally came back to the conversation.
"Then if he is on the list, we have nothing to worry about."
I stood there for the longest as that name was familiar
to me. I'd never forget that damn name. I thought back to
the day a man with that same last name tried to kill me
and had to wonder if there was a connection there. When
I heard the door opening, I hurriedly moved down the
hall to make my exit.

Hours later, I looked at the clock on my wall. Seven
forty-five. Marcel said I had to text by eight. Why would
I go on this date? What would it accomplish? I paced my
front room as I thought. He could give me the answers I
wanted about the man named Sepriani who his boss had
business with. He could tell me if the man was related
to Antonio Sepriani, the man who I had no doubt would
have raped and killed me.

Marcel was the only one who knew what had happened
to me. Was I going to overcome my fear of him as I'd
told myself, or was I going for another reason? I didn't
know. I couldn't answer for certain. All I know was when
seven fifty-five came around, I texted a simple yes to the
number on the card in my hand.

Chapter Six

Marcel

When I received her text, I was at my warehouse crossing off the Dutch South African diplomat and moving the picture of Sepriani into the center of my board. Vincent Sepriani was the father of Antonio, the cat who tried to rape Sabrina. The elder Sepriani was a bad motherfucker, a dude who had been on my watch list after I had killed his son. I knew the day would come where I would have to handle him because he was on my list. But because my boss insisted that before I go after him, I need to train and become stronger in my craft, so I couldn't go after him then.

When I received a message from my boss that Sepriani was coming to Atlanta, I knew that I had to scope him out and make him my priority. Pacing back and forth, I was in my mind trying to figure out how to kill this dude in an unnoticeable kind of way. With the killing of that diplomat, I had gotten ahead of myself because I had forgotten that the state would lock down and go on alert. Authorities would be on the lookout sniffing for any type of bullshit, and I couldn't afford to be caught up in any of that, or in view of Sepriani. I had to play this one smart.

My work as an aide might be able to come in play, though. It was as I was formulating my plan that Sabrina's text drew my attention. A pleased smile spread across my face, and I found myself rubbing my beard. Our date was set; I just had to think of a place to take her was all. My goal was to make her comfortable with me, as well as stop her from being jittery and loose of the mouth about what she experienced. Sometime and some place we would speak about it, but not at work and not in public. I aimed to let her know that because people listen and I did not need any issues with my boss that might also put her life at risk. I wasn't sure that I could save her again if something happened. But shit, what cha going to do? Nothing, but accept the cards that were dealt and take a bullet that can't be dodged. That was good for me, but I knew that wouldn't be good for Sabrina.

The next day rolled around, and I was all set to handle business. Dropping down at my desk, I made a quick call before dealing with Sabrina.

"'Sup, Cel?" answered the voice in my ear.

"'Sup, Diggy? You get that note from the boss?" I asked typing on my computer as I spoke to the air.

"No doubt. He's been spotted in Brookhaven," he said casually.

Diggy was my resident hacker and tech wiz who always helped in the tracking of my most active marks. Like me, he was a young dude who was employed by Senior Giulio. No one but the boss and I knew his locale, and we all respected it being that way considering the type of work he did with his tech skills.

"A'ight. I'm in the street cameras and . . ." I sat watching the images scroll back thanks to an algorithm Diggy developed that he called "Fish Eye."

The program made it easy to spy globally and trail anyone I wanted. I enjoyed it, and I bobbed my head in appraisal as Sepriani's car came in view. "Yeah . . . *That's* what's up, dude! There that rabbit goes. He's at a little fly restaurant. I need to hurry. Thanks, Dig."

"It's all good, man. Holla a'cha," he said before hanging up.

The convenience of him being at a restaurant was all God's. I had to thank Him or Her because He or She must have known it was time for Sepriani to die, and I was happy to be the one to deal the blow. Moving around, I texted Sabrina to wear a simple cocktail dress, something with a little color because I noticed that she was prone to black. I enjoy a woman in various colors, and I figured that today she could be a little different with it. I then told her where to meet me because I had a feeling that picking her up would be too much for her.

While I moved through my crib quickly dressing, I went back to my monitors checking out where the car landed. The area of Brookhaven had plenty of restaurants nearby that I could take Sabrina. The key here again was not to be in the view of my mark. If one was smart enough and paid attention to the killings, they could link up that I was around every time, except the opera murder. This time, I wanted to alleviate that, so as I stood tapping my finger on my desk and with my dress shirt open, I noticed the make of Sepriani's ride.

The sensation of a lightbulb going off in my mind had me moving to my drawer with my phones. Pulling on my gloves, I pulled out a tiny device, then frowned. "Nah, keep it simple, Cel."

Closing the drawer, I finished getting dressed in a simple white, button-down shirt, jeans, and black leather casual dress shoes. I then drove to Brookhaven and waited on Sabrina while keeping an eye on Sepriani's car. I had driven by the Italian restaurant he was at and made a note of his limo chilling in VIP parking. I was still deciding on what to do when Sabrina's car pulled up, then parked.

Walking up to her car, I knocked, then opened her door so that she could get out. For a second, I saw a glimpse of fear, but then it disappeared when she saw that it was me.

"Surprised that you hit me up, Sabrina," I said holding my hand out so that she could climb out of the car better.

"I had some questions, so I'm hoping you can answer them, or there won't be a date," she said gripping my hand, then closing the door to her ride and hitting the clicker to activate her alarm.

A husky chuckle came from me, and I let go of her hand. "I'm not about answering many questions, but I can see what I can do as long as they aren't pressing."

"Pressing?" I heard her say as she stepped up to me.

"Meaning, as long as you aren't stuck on talking about things that don't involve me. People are nosy, and I don't have time for accusations." Glancing down at her, I took in her appearance, "You look beautiful, Ms. Sabrina."

She stood in a soft yellow minidress that flared out, showing her pretty thighs. Her hair fell around her shoulders in waves and was parted in the middle while she kept her face natural with just a touch of lipstick. Sabrina was beautiful to me. I suddenly appreciated her company.

"Thank you, though I feel as if you just put me in my place," she said while holding her purse.

"No, I just wanted to be clear in my thoughts on things. Anyway, let's put all of this on hold. I want you to walk with me to this Italian restaurant across the street. I want you to check out the menu and tell me if you desire what they have. I'm on the fence about my tastes right now," I said while offering her my arm and taking her to the restaurant.

The weather was nice enough to walk, but chilly enough where Sabrina pressed closer to me. I felt like a king for sure. Pride had me poking my chest out as we walked into the restaurant. I had her standing at the side reading the specials in the restaurant while handing her a menu as I scoped the place.

Crowded as it was, I was able to make Sepriani who was standing and heading to where I could see several people were coming out of a hallway where the bathrooms were. It was then that my plan took shape.

Resting a hand against the small of Sabrina's back, I looked over her head, then scowled. "Hey, give me a moment. I need to excuse myself for a second. Left something in my ride. I'll be right back."

Sabrina's brown eyes assessed me as she turned her face up to me; then she nodded. "Okay. I don't think I want to eat here, though; it's too crowded."

"Yeah, me either. I have a taste for the tapas joint across the street, but hold that thought, okay?" I said stepping away.

"Okay," she simply said glancing back at the menu.

Relief flowed through my shoulders, and I moved quickly back outside. Every move I made was calculated and precise. When I scoped out the restaurant, I'd seen that I could easily slip into the restaurant in the backway undetected, so that's what I did. I kept my face down and worked the back door to make it inside the establishment unseen by human and camera's eyes. Quickly, I moved to the bathrooms, keeping a low profile and making sure that enough people went in where I did not become suspect. Stepping into the huge bathroom, I counted the stalls as I stood in front of the mirror. Traffic in and out of the bathroom was going to be a problem as the old man sat in his stall, probably shitting bricks.

That soon was confirmed when he started grunting. Flashing a humorous grin, various dudes quickly finished draining the pipe and leaving the old man and me alone. I took that time to lock the door then and walk two stalls over. Removing my shoes and positioning them in a way that appeared that I was still in the stall, I calmly dug in my pocket, pulled out my black handkerchief, then tied it around my face. I pulled out another, tied it over my head, then rolled up my sleeves.

For this one, I had to be hands-on, and I was down for it and hoped for a good fight. Slipping on my leather gloves, I waited for the old man to come out. A loud flush went down, along with the scent of the bowels of hell wafting through the bathroom. The sound of a latch unhinging, then the swing of his door opening put me in action.

Pushing out of the stall to rush him, I heard him say, "What—" before wrapping my arm around his neck and squeezing through the fat rolls.

This dude was a hefty man, so taking him down was not going to be a simple feat, but it would be a fun one. I rode Sepriani's back as he tried his best to grip me, and I laughed in the process.

"Don't make this harder than it needs to be," I muttered against his ear as he fought me.

I felt his elbow slam into the side of my ribs while he grunted through the spittle that ran down his beefy face. "Who sent you?"

His questions were my fuel, and I said nothing. I just kept squeezing and feeling his energy wane the more I held on. There was no way that I was going to speak to this dude, just in case this attack didn't go my way. So because of that, all he got was my hand over his mouth and nose. I watched him sputter and try to continue fighting me as I suffocated him.

Once his legs wobbled and collapsed under him, I let go of his mouth and let his breathing return to normal. It was then that I dragged him back into the stall, and positioned him back on the toilet. Yanking his pants down, because everyone knew that when a person dies, they always shit themselves, so I wanted to give the old head a little bit of respect.

Chuckling to myself about it, I slumped him in the natural form a person would look like if they had died of a heart attack or from asphyxiation. I then stood back with my chin clasped in my hand while studying him. This was my art, and I wanted to make sure that it was perfect.

My homework on him let me know that he had an allergy to seafood. On my wrist was a simple mixture of water that had been shrimp laden for several days in a tiny spray bottle. Pulling it out, I gripped his jaw, opened his mouth, and sprayed. I knew that if anyone did their CSI shit, it would appear that he might have accidently had traces of seafood in his meal.

That was a plus for me, which is why I clamped my hand over his mouth. I waited for him to wake back up and fight me. Once he did, I watched his throat work, then enjoyed how his bucking eyes rolled into the back of his skull. It was then that I punched him in his throat hard enough to collapse his trachea.

My work here was done. I watched him shake and quake. It took a damn long time, but eventually, all life in his eyes went blank, and it triggered his faulty heart. Waving to his faded spirit, I tilted my head to see art in how dying made his face seem peaceful. I then climbed over the top of the stalls back to my own.

Stepping out with my shoes back on and everything on me back in order, I unlocked the door, walked back into the stall holding my feet up and waited for people to come and go. I listened to conversations; then I slickly exited out the backway of the restaurant.

Once outside, I made it appear as if I was on the cell phone while walking around to the front again with a large group of people. Back inside, I slipped my hand against Sabrina's waist and felt her jump when she turned to see me again.

"Wow, you were gone a long time. What were you getting in your car?" she asked sizing me up.

A playful frown appeared on my face, and I shrugged. "I'm not sure that you want to know, considering I might have to kill you."

Sabrina's eyes became wide as saucers. My arms shot out, and I pulled her into a hug. "It was a joke, a bad one. I'm sorry."

I felt her hands on my chest, and the sensation against me had me feeling very good, but I knew I had to let her go and get out of the restaurant.

"Let's go to the tapas restaurant up the street, and I'll answer a few of your questions," I quietly said, guiding her out.

As we left, no curious screams happened, so I figured that no one had found Sepriani's dead body yet.

Once we were seated and we both ordered, I chuckled at how Sabrina watched me. "Dang, Sabrina, what's on your mind? You've been drilling holes into a brother this whole time. I'm sorry for having you wait as long as you did."

"Well, what were you doing?" she asked with a slightly irritated tone.

The way her face stayed blank, but her eyes were shooting me daggers amused me. "I was getting my jacket, then answering a phone call. It was an important business call with the aide office. I'm sorry about that; I truly am."

"Oh, well, okay," was all she said while shifting in her chair uncomfortably.

I made ready to say something joking and quirky to her, but before I could, Sabrina sucker punched me with her question.

"Who is Sepriani to Mister—I mean, Senior Giulio? I remember that name and—"

"No, you don't," I immediately said, cutting her off. "And back up off of that."

Hitting me with a slow blink, the waves in her hair moved while she shook her head and grabbed her glass of wine. "No. I need to know for business purposes as well as—"

"For things that don't pertain to you. I know he's not listed anywhere on your books, so no," I said in a low, rough tone. "This isn't the time or the place for this, even though we are nestled in an intimate and secluded area."

"You told me that you'd answer my questions if I went on this date with you. That was the stipulation, so honor that," she heatedly whispered.

Sitting back, I ran a hand down my face, then sighed. I just had killed the man she asked about, and now I had to focus my attention back on him without revealing that. Damn, she was persistent.

Dropping my hands in front of me and folding them on the table, I waited for our waiter to finish placing several small plates of savory foods in front of us before I spoke up.

"Is-he-the-same-man-you, ah . . . *handled* back when we first met? Is he? No, is he related in some way to that man?" Each word she said was enunciated in a way that stressed the importance to her.

Once again, it had me sitting back, formulating a careful response. "Where did you even hear that name?"

"It doesn't matter, and I'm asking the questions, not you," she snapped back.

I noticed that her hand holding the wineglass slightly shook as she hastily downed the red liquid. Shorty was getting her liquid courage, and it had me being very cautious.

"Yes, he's related. He's the father. That's all I got for you," I said with a quiet, even tone.

My face held no emotion; it was just a stoic blank expression when answering her. I wanted her to understand that I wasn't lying and that my voice was low so that no one could accidently hear us.

"Is he working for Giulio?"

There was a slight panicking tone to her voice when she asked that. I immediately knew that she was on some PTSD flashback shit, and if I said the wrong thing that she might fall apart, so I opted to keep my response simple but truthful.

"No, and you don't have anything to worry about with him," I said leaning over the table and gently taking her glass from her. "No worries and no threats, I promise you that."

Sabrina's stare held a fearful glaze to it. But once I gently said that she had nothing to worry about, that panicked gaze shifted to stare me in the eyes, then soften with relief. After that, our date went well, even as I noticed an hour later the many flashing lights flickering in the windows outside our restaurant.

Chapter Seven

Sabrina

As the weeks went on, Marcel and I went on more dates. It was a tricky kind of relationship he and I were building. But I found myself drawn to him more and more as time went by. For some reason, we felt it was best we kept our relationship on the low. Wait. I have to laugh. I said *relationship*. I wouldn't call what we had a relationship. No, not at all. It was more like a game of tag.

One day, I was it, and one day, I wasn't. I couldn't take Marcel's abrupt absences. After our first date, he disappeared for two weeks. I kept myself busy fixing the Giulios' books. Since they already owned adult entertainment clubs, rated-X video stores, and casinos, I'd convinced them to shut down the car wash as it was a typical way to launder money. I convinced them to do the same for a few of the Laundromats. Once that was handled, I told them to invest in property as in apartment complexes, duplexes, and even some house rentals. That way, they wouldn't look like the typical Italian smart guys who thought they were pulling a fast one on the government. I also convinced Senior Giulio to update some of the bistros. At least the financial system and some of the cooking apparatuses. He wouldn't allow anyone to change the front of the place—the dining area. I respected that.

I think I got so good at working for them because they respected me. They questioned me a hell of a lot, but they respected my intelligence. I wanted to ask where Marcel had gone but didn't want anyone to know he and I had gone on a date, or that I was a little worried about the asshole. I was watching the news one night and saw that NBA player Paul Watts had died in a car accident out in California. The fool had fallen asleep behind the wheel of the car. People were mourning him like he was the pope or something. Personally, I thought he was a coon-ass Negro because he thought he was better than those less fortunate than him, but that was neither here nor there.

Marcel showed back up out of the blue after his first disappearance. I wanted to be mad at him, but I didn't know for what. I wasn't his girlfriend. It was just that on our first date he had been the perfect gentleman. I didn't know what I was expecting, but it wasn't someone who could discuss a wide range of things. We went from politics to the racial tensions looming over the U.S., all the way back around to sports. I guess I shouldn't have been too surprised. I had to admonish myself as I'd been stereotyping him. He made me feel so comfortable while we were on the date that I almost completely forget he had threatened to kill me. I said *almost* because it was still in the back of my mind from time to time.

Still, I did give him a bit of the cold shoulder once he returned. But that didn't last long at all. By the time he sent flowers to my door three times and promised to make it up to me, I was over it. Growing up, I'd been one awkward-looking girl. But by the time I hit 20, things started to change. My body filled out. My clothes fit better. My 'fro was thicker and longer, and men started to pay attention. Now, I wouldn't say I was a virgin, but I'd only had sex with two men. The first time was awful, and the second time I'd rather forget altogether.

I said all that to say that I wasn't used to a man like Marcel taking an interest in me. I expected him to be like my father as in wanting something light, bright, and damn near white on his arm. I had no qualms about it; just speaking my mind. It was no secret that the darker the black man, the lighter he wanted his woman to be.

On our second date, Marcel invited himself into my home so he could cook for me. That was a good night too. Daddy was right. He did make the best damn steak this side of the Mason-Dixon Line. Not to mention he had a way of looking at me that made me remember that I was a young woman who still had hot blood pumping through my veins. He had a way of making my nipples hard and underwear wet without ever touching me. I'd never tell him that, of course. He was arrogant enough.

By our fourth date, I knew he hated popcorn because he didn't want the kernels to get in his teeth. He listened to classical music when he was stressed, and he hated to be touched when he hadn't invited a person to touch him. He'd taken me to Centennial Park so we could ride on that big Ferris wheel. Yes, there were times he disappeared to go to the bathroom and would find me thirty minutes later, but I didn't complain. I was doing something that I hadn't done since my father walked out on my mother. That was . . . enjoy life.

Our sixth date rolled around, and Marcel was nowhere to be found. He stood me up. I had to admit my feelings were more than hurt. I'd taken care in the way I'd dressed. He always made a joke about me wearing black all the time, so I chose something colorful. I chose a cream, backless dress with specks of purple since purple was his favorite color. He always complimented me on my hair, but I got more praises from him when it was curly or in its most natural state. So I let it fly wild and free. I was excited to see him because no matter what was going on around us—from some woman attacking Leo who claimed he had killed her son a week ago to my father being accused of sexual harassment by a schoolteacher— Marcel found a way to take me away from it all.

We had been intimate without having sex. Over the course of our time being together, the fear Marcel had spiked in me from the moment we met had subsided. We'd kissed, hugged, touched, and spoke about what the possibility of what our being together meant so I'd thought things were going good, but I guess I'd been wrong. That had been two weeks ago.

"Sabrina!"

I jumped and snapped my head around at the person who had called me. My mother was scowling at me. My twin sisters, Jimma and Jana, had amused smiles on their faces. I was quite sure it was noticeable that I didn't mention the three often. They wanted as little to do with my father as possible, so they often chose not to travel to Atlanta. When my sisters moved up North, one to Pennsylvania and one to New York, my mother chose to leave with them, settling in Manhattan to be an in-home nurse to the wealthy.

Mama was still beautiful in her older age. She fixed her dark skin with the perfect touch of makeup; her natural hair pulled back in a neat bun. She had on a nice blue pant suit that accentuated her voluptuous frame. We all sat in Giulio's as I picked it so I could see if Marcel would miraculously show up.

"Yes. I'm sorry, did you ask me something, Mama?" I asked.

"Yes. I've asked you twice if everything is going okay with you here. Lots of bad energy seems to be floating around Atlanta. First, the mayor dies. Then a diplomat is assassinated here, not to mention I just don't like this place."

"Mama, you don't like this place because Daddy is here," I told her.

"Isn't that all the reason needed? No matter where that man goes, or what he has his hands in, it always goes bad."

"Mama's right," Jimma chimed in.

She was the oldest and sterner of the twins. She had her long, brown hair pulled back into a sleek ponytail. Hazel eyes against their dark skin always made them stand out from the crowd. Both were very prominent attorneys in their field; Jimma a criminal attorney, and Jana, a corporate lawyer.

Jana added, "She sure is, and he has you wrapped around his finger because you're the baby and don't know what we do."

"Working for Daddy isn't going to turn out well for you, little sister," Jimma warned.

"If he does anything to cause my baby harm, I'm going to see to his demise personally. Trust me on that," Mama spat out venomously.

They were talking, and my mind was on Marcel, stuck on Marcel. Where the fuck was he?

"Daddy has been very helpful in my career here," I defended my father.

"Helpful?" Mama scoffed. "He has you working for Giulios, who are connected to the Seprianis, who are connected to the mob, who are connected to only God knows what. Exactly how is *that* helpful?"

There was that name again, but since the day Marcel assured me I had nothing to worry about, I hadn't worried at all.

I shrugged. "I don't know anything about that, Mama. I just make sure the books for their businesses are run efficiently and legally. For as long as I've been working for them, I've neither seen nor heard anything illegal.

And Leo is the interim mayor, for crying out loud. Daddy is on his way to becoming chairman on the Fulton County Board of Commissioners."

"Girl, the government are the biggest crooks there is, and it shows since a Giulio and your father are both apart of the government here," Mama chided. "You best keep your wits about you, girl. If you end up in prison, I will beat you to death, you understand me? No child of mine will have a criminal record."

"Yes, ma'am," I replied.

When Mama was going off on a tangent, my sisters and I had learned a long time ago to say "yes, ma'am" and keep quiet.

"How is that damn Katrina doing?" Mama asked.

I glanced over at my sisters and then back at Mama. Didn't know why she wanted to know about the woman who used to be daddy's mistress who was now his wife.

"She's fine, I suppose."

"Your daddy beat another baby out of her yet?"

I choked on my wine. Mama had to pat my back.

I grabbed a napkin to catch the spittle and slobber hanging from my bottom lip.

"Excuse me?" I barked.

The twins chuckled.

"Daddy beat Kat so badly once, the baby she was carrying fell out of her into the toilet," Jimma told me. "She miscarried."

Jana jumped in, "And he did that while she was the mistress. Who knows what he's doing to her now."

I was sure my face held the terror that I couldn't find a way to voice at the moment. There was no way I could believe my father was that kind of evil.

"I tried to warn that damn girl when she thought she was getting one up on me by being his mistress. Tried to tell her your daddy was the devil incarnate. Even tried to beat it into her myself that she was going down the wrong path, but she wouldn't hear me," Mama said.

Kat's words that the Lanfairs had been kicking her ass since the day she met them made more sense now than ever. I felt sorry for her, but she brought it on herself, I suppose. As the night went on, my mother and my sisters wanted to spend some time in Atlantic Station. They loved to shop, and Atlantic Station was like a shopping haven for them. From there, we headed to Phipps Plaza and then Lenox Square. I found it funny that they all had only flown in for the day. I found it even funnier that Daddy called to speak to Jimma and Jana, but when I asked if he wanted to speak to Mama . . . That was a different story.

"I'm busy. Ain't got time to tongue wrestle with the devil's mistress," he let fly.

"Well, since she considers you the devil, I don't understand why you wouldn't want to speak to her since she's your mistress."

Daddy hung up on me. Mama laughed, and the twins high-fived me. Regardless of what we all thought of Daddy, Mama still deserved some kind of victory. Daddy had indeed done her wrong, and for that, I would always hold some disdain for him, although not as much as Mama and my sisters.

A few hours later, they were gone, and I tiredly walked into my apartment. And, yes, Marcel was still on my mind. I could have easily texted him except for the fact he told me the number I'd texted before was no longer in service. He never kept a number long, and, this time, he left without giving me a new one to contact him on. He said he didn't need a digital leash. I cursed him to hell for that.

I cursed him the whole night until I fell asleep. I'd gone to sleep with my shades open, so the moonlight could bathe me in its essence. So, when I woke up to them closing, I knew I wasn't alone. I turned onto my left side in my bed. The covers rustled as I did so. I stared into the darkness chewing on my lip to stave off the nervousness I felt.

"Where have you been?" I asked. There was no malice in my tone. For as angry and hurt as I had been before, now I was secretly elated. No, more like I was relieved. Relieved he wasn't dead or hurt. Relieved he was whole, safe, and sound. And relieved he was back with me.

"Out. Had to handle some business," Marcel said.

Because it was dark in my room and silent, his voice boomed like surround sound. I welcomed it, even if I didn't like the vagueness of his answer.

"Do you have a wife or something somewhere? Some kids? If I'm going to play second fiddle, at least give me a heads-up."

He chuckled easily. I heard him yawn, which meant he was tired. I heard when he clicked the sensor, so the shades opened again. The moonlight illuminated the room like the sun rising on a new day.

"No. I told you, I was handling business. Was out of the country."

"What kind of business did you need to handle outside of the country?"

"You ask too many questions."

"And you answer too little."

"Did you miss me?" he asked.

"No."

"Liar."

"Among other things."

He chuckled again. I was quite sure he remembered the last time those same words were spoken, only *I* had been the one calling *him* a liar. There was silence between us for a few moments. I could feel and hear him moving closer to me. When he was standing on the right side of the bed, my heart rate picked up a bit. The covers moved, and my spine tingled.

"Did you shower?" I asked him.

"Before I came."

"How long have you been back?"

He slid in bed behind me. His chest was bare, but he still had on his jeans and socks. When he wrapped an arm around me, all was right in the world.

"A few hours," he said after kissing the back of my neck.

I closed my eyes and inhaled deeply. His scent blanketed me. I'd missed it. Just like before when we had lain together, our breaths synchronized. It was a soothing and calming ritual we had. I had so many questions, but I knew he wasn't going to give me a straight answer. After a few minutes, I turned in his arms so I could face him. His eyes were wide. Before I could launch into a diatribe, he kissed me. Slow at first, nibbling on my bottom lip, then the top one before letting his tongue trace the outline of them.

I relinquished all control I felt I needed to have at the moment. When his tongue sought out mine, my breathing hitched. My hand traveled up the muscles in his arms, then over his shoulder and down his shoulder blades. The velvety feel of his tongue against mine hypnotized me. Wherever he had been or what he had been doing became obsolete. His fingers played a beat up my spine; then his hand cupped the back of my neck, bringing me closer to him. He slid his thigh between mine. The friction he caused to my sex made me squirm around while his hand traveled into my hair. I could feel moisture pool into the purple lace boy shorts I had on. Just when I thought he was going to kiss me senseless, he eased back. He was gazing at me when my eyes finally fluttered open.

"I told you, you missed me," he said, arrogantly so.

I ran my hand over the waves in his head, then smiled. "Don't leave me again."

"I won't make you those kinds of promises."

My heart dropped a little bit, but I understood his position. "Will you at least get a permanent phone?"

He brought his hand around to cup my ass. "I'll consider the option."

"Either that or hear my mouth every time this happens."

He chuckled and said, "I'll take my chances. Businessmen such as I only need a phone every once in a while."

"So how will I contact you . . . let's say . . . if something happens and I need you?"

"Are you expecting something to happen where you will need me?"

I couldn't readily answer that question as I really only wanted to be able to pick up the phone and call him whenever I wanted. I didn't think it would be a good idea to tell him that as Marcel didn't seem like the type who wanted anybody to keep tabs on him. I cast my glance down; he hooked his finger against my chin and made me look back up at him.

"I'll always be here; even when you don't see me, I'm here. And even if I happen to be in another state or out of the country, my presence can and will be felt," he reassured me.

I smiled, then kissed him again. I moved my hand down his chest and abs, then went to move them around his waist until he winced. I jumped back.

"What's wrong?" I asked.

Marcel moaned out a bit, then slowly rolled onto his back. For a minute, I thought I'd done something wrong. He growled out, then slowly sat up. Punched a fist into my bed with one hand while his other arm wrapped around his waist.

I quickly stood, then pressed the remote to turn the light on in my room. I moved around the bed to stand in front of him. Obviously, he was in pain. It was only then that I noticed the purple and blackened bruise that adorned the left side of his abdomen. He had his head down, forehead creased in apparent pain. I also noticed his knuckles were battered and bruised as well. His skin was dark, so for bruises to be visible meant he had been in one hell of a fight.

He looked up at me; then I saw the stitched cut on his jaw. The part that had been hidden by the pillow.

First, I gasped. "Oh my God, Marcel, what happened to you?" I squeaked out.

"Comes with the territory," was how he answered before standing.

"Comes with the territory? And what *territory* is that? The kind where you get your ass kicked?"

I think at that moment, I realized I'd started to care about him way more than I cared to admit.

Marcel looked at me and grinned. "You should see the other guys."

He was making light of the situation. I followed him as he stalked into my bathroom, then invaded my medicine cabinet.

"Got something in here other than this store-brand shit?" he asked tossing around bottles of Tylenol and Advil. I stared at him for a long time. "Sabrina, I'm in pain. Help me out, baby."

I moved over to the medicine cabinet and closed it. "Yeah, come out here," I said as I walked out of the bathroom.

I went to my closet and pulled down a small black traveling bag. I looked inside until I found some Vicodin and Percocet from when I had a root canal, then tossed the bottles to him. He didn't say anything. Popped the top to the Vicodin and poured three in his mouth from the bottle.

"Thank you," he said, then pocketed the bottles. "I'm keeping these."

I shrugged. We watched each other silently. "Did this happen to you while you were out of the country?"

He sighed. "For this to work, you're going to have to stop asking me those kinds of questions."

I stared him down as I was sure he knew that response didn't sit well with me. Still, I responded, "As you wish," then left him in the closet.

I turned the lights out and crawled back into bed. I'd never seen his house, couldn't ask who left the bruises on him, and didn't know where he disappeared to from time to time. It was safe to say I knew right then we wouldn't have a typical relationship. I didn't ask him anything else about what had happened to him. Just like I was doing more than financially advising the Giulios, that was the night I figured out Marcel's job entailed more than being an aide and a cook. I didn't know to what extent, but the pieces were coming together. And as time went on, they would continue to fall into place.

Chapter Eight

Marcel

After taking out Sepriani, my schedule had become busy. Using my cover as an aide, once clearance to travel by plane came back, I had to leave. Paul Watts was out of the city in Cali, so I had to trail after him and use that moment to cross him off my list. After that, I got a notice that another hit of mine was active in Dubai, so I flew to Paris. Checked off some others on my list, then made my way to Dubai.

Another reason why I was gone so long was that I was laid up in a hospital. My last mark was a beastly motherfucker. He broke my young ass down and made me work for my kill, which was all the more fun for me. Dude cracked my ribs, cut my jaw, left the imprints of his fists in my sides, and had me close to death. However, what I did to him was worse. Gruesome, bone breaking, but I won't go into all of that.

After disposing of my mark's decapitated and chopped up body, I then went to the hospital to heal up a little. I wasn't at any ordinary hospital, of course. I went to where people like me could hide and not be questioned, which wasn't your typical mom-and-pop's clinic. The doctors who ran the place were the best in their field, hired by people like boss to keep things low-key and unassuming. From the outside, it looked like a hotel, but just beneath the surface—underground—was a state-of-the-art medical facility like no other.

Once I rested, I flew to France, chilled, drove to Norway, chilled, took the train to London, chilled, and then flew home. Had to cover my tracks. Of course, I found my way in Sabrina's arms too, but as she said, everything wasn't perfect or good, but when it was, it was all that mattered.

As time passed, I took her to my crib. Not the warehouse—never there, but the place I laid my head down and tried to live as if I had a normal life. The day that happened was a good one. I believe it was maybe two months or so after we had been doing our thing.

"Why haven't you brought me to your place before, Marcel? This place is nice," she said.

The way she expressed her enthusiasm always made me feel good and always amused me too. It had me walking up behind her to slide my arms around her waist while she stared at the skyline of my place. Dropping my head, I kissed the back of her neck right where her hair stopped. I enjoyed that spot. It always carried a light lingering of her perfume, and it always calmed me.

"You know why, baby. Busy, and I like to visit you. It became a routine that was ours," I said, letting her go. "This is my spot. You can make it yours and take it in while I go chill on the couch."

"Oh, so you're not going to show me around?"

While watching Sabrina, I chuckled because she had her hands on her hips and had the nerve to furrow her brows and give me the upset face.

Again, it was why I enjoyed her presence. It was the little things, and it had me reaching out to tilt her head up by her chin to kiss her.

Feeling how easy it was now and how good it felt to have her soften for me, to feel that heat rise between us made me grin against her lips.

I stepped back and waved my hand in a sweeping gesture. "Nah. See, I just figured, since my bedroom is viewable because this is a loft, and behind you is the second bedroom, and behind me is the massive bathroom and shower, that I had nothing to show you."

I moved to stand close to her with our shoes touching while staring down at her, "My place is simple. Chef-style stainless steel kitchen. Sunken living room. Closed off elevator and parking garage below. Not sure what else to show you, unless you're trying to see my bed."

Sabrina gave me a slick smirk, then blushed only for me as she reached up and caressed my jaw. "Just your place and I like it."

Taking the time to incline slowly toward her for a kiss again, I reached out to tuck her hair behind her ear. "You sure?"

Always feisty, my baby flicked her hand out to pop me on my chest. I checked out how her face lit up in humor while she laughed at me.

Looking past me and pointing toward the kitchen, I chuckled as she said, "Since you're my host and tour guide, where're your snacks? I mean, may I have some chips, fruit . . . something?"

Since being with her, I became used to her prissy spurts. Whenever I was with her, I learned that she looked forward to whenever I decided to jump into the kitchen. The sentiment made me feel good and fed my ego because she knew that I had a passion for it. Sharing that real part of me and watching how she enjoyed my food always gave me a sense of pride as a chef and as her man.

"Go sit, baby," I said laughing, then led her to my living room. As I headed to the kitchen, I told her, "I'll hook you up with some wave."

"Wave?" she repeated as she sat.

"Swag, sweet treats, stuff." Now in the kitchen, I rolled up the sleeves of my shirt, then went through my cabinets.

I pulled down some plates, then went into the refrigerator looking around. Red wine was Sabrina's favorite, so I grabbed that with some glasses, setting them to the side. Searching through the refrigerator, I threw some stuff together. Fruit, cheese, some meat, pita bread, hummus, pickles, and carrots were all placed on a platter for her.

Our time of intimacy together was good. We relaxed, watched movies, talked about stupid stuff, then when the mood hit, we spoke on political things as well, especially what was going on with the Giulios and her father. It was while I was going upstairs to grab her one of my shirts to sleep in since Sabrina didn't want to leave, that things got funky. While I was in my walk-in closet, the sound of my work cell went off, causing me to grunt aloud. I had told Sabrina that I didn't like to be tethered to a cell, but that was far from the truth. I had one cell that had to be linked to my boss.

That annoying ring drew me out of my closet and to my nightstand where I had it in a drawer strapped to the underside of it. Pulling it out of its sleeve, I hit answer and stepped back into my closet. My life was important to me. So was keeping my identity to myself. I had to make it a priority to keep Sabrina from ever finding out the real deal.

Listening closely, I heard several coded messages come my way, and I stored them all to memory before hanging up. Exhaling, I stepped out of the closet with a shirt, running into Sabrina. She stood there looking sweet faced and beautiful with many questions floating behind her eyes. Dropping my head, I rubbed the back of my neck, then looked back up at her.

"Work is calling. I know that it's late, but I need to leave," I said with a toneless voice.

Checking out how she just stood there watching me, I assumed that she was about to go off on me, but she didn't. She nodded, then turned to head back down to the main level of my place.

I caught up to her on the stairs where I reached out to grab her arm gently. "I'd like you to stay here."

"Okay," was all she said in a strained, quiet tone.

Damn, I could feel the vibe coming off her. She wasn't hitting me with anger, but there was a lot of disappointment, along with a feeling that she wanted to question me. I had hoped that we didn't come to this, so I was doing all I could to keep her from walking down this road of my real work. I saw that she still had that peculiar look on her face as she hovered near me.

As I got ready to turn, she stepped forward, then paused and turned to look up at me on the steps. "Take me with you. I want to get some air."

"I can't do that," I said, finality in my tone.

Dipping back upstairs, taking them two at a time, I tossed the shirt on the bed and sat down to put my kicks on and switch out my top for a black, long sleeve compression shirt.

"Marcel," I heard her say while I moved around my room.

I could see Sabrina from the corner of my eye watching quietly, and it made me nervous suddenly.

"I can't do that, Sabrina," I said again, putting more bass in my voice.

Yelling at her and getting heavy handed with her was something I didn't want to do. I wasn't going to put my hands on her ever, and I wasn't going to batter her with words to the point that she shrank away, but fuck, I had a hardheaded woman on my hands. Since our time together, it had been crazy how easily I had shared half-truths about my life, so much so that I had told her things that just didn't add up to the life of an aide. The fact that she never vocally questioned it amazed me and had me digging her even further. However, now, I could sense that something had changed just that fast between us.

"Yes, you can, so take me," she said coming to my side. "It's as simple as that. You're just doing some aide work, right?"

Clearing my throat, I moved past her, down the stairs, then to the door, while grabbing my coat. "Yeah. But I'm not taking you. Damn! You'll be good here, I promise."

As I gripped my coat, Sabrina was hot on my heels, and I knew that there was no shaking her.

"I'll be good with you; I promise you that too. Let's go," she said, ignoring me completely.

"Shit, Brina," I spat out, shaking my head and walking through the door.

I knew that yelling at her had shaken her a little, but her determination had her following, and I didn't have the time to break her spirit and cause a huge blowup, so I let it slide. I just knew that I had to think of how to divert what I had to do because she was not giving up. Especially, no matter how many times I said stay at my place. The more I yelled, the more it only pushed her to come with me. Which is exactly what happened.

We were both in my car when I whipped it over several lanes and had us heading to Giulio's. The cords of my mark had me needing to be in the same area, so I figured that I could head to the restaurant and have her chill there while I "excused" myself to Senior Giulio's office, then crept out the backway. That was my intent, and I felt good about that as we pulled up.

"I'm going to be a minute while grabbing some things from the boss's office," I said while guiding her inside. "You just chill in the dining room, and I'll get you when I'm done."

Still sizing me up, Sabrina took my hand and squeezed it. "Okay. Don't take too long, though. Being here off-hours always make me think about working."

Chuckling, I kissed her lips and let her hand go. "I promise I won't be too long. Just sit back and relax. I can get you wine if you want."

"Sure, that would be great," she said pulling off her coat and sitting down while nervously looking around.

Nodding my head, I went to the back and grabbed one of the best red wines we had. The killer in me thought about lining her drink with a sleeping agent, but I had left that back at the crib, so that was out of the question. Setting the empty glass down, I poured some wine, then set the bottle down.

"I'll be back," I said with a gentle smile.

I headed to the office, stepped in, closed it, and locked it. After changing out of my clothes into something to blend in with the environment where I was going, I tapped on a panel, slid it to the side, then walked into a dark corridor. Closing it back, I followed the narrow passage to a hidden door behind a wall of ivy. Once outside, I headed to the car, climbed in, then pulled off. I flipped on some music to get in the zone. Drake spit a hook that had me nodding my head. Making it away from Giulio's, I turned to a neighborhood called Red Hooks. Slowing down, I glanced around, parked, and got out of my ride. Popping the trunk, I dug and released a lever that let a drawer slide out. A handgun with several silencers lying beside it greeted me, along with a hunting knife.

Taking them both, I closed the trunk, then jumped back, pointing my Glock. In front of me was Sabrina. She stood staring at me in fear and confusion. While noticing her, I saw her hands shaking, and I inwardly cursed, dropping my gun and looking around.

"How'd you get here?" I asked, snatching her by the arm and moving her back to the side of the car.

Pulling her arm from my hand, she looked up at my face, her eyes blazing, and she hissed low, "I knew that you weren't coming back when you said that. Knew you were trying to trick me, Marcel, so I went to your car and got in the backseat. You were so busy trying to get me in the restaurant that you left the doors unlocked. I lay down and kept quiet, just watching you."

Exhaling, I pushed the side of the door, then moved back. Music was going on at a club a block away from us. The club had an outside dance floor which was often more crowded than the inside. It was where I needed to go, and now I wasn't sure if I was going to take down my mark. This kill was on a time frame, and Sabrina was fucking it up for me, which was apparent because I should have caught her in the back of my ride.

She had me fucking up.

"I don't have time for this. Stay here," I ordered in a harsh voice.

Tugging at the cap that was on my head, I pulled it down where it covered my face. Running with a low gait, I held my gun close to me and waited near a car. In this area, cameras didn't exist, so I knew that I could go at this guerrilla style with no problem, except that there was a problem. While I waited, I saw Sabrina in the distance. She kept herself hidden, but I still saw her watching me.

This part of my life was never supposed to cross over with her. We had been doing so good, now . . . Now, things were going to change drastically. Rough, strident laughter began, and it had me peeking over to see my mark in the middle of a large crowd on the outside dance floor. Nigga was cackling and shit, with the scent of blunts saturating the air. Feeling anxious because Sabrina was here, that fact had me pissed and had me pushing off the car. Kneeling, I unloaded my gun on the people in the crowd.

My orders were to spray rain and make it look gang related while singling out my main target. As I shot off rounds, I saw who I was after. Glancing back over my shoulder, I shook my head and got up, then rushed my mark. Hunter knife in my hand, I tackled him and slammed the blade in his skull. Surrounded by fallen bodies, blood was all around me. Some survivors screamed, and I kept slamming that blade in the guy's head before leaving it there on purpose as a symbol. Quickly standing, I took my gun to finish off the few that were still alive, and then ran off in the opposite direction of where I came from.

Finding a place where I could stand in the darkness, I tried to catch my breath. The whole time I was thinking about Sabrina. I knew she had to see the gore that I left, and I wondered why today had to be the day she would stumble onto my truth. Anyone with a sane mind would not be around me and would try to go to the authorities—and I couldn't have that.

I took a back route to get to my car. Once I made it there, I saw that Sabrina was gone; that is until I glanced in the car where she lay covering her face in the backseat. I pulled off my cap, wiped off the blood on my face, then pulled off my gloves. Popping the trunk, I tossed it in the open plastic bag in the back as I pulled off my shirt and tossed it in there as well. I stood outside in an open area undressing, grabbing water bottles and pouring it on me to cleanse my skin. Once done, I pulled out the fresh clothes that I always kept in the trunk.

After that, I took my gun, reloaded it, slid it my pants, and closed the trunk. Hopping in my ride, I said nothing as I turned my rearview mirror to focus on Sabrina's quiet form.

"I'm sorry, baby. This is the last thing that I wanted you to see," I said, keeping my voice even and in control.

My choice in words and tone had to be carefully given out to keep her from flipping on me and making things messier than they already were. The soft shift of her body had me watching her sit up. Wetness coated her cheeks and sprinkled in her long lashes. A gut pain had me slumping my shoulders and bowing my head.

"You really . . . really weren't supposed to see or know about this," I said, more so to myself than her.

The touch of Sabrina's hand on my shoulder had me running my palm down my face as I held the gun that was holstered in my back, now on my lap. I turned and stared into the face of a girl I had once saved and now had to take out.

"I love you, Marcel. I didn't see anything. I don't know nothing, and I didn't hear nothing," Sabrina said, her tone thick, but voice light.

"But you did, baby. I know you did," I said slipping my fingers over my gun.

"I turned when you stood up. I couldn't watch. I just couldn't watch," she said through her tears.

"Still . . ." I muttered staring into her eyes letting the silence fill up the voice of the pain we both were feeling.

When Sabrina's hand dropped, and she slid back staring at me with a solemn gaze, the quiet between us spoke for us and said what we both knew. That we were done. Gripping my gun, I turned to get a better view of her beautiful face one last time.

"I love you, baby," I said, surprised at the feeling I hadn't experienced since my family died.

"Damn," was all I could say as I knew how the rest of the events had to play out.

Chapter Nine

Sabrina

As I gazed unapologetically at him, I caught a glimpse of the gun in his hand. I knew what he was saying without him even having to say the words. His repeated apologies were not really for the fact that I'd found out about a part of his life that I shouldn't have. No. His apologies were for the fact that he was going to have to kill me.

Many would question how either of us could feel emotions for the other so strongly when we had just started dating, only two or so months in. No official title had even been placed on us, but if you thought about it the way we did, we'd had a connection to each other years before actually dating. Call it the laws of attraction. The universe brought me back to him and him back to me. Was it destiny? I didn't know. Fate? I couldn't call it. All I knew was, he had raised his gun dead center between my eyes.

For the first time in a long time, I wasn't afraid of him killing me. He told me he loved me. I didn't even think he knew he'd said it. He was zoned out, somewhere in his own mind thinking about whatever it was he thought about during times like this. To be honest, technically, I'd never actually seen him kill anyone. I'd heard an arrow whizzing through the air, and the next thing I knew, Antonio Sepriani was dead. I'd heard gunshots but didn't see Marcel pull the trigger. I assumed he did because when he walked into the crowd, shots rang out. His back was turned to me, so I couldn't say for certain it was him who had done the shooting. And I had no idea what he had done when he dropped down to the ground because, by then, I was already running back to his car.

Nervous tension settled around us.

"You're going to kill me?" I asked him.

"Goddamn it, Sabrina, why couldn't you just stay in the restaurant?" he snapped.

It would be the first time he had ever raised his voice at me. The first time I'd ever seen the look of utter disgust on his face when it came to me. The first time I knew that his urge to kill me was strong.

"Because I'm stubborn. Because I wanted to know more about you than you were willing to tell me."

He closed his eyes, then inhaled and exhaled hard. "Your incessant need to know is going to get you killed."

My voice was shaky when I asked, "By you?"

My question seemed to anger him further as he turned around and beat the steering wheel while aggressively groaning under his breath. After he was done taking out his frustration on the inanimate object, he cranked the car and sped away. I had no idea where he was taking me. No idea what he intended to do. For as much as I cared about the man, I wouldn't allow him just to kill me if he planned on taking me somewhere to do it. That was how being near him these days made me feel. Marcel made me feel like I could take on the world. I needed that. I needed him. Before him, I simply coasted through life. Marcel gave me a reason actually to live it. While it would hurt me to do so, I had every intention of fighting for my life.

But to my surprise, my worst fear didn't materialize. Marcel pulled up to the front of my high-rise. Valets rushed around to the driver side, anxious to make a tip. He waved them off.

"Get out," he told, more like ordered, me.

"I don't want to. I want to talk—"

He whipped around so fast my words got stuck in my throat. I gasped and leaned back. His eyes were red and, at that moment, I realized I'd crossed a line from which there could be no return.

He snapped, "Get.the.fuck.out."

I still had tears in my eyes, and his tone of voice just made them worse. I opened the door and placed one foot on the cobblestone ground.

As stupid as it sounded, stubbornness was rooted in my DNA. So, of course, I couldn't just get right out of the car.

"Will I see you again?"

"Oh my fucking God. Sabrina, no. Get out."

I got out of the car, then slammed the door. I turned around to get one last look at him, but he was already speeding away. People watched me with curiosity and some with pity. I was sure they all wanted to know why I was crying, but I'd already made a fool of myself once that day. I'd no intention of doing it again. I rushed onto the elevator, then headed up to my place.

I lollygagged around the rest of the night, hoping Marcel didn't mean it when he said I'd never see him again. Part of me wished and hoped he would change his mind and find a way into my home without me knowing like he had done before. But no such thing happened. I realized that I'd messed up a good thing before it had started. That was why I said that day he had killed me. A little piece of me died when I realized he was gone and never coming back.

Four weeks later . . .

"Today marks a good day in the city of Atlanta as Interim Mayor Leo Giulio congratulates his good friend and avid campaign supporter, Othello Lanfair. A private investigator uncovered an elaborate scheme by Lanfair's opponent, Joe Peppercorn, to tarnish Lanfair's image. As you know, Lanfair is going after Peppercorn's

seat as chairman of the Fulton County Commissioner's office."

I watched in silence with everyone in Giulio's as Channel 2 Action News reported. We'd all gathered around the TV, anxious to see how the news would spin the events. Daddy's face appeared on the screen.

"I'm smiling because these unfounded allegations have been declared null and void. For Ms. Carthan to become a part of a devious scheme as such not only paints Peppercorn in a bad light, but she's singlehandedly made it harder for any woman who is a true victim of this kind of crime. Women have a hard enough time as it is getting people to believe them when they are sexually harassed or sexually assaulted. I'm disgusted by the length Peppercorn has gone to win this election."

Cheers erupted in the restaurant as Leo patted Daddy's back. Daddy actually looked as if he believed what he was saying. This was a major win for him. The fact that Peppercorn had been found to know the teacher accusing Daddy of sexual harassment had been a plus for us. Then for Daddy to use the fact that women have a hard time getting justice when reporting rape and sexual harassment sent his chances of winning the office through the roof.

With Leo seen shaking his hand and smiling along with him, it was indeed a good day on this side of Atlanta. Kat was all smiles. Leo's wife Machonne was applauding as if she had just won an election. Leo's wife was insolently black. She wore her hair natural and often boasted of the fact she was pro-black, which drew the ire of the Republicans in office. The place was packed with supporters. The smell of food permeated the room. Several times, I'd snuck away to the kitchen to see if Marcel was there. I'd done that for the last four weeks. When I wasn't working my legitimate job and had to keep track of the Giulios' finances, I always looked for him, but I never found him.

I mindlessly picked at my food while utensils clacked and clattered against plates and bowls. Daddy noticed it and asked if I was okay. I wasn't but lied and said I was. After a while, I got tired of the politics talk and excused myself. I got home in record time, where I showered, grabbed a blanket and a book, then settled down for the night.

As the weeks went on, I started to get used to Marcel not being around. There was no number to call. I thought about just showing up at his place but then thought better of it. My life had gone back to the way it was before I met him. It was routine; work and home. I'd never been a socialite, unlike my twin sisters. I didn't like hanging out. Was a loner. Didn't have too many friends, and the ones I had knew not to ask me out. More than likely, I'd turn them down. I was an acquired taste, and not many people were able to swallow it.

November 1st rolled around. Election talk was in high gear. Daddy was campaigning hard, had become the face of women's rights. I laughed so damn hard at that irony— especially since he had smacked Kat and since Mama and the twins told me he had beat a baby out of Kat at one time. Leo had made it known that once the election for mayor in 2013 rolled around, he was throwing his hat in the ring as had been the plan all along.

Things were going well until the Feds raided the restaurant and Laundromats. Agents from the IRS's Criminal Investigation office invaded the Giulios' life like a hell storm. Acting U.S. Attorney Ramon Parker, of the Northern District of Atlanta, had a hard-on for them. They were going back years in their investigation. It wasn't a good look for Leo who told my father to distance himself for the sake of the overall plan.

"You let me worry about this end," Leo told Daddy one day in his office. It was a day after the Feds had raided the place.

"You sure about this?" Daddy asked.

Leo nodded. The stress lines were creased into his forehead like they had been drawn there.

"I'm positive. Stay the course. For the sake of the whole agenda, just put distance between us. I'll figure out how this is going to go."

He sat behind his desk, hands steepled in front of his mouth. The restaurant was still operating, as Senior Giulio was a proud man and refused to close the doors. I'd just walked in with all the files in my hands. I laid ten black books on his desk. Now it stood to reason as to why the Giulios brought me on so soon. They must have known the Feds were coming for them.

"I'd already taken the liberty of cleaning up the files as far as ten years back. I'm glad I did. It was a tricky thing to do, but I got it done. Now, everything will not be peaches and cream because we don't want it to be perfect. We want a few discrepancies, but we want them to be minor," I told him.

He nodded, a frown still etched on his face. "And you're sure about this? We got nothing to worry about?"

"No, Leo. I know what I'm doing," I said, more aggression in my tone than I had wanted there to be.

He snapped his head up and looked up at me. At first, I thought the frown had deepened because of my tone of voice with him, but I turned around to see the federal agent over the case stalking down the hall. He was a black man. Cute in the face, caramel complexion, and stocky build. Chewed on a toothpick and was always smiling like he knew something you didn't know.

"You seem so sure of yourself, little lady. Sherman and Hughes pay you top dollar in their firm, I heard," Agent Stokely said to me, referencing the financial advising firm where I worked.

I wanted to tell him I was indeed sure of myself but didn't readily want to speak to a federal agent or any officer of the law, for that matter. My sister had always told me to remain silent in certain situations, even if it was mundane talking.

I grabbed my clutch from my father's hand, then looked at the agent. "Agent Stokely, if you wish to speak to me, you can do so through my attorney, Jimma Lanfair. She'll be more than happy to set up a time and date where she will accompany me wherever you need me to be," I told him.

I didn't give him time to respond. I tucked my clutch under my right arm like the lady I was and dipped. Danny was my shadow as my father didn't want me to go anywhere alone. He was afraid of me being followed for some reason. Danny opened the back door of the black Navigator for me, then helped me inside.

Something about Danny had been off as of late, as well. I would catch him watching me. I mean, it wasn't unusual for him to watch me as he was told to do so by my father. But sometimes, the look in his eyes prickled my skin.

Danny followed me while I went to Whole Foods to grocery shop. His presence normally annoyed me. On this day, I didn't care that he was around. People watched us wondering who of importance I was. Most of them had no idea or didn't care one way or the other that I was Othello Lanfair's daughter. But because Danny had an earpiece in his ear, wore an all-black suit, and refused to let anyone get within a few feet of me, they all stared and whispered.

Once I'd gotten what I needed, he took me home. I kicked my shoes off at the door. Checked my messages. Jimma had called. Told me I needed to answer my cell. I checked my purse as I hadn't heard it ring. When I noticed it wasn't there, I went to my bedroom to find it lying on the bed. I stopped in my tracks. Not because my phone was on the bed, but because underneath it lay a lilac. I spun on my heels. Blood pressure spiked instantly.

"Marcel," I called out.

I was hoping, wishing, and praying he was there. I rushed to my walk-in closet and looked around. Lilacs had been his mother's favorite flower and, ironically, mine as well.

"Marcel, are you in here?" I called out again.

I knew I probably looked like a fool spinning on my heels, wringing my shirt and biting down on my bottom lip. The locks turned on my door, and my heart beat ferociously against my rib cage, only to be deflated once I saw it was Danny. Gun in hand, he came in looking for anything that didn't feel as if it didn't belong.

"You okay, Ms. Lanfair?"

I blinked away tears of disappointment. "I'm fine, Danny. Thank you."

"I heard you yelling," he said, baritone deathly laced with intent to kill had I not been okay.

"I'm okay. Do you know if anyone has been in my place?"

"Mr. Lanfair was earlier. Said he noticed you hadn't been yourself. So he stopped by to check on you, but you had already gone. The cleaning crew stopped by as well. You sure you're okay?"

My heart deflated a little more. Daddy knew my favorite flowers were lilacs, so it made complete sense that he left one on my bed. I felt so foolish that I could have screamed. Instead, I simply nodded.

Danny gave me a look of skepticism before touring my penthouse to be certain. Once he was satisfied that I was indeed okay, he left again.

There I was damn near six weeks later still wishing, looking, hoping, and praying Marcel would come back, and he hadn't. I felt stupid. Figured it was high time I got over the man and let well enough be enough. I talked a good game. Gave myself a good pep talk while putting away groceries. Even still, echoes of the dates we had and times spent together lingered in my mind.

I was just getting into a good sleep when I heard the locks to my front door opening. I figured it was just Danny doing his nightly walk-through. He did that from time to time, especially when Daddy felt the need to have him guard me on a twenty-four-hour time frame. It

annoyed me that he had easy access to my home in such
a way. I threw my covers off me and stormed into my
front room, set to tell Danny he could no longer just walk
in if there wasn't an emergency. I wanted him to call me
first before invading my privacy as such. Or I could have
simply been in a funky mood because I knew life had to
go on without Marcel.

"Danny, you can't just barge in here like—"

My words got lost in transmission. The man standing
in my front room wasn't Danny. Butterflies took resi-
dence in the pit of my stomach. His facial hair had grown
out a bit more, but he looked the same. Suddenly, I felt
conscious of my appearance. I had on a simple white,
extra long tee shirt and nothing else. Hair was probably
all over my head as I hadn't cared enough to tie it down.
Breath was stale since I had been lying in bed for hours.

Meanwhile, he stood in gray sweats, a fresh pair of
white kicks, and a thick, black tee shirt that hugged the
muscles in his upper body. I couldn't read the look on his
face and didn't know what to say to start the long-awaited
conversation I'd wanted to have with him for weeks now.
I went from being remorseful about the place I'd put him
in to being angry that he just walked away so easily. I
would go from wishing he would come back to cursing
him to hell, swearing he could stay where the hell he was.

I opened my mouth to say something, but he held up
his hand to stop me. "Don't, Sabrina. If you say the wrong
thing, it's going to piss me off," he said.

I'd missed his voice so much. That deep, penetrating
timbre always did something to me. Still, I needed to
speak. Needed him to know some things. I had to get
some shit off my chest.

"I—"

I backed away a little when he stepped closer to me as I
didn't know what this visit meant. But the look on his face
told me I needed to be quiet. For as badly as I wanted this
to be a social call, the last time we had seen each other

the threat of him killing me was ripe. Obviously, since he was in my place and had come through the front door, Danny wasn't posted out there anymore. He stepped closer. I stepped back again.

"What do you want?" I asked him, timidly.

My eyes scanned the room for anything I could use as a weapon, if need be. When he stepped closer this time, I tried to back away, but he reached out and grabbed me. The soul-stirring kiss he planted on me told me all I needed to know. I was scared. I was confused. I was elated. I was so many emotions wrapped into one that I forgot to breathe as he kissed me. His hands gripped my waist, then snaked around to grip my ass so tightly it was painfully pleasurable, causing a shiver to dance up and down my spine.

Both of my hands came up to cup the back of his strong neck. He smelled so damn good. Just as I remembered, but richer this time around. That woodsy spice of a scent tickled my olfactory senses and gave me the comfort of familiarity. I kissed him with just as much fervor as he kissed me. . . . Tongues touching and dancing eagerly as we devoured each other. I didn't even realize he had backed me into the minibar in my front room. Not until he lifted me, then set me on top of it. Yes, my naked ass was atop the cool granite surface, and I was sure there would be a wet spot left there when I moved.

I had so many questions. It was just in my nature, but at the moment, I couldn't think of one to ask him. I could sense him stepping out of his shoes. We only broke the kiss long enough for me to help him pull his shirt over his head. It dropped to the floor in a swoosh. Next came his sweats and boxer briefs. I realized that Marcel's sleight of hand was something to be reckoned with. I hadn't seen him pull the golden-wrapped condom from his pocket, and while he kissed me, he expertly ripped it open and placed it on.

I was so aroused—wet and horny—that foreplay really wasn't needed. He lifted my bottom from the bar, then worked his way inside of me. It was a slow task as he was well endowed, and it had been awhile since I'd had sex.

"Ooh," was all I could say, followed by my hiss and my nails digging into his arms.

"You can talk now," he told me in a low, guttural tone. . . . One that told me he was being sarcastic. No way had he expected me to talk when his dick was causing me blinding pleasure. My thighs quaked uncontrollably. My back arched against my will, and the only conversation going on was between our bodies. Marcel switched between fucking me long, hard, and deep, to a steady beat that rocked my soul to the core. He pushed my shirt over my breasts, palmed one while his mouth sucked the nipple on the other. The stimulation was almost too intense for me to handle. I'd never had sex that sent electricity through every molecule of my DNA.

I rocked my hips back against his. My orgasm was so close I could taste it. His dick swelled inside of me. The more I moaned, the more I threw back every thrust he gave to me, the harder he became. But it wasn't until he isolated my hip movements, made me stop moving so he could control the show, that I lost my mind. I moaned, and probably even screamed, so deep and melodious that I was sure the neighbors knew his name. It wasn't long after he took me on a natural high that he came crashing down with me.

It took us awhile to get ourselves together. Once the high of the sex started to dissipate, we still had to talk about the elephant in the room. On steady, but clearly tired legs, he took me to my bedroom. It was only when he laid me on the bed that he removed himself from me. I watched as he moseyed to the bathroom. Heard the water running and knew he was probably cleaning himself up.

Was pleasantly surprised when he brought out a warm, soapy towel to do the same to me. Afterward, he crawled into bed behind me.

Silence serenaded us as the moon played voyeur.

"You placed me in a bad situation, Sabrina. You're supposed to be dead," his deep voice rumbled. "You were never supposed to know that side of me."

I swallowed, body still humming from the sex we'd had. "I don't know what you're talking about," was my answer.

"Yeah, you do."

"No, I don't."

He turned me over to look at him. "I know what you're trying to do; trust me. I get it, but for us to do whatever this is we're doing, we have to be up front. You know what I did."

I shook my head. There would be no way I could—or would—ever admit it, to him or anyone else.

"No, I don't know anything. As far as I know, you're an aide to Leo Giulio, and you cook in his kitchen. That's all I know. That's all I'll ever know."

We stared at each other for a long time. I had no idea what he was thinking, but that was the night I saved my own life. For as cruel as it sounded, if I had admitted to seeing him do anything, even after he had fucked me, I would have gone to sleep and never awakened again.

Chapter Ten

Marcel

My grandmother would say that people get in you when you least expect it. If you can't get them out of your system, then it ain't meant for them to stop being a part of you. With Sabrina and me, that adage ran deep and true. Killing my wife, metaphorically speaking, had killed a part of me. A part I had never told her about. My family. Yeah, I had off the cuff told her about how my mother's favorite flower was a lilac but speaking about them all in detail never ever came out of my mouth. There were too many pieces of me that were off-limits, so I thought.

I found that the longer that I was with Sabrina, the easier little things would slip out. When they did slip out, though, I always made sure to keep it contained and not let it be anything about my "business," especially after she learned the truth about me. My time away from her was fucking hard on a nigga; something I wasn't used to. I felt like I was too young to be digging her like that; yet I was. I wanted her the moment I saw her the second time around, and I had been accepting of it. But when I told her I loved her in the back of that car, yeah, that all changed the game for me.

I really wasn't speaking to her. In front of me was my family. It was them that I was telling sorry to for losing their lives back in the day. It was their spirit that I was communicating with in explaining why my hands were covered in blood, the kid that they raised to be more than what I was—a killer, a mercenary for crime lords. In Sabrina's eyes, I was even speaking to her younger self. I didn't want her seeing that side of me, didn't want her tarnished, but now she was.

I felt like I lost her to the game, which was one of the reasons why I left as I did. Dropping her off at her place, I drove home, packed up, and then drove to South Carolina. After that, I paid for a bus ticket to drive me to Maryland. Then from there, I took a train to DC. Essentially, my movements were done in a way that would not allow for a clear-cut trail. After everything that had happened, I wasn't sure if Sabrina had gone to the police or not. I was literally playing with my life, but I just couldn't bring myself to harm her. All I knew was I needed to go home and visit the graves of my family, and that was what I did.

Everything I did while back in DC, I took old school. I slept on the streets, in shelters, and in abandoned homes, to bide my time. Afterward, I went to the graves of my people and communed with their spirits. It was crazy. They were the only ones I spoke all of my truths to and all of my pains. I washed my blood off my hands with the dirt of their graves, metaphorically speaking. Being with them was my counseling, and usually, I did this once a year, but after leaving Sabrina, I found myself back before schedule.

Once I dumped my truths on them, I flew out of DC and went to Florida where I stayed low-key doing some work and cleaning up small hits on the list just to ease the time. Through it all, Sabrina stayed on my mind. We had no real relationship, but shorty had me feeling her on a level I wasn't truly ready to accept yet. That was exceedingly clear because I had let her live. That wasn't part of the game. I had others, who knew nothing about what I did. Only one time did I have to take care of one of my partners because they stumbled upon something they shouldn't have, which was back in Vegas.

Tracy Moore. Baby girl was thick like a milkshake and a pretty sista who had a habit of fucking snooping. That's what ended up getting her killed. Her pretty face, phat ass, and gift of sucking dick couldn't save her for shit. After I dragged her in the bathroom, banged her head against the shower wall, then snapped her neck, I made her death as pretty as possible in respect for the little bit of a relationship we had. After that, I sent flowers to her funeral and flew to Italy.

Killing was my life, and, yes, there were parts of it that gave me pride; there were also parts that no sane man would allow to be shared between the people of his family. I had slipped, and I didn't know what to do besides what was natural, and that was to end Sabrina.

As September rolled into October and October into November, I kept my eyes on the news. I saw nothing about me being linked to the kills in Red Hook. I flew to South Africa, chilled a few weeks, killed some more, mingled, fucked, and still saw nothing in the news. Sabrina had kept her mouth shut, and she had made herself a permanent occupant in a part of me that I had thought long dead.

It was because of that that I came back to the States and Georgia to see her. I also was still weighing killing her. But when I stepped back into her world, when I saw her, once again my mind flipped on me and changed. I ended up digging that kitty out and made my choice, right then and there. It would be another two weeks before I verbally said what that choice would be, and, no, I wasn't asking her to be my wife.

We were nowhere near ready for that at that time because I wasn't about to fly off to Paris or some shit and propose to her after leaving her out to dry so many damn times. Nah, we needed to be on the same page for a question like that, and as I said, we weren't ready. We were young and trying to see what this even was. I mean, a brotha had casually said that he was going to kill her too many times to be popping the question.

But, yeah, we were chilling down in Midtown dodging her handler Danny. I pulled her to some steps hidden off the side of one of the buildings. I held her as she sat on my lap, and she sipped on some Starbucks. A white mocha latte, I think it was. Her nose was a little red from the strong chill we had going on in Atlanta, something that usually didn't go down, but how fucked up the climate was, I wouldn't be shocked if a blizzard hit us hard any time now.

"Brina, been thinking that as long as you keep seeing things as you do in regards to me," I found myself saying while I watched cars go by, "I'll be good with that and won't do anything reckless because you have me trusting you."

The sudden shift of her body against me, the sensation of her tensing up at my words had me studying her presence. My arms found themselves wrapping around her snuggly. Not too tight, but just right. It had me remembering how good she felt against my hands when they gripped and held on to her as I pumped in and out of her. We were on some animalistic shit the first time we fucked. It was like on the cusp of something soft and slow on her behalf as well, but through the whole experience, Sabrina felt good to me, like I knew she would.

My palms itched in remembrance of holding her ass in my hands, sliding over the small of her back, then upward to feel her breasts swell in both my hands. Shit was candy for me, and while I remembered all of that, it left me with a weird feeling that I finally realized what it was.

"You make me want to protect you, not that you need it, but I'd fuck a bitch up if someone came stupidly at you. That's why I'm telling you this. If you can honestly tell me that you can be good with all of who I am right now, then I'll believe it, and we can keep on learning each other, a'ight?" I added knowing that she had to be thinking I was a crazy nigga.

I mean I was. I honestly was. I was a liar, a manipulator, and a killer, but above all of that, I also was a man who was once raised in love and understood what that looked like because I had seen it. I knew respect, and I knew loyalty as well. So, I was offering her a little of that in trust that she would not betray me and since I was damn good at reading people; then I'd wait and see if she would give the same in return.

"All right, Marcel, I meant what I told you before, and you leaving me like that hurt me deeply. I need your spark, strangely, so I'll keep seeing things as I do. I promise," she whispered against my neck while hugging me. "Just don't leave again without giving me some type of link."

Seeing things as she did meant she hadn't seen anything at all. Here we were building on whatever this was we had, and she already hit me with the first boundary for us. I wasn't sure that I knew how to do that yet, but because she was trusting me, I figured that I could attempt to make a small move toward what she needed and introduce her later to a burner phone. As I hugged her, I told her that I would and spent the rest of the day with her relaxing, and we managed to get some good sex in there too.

Several days later, I was sitting in front of Leo Giulio. Initially, when he had gotten married, I was a little shocked by that. From all the flirting Leo did, seeing him wife someone made me laugh because it was all a ploy, in my opinion. He might love his woman; I didn't know. Didn't care; wasn't my business. But the woman he had on her knees before I came into his office let me know that he was still doing him and not giving a damn about anyone.

"Good to see you back, Marcel," he said, leaning back while swirling a crystal glass of something clear and brown in it.

Arms crossed, I nodded. "You know me. With the work I have to do for your campaign and representing your office, there are times when I must travel, and that traveling has come to an end for now."

A slick smile spread across his face, and bright white teeth flashed me as he gave a hearty laugh. "Exactly, and the work you've done for me was spot-on and much respected. Thank you for your dedication to me and my vision."

"Of course," was all I said.

Chilling in a large chair, I rested back with my elbows on the arms of the chair; legs stretched out in a black suit staring across at my handler. He had a strange look in his eyes as if he were calculating something which was how he always looked. It was as if he always needed to be ahead of the game, but that wasn't my problem.

"What do you need of me?" I asked, waiting on his catch to why he called me in his office.

"As you've heard, a lot of changes have been going on since you've been gone. Father is in Italy, while my mother is doing tours of Europe. Which leaves me—"

"As my boss. Got it before you said it. What do you need?" I said interrupting him.

Dude didn't go through the proper channels, so I was a little ticked off about it.

Leo gave me a look, one where his eyebrow raised up sharply, and the corner of his nose wrinkled up as if something stunk.

I watched him thumb his nose while taking his time to answer me.

Me? I just sat there with a blank expression waiting. They thought I was their dog to call and snap fingers at, at will. I was, but I wasn't, feel me? Through it all, I deserved respect, but, of course, I never verbalized it unless I felt like it. I let my actions demand respect at all times. Unfortunately, Leo sometimes forgot that I wasn't a mindless minion. During those times, I often had to buck at his ass if he pressed me.

Tension rose between us until Leo gave a guttural sigh, then reached out to pour from his crystal decanter into his glass. "The IRS is sniffing. It's time we dumped something which brings me to why you're here. My father knows that you have a love for the old place, cooking and all. I don't want anything to do with it considering that holding on to a place linked to criminal activities will only tarnish my reputation further."

"What does that have to do with me?" I asked ready to get to the point already.

"We're reluctantly letting it shut down. After six months, the place will be bought in your name, along with the title given to you. Do with it as you want," he said as he took a deep gulp of his drink.

The clicking of ice in his glass fell in rhythm with the ticking of my jaw. I sat there assessing the situation. Running the bistro was the last thing on my mind to do. Dropping this on my lap was interesting, though. I wasn't sure if I was ready for such a thing, but since niggas were dropping shit on me, it didn't hurt to listen and contemplate things.

"But I'll have to stay linked and tied to your family? I'll owe you all?"

Yeah, I needed to know what the trap was.

"Now we get to the business." Leo grinned like a Cheshire cat and smirked. "No, we'll have no ties to your business, although The Family will continue to use your other services, of course."

He gave a knowing chuckle because we both understood what that meant.

"The old man was reluctant in closing it; however, he felt adamant about giving you the place and land around it. He believes that you, of all people, will love the place as he did and will keep the business going," he explained.

I sat back thinking about all the times his old man would get on my ass about learning every level of the business. He made me start from the ground up with cleaning the outside and inside of the restaurant. That meant picking up trash, cleaning bathrooms, sweeping, fixing whatever was broken, painting, etc. After I mastered that, I was elevated to kitchen duty where I was the bus boy. From there, I helped plate food. Then from there, I was a greeter, then waiter, then back in the kitchen to where I rose up to become head chef. My lessons continued even after that with learning management as a means to understand how to keep the place running. I never realized the old man was grooming me to take over, not some kid he picked up off the street who he found digging in his trash. Now, it appeared that I'd be a businessman.

"What do you say?" Leo asked while swiveling in his chair in a slow rock.

Reaching up in thought to run a palm over the waves of my hair, I leaned back, then exhaled lightly. "What do I think?"

Leaning forward, I clasped my hands in between my legs and leaned on my thighs. "I want it in clear paperwork, and I want time to read over everything. I want it laid out that this joint will be mine and mine only. I want to be written in a clause that none of you can enact some type of grandpa clause on me and that you can't make me use my place for your family business. If that's spelled out, then we'll see what I say."

"Pops thought you might say that. Here," he said, sliding a packet to me over the desk. Leo leaned back pressing his pointer fingers against his lips. "Read it over, and I'll speak to my lawyers to make sure everything is in black and white, clear on all fronts."

Swiping up the paperwork, I locked my gaze on him. "Now, what else do you want?"

The deep, amused chuckle from Leo hit me. He was a cunning motherfucker.

"You have more work to do for us," he casually said.

Now, this is the moment that I decided to press my game. "No, not really. I have one last case to handle for you all, and then we come to the renegotiations of my contract with The Family. I'm now my own boss, especially with how the Feds are on you all. Agreed?"

Leo twitched in his chair. His eyes narrowed; then he gave a deep frown. "Agreed."

"Exactly. Your father and I will speak about how my terms will be laid out now with you all doing further business with me, but as of now, I am my own man." Grinning wide, I rested my ankle on my knee. "Now, my price grade goes up. If you all can accept that, then I will happily send a new contract your way. I thank your family for training me as you all have, so I owe you all that much."

I quickly added, "Besides, it was your father who told me that this day would come, that I would receive something benefiting to me, a gift from him. Once that happened, my shackles to you all officially break free."

Silence settled between us, and then Leo shook his head, abruptly stood, then smiled at me. "I always knew that you were smarter than you looked."

"Of course, I'm smart. I graduated the top of my class at Georgia State, communication my main. But you forget, I double majored in political science, my man," I said with a slight smirk.

"I stand corrected. Dad always thought of you as another son, the one lost to him, and I did too at times. You're cunning, and I appreciate that." Standing in front of his massive bay window in his office, Leo placed his hands behind his back. "I'll send everything to you. Until then, you're only my aide. Othello Lanfair and I are distancing ourselves from each other as a necessary means to a fucked-up situation. I need you to be the intermediary between us since you're my aide, understood?"

Being the intermediary worked out for me, but I wouldn't let Leo know that. By working close to but not too close to Mr. Lanfair, I'd now have even easier access to his daughter, so I was down for that.

"A'ight, I'll do what I can," I said.

"Good, because your work as a chef is on hiatus since the restaurant will be closed for a few weeks, and we can't do shit without the Feds crawling up our asses. This Family can't afford to lose an asset like you. We'll be in touch," he said turning to focus his attention my way.

Standing, I headed to the door of his office and opened it, then paused. "You're right. The day Senior Giulio passes is a day that I'll mourn. I'm honor bound to him; that's all. I'll work that all out as always. Respect, man."

With that, I walked out and headed to my spot where I usually sat to throw off the Feds who followed me. I had a new future in my hand, with two paths that I now had control of. I was a killer and enjoyed being a professional hit man. I could walk away from it after crossing off my last hit for the Giulios or I could make this a permanent thing and truly take this global. Then, I also had the opportunity to take on the bistro and turn it into something incredible that honored the old man but also brought it up to date with my style and how I wanted things. I'd bring in legit money this way and not just killer money.

I wasn't sure what I would do, but looking over the paperwork, I saw everything looked on the up and up and nothing misleading. Damn, I really respected that old man for this. When I lost my family, and he heard my story after I shared some of it with him, he got me. Took me from the gutter in my depression and fear and turned me into a new kind of beast. In this path, the man was giving me power. Part of me knew that Leo might feel some type of way about it, but I also knew that he respected it. I mean, I was their personal cleaner. I helped Leo out in situations that his pops didn't even know about, so if something did happen to the old man, I knew Leo would always seek me out for work, and by doing so, I'd always have money and work.

But yeah, I needed to think this out and make sure I did the right thing.

As my day shifted to night, I went on to my business. I hit up Sabrina and spoke some nasty shit to her, told her to pack her bags for a minitrip to St. Croix, and then I headed out to take out the last mark, some white dude named Jason Hobbs. He had an addiction to weed, black culture, and black dick. He also had a problem with leaking people's business as well, from what I learned. Pulling my skullcap on, I moved out and handled business; hip-hop thumped through my speakers as I began to think about my future, something I never had the opportunity to think of since the death of my family. It was a new day, and I was digging it.

Chapter Eleven

Sabrina

December 2011 . . .

We never made it to St. Croix. At least not when he had planned it. Shit in our lives got pretty hectic after we decided we were going to do that thing called love. A killer and girl like me shouldn't have even entertained the notion of being together. But Marcel and I had always gone against the grain. Not everyone was happy for us, though. . . .

"Excuse me," Daddy said as he blinked rapidly and made a face that suggested he couldn't have been hearing what he thought he'd heard. "This guy?" he asked pointing at Marcel. "*This* is who you're dating?"

I was baffled by his response. Upon first meeting Marcel, the night the mayor died, Daddy was all smiles, patting him on the back, asking him his thoughts on things. And now, when I reveal that Marcel and I were dating, he appeared to be dumbfounded. Marcel hadn't liked the idea of me exposing us yet. Said that we should have waited, but I knew my father, or so I assumed. He'd invited me over to his place as he was throwing a private dinner.

Leo decided not to attend as he and my father were still putting on the front that he had distanced himself. Marcel had come as a representative, and once all the other bigwigs had left, only Kat and Daddy's guards remained. I didn't see a problem with telling my father that I was seriously involved with someone. I just didn't expect him to turn it into a spectacle.

"Yes. He's who I'm dating," I finally responded after the wave of embarrassment wore off.

"He's a cook," Daddy spat.

He didn't seem to care that Marcel was still even in the room.

I glanced at Marcel who hadn't said a word. He was dressed in a navy-blue suit with a gray dress shirt and gray wing-tipped dress shoes. He truly looked the part of an aide. There was a strange look in his eyes. One I couldn't read.

"He's a chef, Daddy. He's smart. He has degrees, and he's an aide to Leo—"

Daddy waved a hand to cut me off. "Sabrina, let's call a spade a spade, shall we? All the degrees in the world and he'd *still* be relegated to the kitchen like the field Negro he is," Daddy spat venomously. "You mean to tell me the pickings are so slim in Atlanta, you've settled for *this?*" he asked, pointing his thumb at Marcel.

My eyes widened. Kat shook her head as she chuckled and sipped her wine. I got ready to speak, but Marcel laid a hand on my shoulder to silence me.

"I'm sorry, Mr. Lanfair, I'm a bit confused. So, I'm good enough for you to ask my opinions on certain things, but not good enough to date your daughter?" he asked my father.

Daddy stood up. Back straight. Shoulders squared.

"Just what is it that you think you could offer her? What kind of future does a cook, who is an *aide,* have to offer my daughter? Her credentials and work ethic alone show you're beneath her in every way. She comes from good stock, and you come from *what,* exactly?"

"Daddy, stop it," I jumped in.

Marcel chuckled sardonically. "Good stock, huh? It was my work ethic that took me from being homeless to working for the Giulios. My work ethic ensures that I've kept a steady flow of employment since that time. I went from sweeping the Giulios' floors to running the restaurant. So, my work ethic isn't the problem. I think the reason you have a problem with me dating your daughter is because I'm a reflection of you."

Daddy scoffed. "*Me?* You, a reflection of *me?* In what life? You can't possibly mean you're a productive citizen—"

"Nah. I'm more like the *other* side of you. The side underneath the slimy façade. The side that's criminal and a snake. The side that's going to win you the election."

I could feel when the mood in the room darkened. The tension that took over the once jubilant atmosphere was evident in the way Daddy stared Marcel down. Marcel didn't seem to care one way or the other. There was a slick smirk on his face that said he welcomed the challenge Daddy threw at him.

"Leo told me about you. Your parents came from a hood in Washington. They were no more than the bottom of the barrel, just like you are now. And for you to think you're worthy of more than my daughter's ass to kiss is a mind fuck I'll never figure out."

"I can assure you that I've kissed your daughter's ass plenty of times, and each time she's loved it."

Daddy stormed over to stand face-to-face with Marcel. I stood, and Kat rushed to stand behind my father, her hand on his chest urging him to stand down.

"You dare stand and insult me in my own home?" Daddy roared.

Marcel didn't back down. I stepped in between them.

"Stop," I pleaded. "Daddy, it is what it is at this point. There's nothing you can do about it. I love him—"

Daddy looked as if he was about to have a conniption. "You *love* him? You don't know what the hell love is. You're a feeble-minded child who's been coddled all her damn life. This nigga is nothing more than a low-life thug!"

I said before that my daddy had always hung with the
hoods and the thugs back in New York. He grew up in
Staten Island. Still, any time I heard the hood in him
jump out, it always shocked me.

"You want to call me a thug when you keep company with
the most hooligan of them all? How fucking hypocritical
of you!" Marcel snapped back, although there was a bit of
sarcasm in his tone. "I'm leaving," he said to me afterward.

"No, baby, don't leave," I rushed out, grabbing his hand
as I tried to stop him.

"No, let him go. The best thing he could do for his own
safety is get the fuck up out of my house."

Marcel had turned and was walking away. However,
I knew that the fact Daddy had threatened him rubbed
him the wrong way.

He turned slowly, eyes narrowed at my father. "Is that
a threat?"

I saw when Danny moved closer to my father. I didn't
want this. I hadn't planned for any of it to blow up in my
face, but it had.

"Marcel, please," I whispered. "He didn't mean it. He's
been drinking. . . ."

Marcel frowned as he looked down at me. My eyes
were watering, and I had my hands on his chest.

"I told you," he said to me.

I knew what he was speaking of without him even
having to say it. "I know, and I'm sorry."

Daddy's voice thundered, "Don't you dare stand in my
home and apologize to this cretin! Let that nigga go."

Marcel inhaled, his jaw twitched, and lips turned down
into a scowl. "I'm leaving. You can stay or come with me.
Your choice."

"Baby, please."

"Not going to stay somewhere I'm not wanted, Brina."

Daddy tsked. "*Brina?*" he muttered under his breath.
"Stripping her of her name. Sooner or later, he'll strip her
of her class."

I whipped around to face my father. "Stop it! You don't have to be an asshole. You don't like us dating? Fine. But don't be a prick about it."

Before I knew it, Daddy had backhanded me and snatched me by my arm so fast, the strength and swiftness of it lifted me inches from the floor. I screamed out in shock and pain.

"Othello," Kay yelled. "Baby, stop it!"

Before I could get my balance and realize what was happening, Marcel had knocked Daddy's head back, then slammed it down on the small table where we were standing. A gun was in his right hand pointing at Danny who was about to come to Daddy's aid. I'd fallen to the floor, face burning, ankle twisted I was sure, but I hopped up, rushing over to Marcel.

"Back up off me, Sabrina," he snapped while pressing Daddy's face harder into the table. I stopped in my tracks. Marcel whispered to my father. "It's one thing not to like me because you feel I'm not good enough for your daughter; it's another thing altogether to put your hands on her in my presence. And the only reason I haven't killed you is because I know it will hurt her. If you *ever* in your life touch her again, nigga, I *will* kill you."

He picked Daddy up by the collar of his shirt, then slammed his head down on the table again. Kat was crying and pleading for Marcel to let him go while Daddy moaned out in agony. I was too scared to move.

Marcel kept his voice low, aggression laced with each word he spoke. "I want you to listen to me and hear the sincerity in my voice. She is *not* your wife. You will *not* treat her like she is your punching bag. If she ever even *hints* that you have looked at her the wrong way, I will end you in the cruelest of ways that no one will even be able to identify your body. You get me, motherfucker?"

I knew Daddy was too prideful to respond, but judging by the way he had his lips balled, it was clear he understood exactly what Marcel had said to him. Once Marcel let him go, he stepped back and placed his gun back in the holster I didn't even know he'd had on until he'd aimed it at Danny.

"Get out of my house," Daddy yelled.

Marcel nodded once, smugness written all over his face. "Gladly."

I grabbed my purse and my coat. "You're leaving with him?" Daddy belted out.

"I am. You had no right to say any of the things you did to him. And to put your hands on me was the lowest of the low."

My father was incredulous. He shook his fist as he spoke, "If you leave with him, you're done. I will never lift another finger to help you. All those clients, good and bad, will disappear. The penthouse—everything. You're done if you walk out of here with that man!"

Marcel was already halfway to the door. I couldn't lie and say my feelings weren't hurt because of the turn of events. I would never have thought my father would behave in such a way toward me. And to put his hands on me? It hurt my soul that my father would throw me away because I chose to love someone he didn't feel was good enough. And while I appreciated everything my father had done for me, I wouldn't be beholden to any man—father or not.

"I love you, Daddy, and it's a shame we've come to this," I told him before rushing out the door.

I could still hear him yelling as I searched for Marcel. He had just pulled his car around to drive away when I saw him. He stopped the car and reached over to open the door for me. I hopped in and never looked back.

The plan had been for me to stay at Marcel's place that night anyway. When we got there, he walked into his bathroom, then came back out with cotton balls, alcohol, and peroxide. Tears slowly inched down my face as he took the time to nurse the small cut one of my father's rings had left on my face. I knew that if I called my

mother and told her what he had done, she would be on
the first flight to Atlanta raising hell. I couldn't believe
my father had hit me. Couldn't believe he and I had come
to this all because of who I chose to love. For crying out
loud, you would have thought I'd just told him I was
getting a sex change.

"If he puts his hands on you again, I'm going to kill
him," Marcel said to me.

There was no need for me to question if he was serious.
I knew he was. I could hear it in his tone.

"I know," I said.

"I would tell you some sap shit like you don't have to
lose your father for me, but fuck him. When he put his
hands on you, all bets were off," he said.

I lay my head on his chest, then wrapped my arms
around his waist. I smiled through the tears when his
arms closed around me. I couldn't even formulate a
response. I was hurting, emotionally and physically. My
arm still stung from where my father had grabbed me.
Face throbbed so badly I had a headache. I didn't know
what all this meant for the future, but I knew that as long
as Marcel was there with me, I could handle it.

"Senior Giulio has given me the restaurant," he spoke
up after a while.

I lifted my head to look up at him. "Explain," I said.

"There's no need to explain it, baby. Once I look over
the paperwork and accept it, Giulio's is mine. I can do
with it what I want."

A part of me wanted to tell him to be careful. While
Leo had never been problematic toward me, I still didn't
trust the man. I didn't know too much about his father to
speak ill of him.

"What's the catch?" I asked.

"As of right now, nothing. The old man gave it to me
because he knows Leo wants nothing to do with it. Senior
Giulio is an old-world-type Italian. Big on family and

legacy, but he also knows that nigga Leo got other shit going on and would let the place fall by the wayside."

"So what are you going to do?"

"I'm going to take it. Turn it into something legit."

"Does that mean . . ."

"Does it mean what?"

"Does that mean you're going to, you know, go legit in all aspects of life?"

Marcel gazed down at me for a long time. Flickers of emotions danced across his face, then settled.

"I'll never make you those kinds of promises," he answered.

I nodded and lay my head back against his chest. We stood that way for a long while. Holding each other and lost in the thoughts of our minds.

Days after turned into weeks, weeks into months. Marcel and I stayed up under each other. Not in the sense that we were always at home screwing, although we did that a lot. No, see, my father held true to his threat. In mid-February, my boss fired me from my cushy desk job at the firm. All Leo's friends paid me for services rendered, then told me to vamoose. I got home one day and found that the locks had been changed on the doors of my penthouse. That was all well and good. I'd already looked into purchasing a loft in Midtown. It wasn't the upscale crib my penthouse was, but it was mine.

I was out of a job, but I didn't care. Leo had kept good on his promise. After Marcel had gone through the contract and had one of his lawyer friends to look at it, he and Leo signed the deal, and the keys were given to him. It took us until May to get into running the place because the Feds had to finish their investigation. Luckily, no matter how hard they looked, they found nothing. Senior Giulio had kept as much criminal activity from Giulio's as he could.

Once I saw the passion in the way Marcel went about renovating the place, I wanted to help in any way I could. So I did. Number crunching was my thing. While he took care of other things, I set out to get the finances squared away. Working for crime syndicates had padded my pockets well. The same could be said for Marcel. Between getting bank loans to make the place look legit without having to answer questions on where we got money, we each brought extra money from our bank accounts too.

Mama thought I was nuts to put my money into a business with a man I hadn't married. I had to remind her that she had been married to Daddy and still couldn't trust him.

"I like the boy; don't get me wrong, baby. It's just that something about him rubs me the wrong way. Like, he's got secrets. Bad ones," she told me one day as we spoke on the phone.

She'd already met him and had taken it a whole lot better than Daddy had.

"We all have secrets, Mama," I said.

I would never tell her that she was right. My baby *had* secrets . . . lots of them. Just two nights before he had left and hadn't come back yet. In the last five months since we had been fixing up the bistro, he hadn't gone a day without being at my place or me at his. It had been a long time since he had disappeared for work. I had started to get used to him being around. Started to think that maybe he had left that old life of his behind. I had worry lines etched in my forehead as I watched the clock. The burner cell he'd given me hadn't rung. I was in my loft, feeling like shit and wishing my mother would stop talking. Not because she was getting on my nerves but because my head was spinning, and it felt as if I was coming down with the flu. It had been that way for at least three weeks.

"Yes, we do, but Marcel looks troubled a lot. Like he's seen the devil, had dinner with him, picked his brain, and then came back up here with us normal folk," Mama said.

"He's had a hard life. Was homeless for a long time, so I imagine he has seen some things."

"I guess, baby. I guess. Just be careful."

"Mama—"

"No, now listen to me. I'm not saying he treats you bad because I can see he doesn't. I've never seen you more alive than now, but I'm saying . . . Sometimes a man can drag his demons with him, and it can cause you grief. He may not even be intending to. Just be careful is all I'm saying. I'ma say a prayer for y'all. Feel like y'all needed it. Especially with your daddy still shitting bricks about who you dating like who you fucking gon' make his tricky dick ass come. Anyway, let me get off here. Love you, baby, and tell Marcel thank you for my new coffeemaker. Love that there thang. Makes me twelve cups of coffee, it does," she said, then giggled.

I was about to say I would tell him when the bottom of my stomach felt as if it was about to come up through my mouth. I dropped the phone and ran to the bathroom. With the way I was heaving, you would have thought I was vomiting up my intestines. Instead, green, slimly bile plopped into the toilet. After there was no more bile to come, I dry heaved for what felt like an eternity with nothing coming up. I was so tired that I couldn't even stand. My head was on the toilet, and I felt as if I was dying.

It didn't take a genius to realize I was pregnant. Had found that out earlier when I'd taken a home pregnancy test. Between Marcel and me trying to fix the bistro up to his liking and fucking like jackrabbits, condoms had become a thing of the past. Yeah, we did all the necessary shit like getting tested for STDs and HIV. Still, he didn't suspect I thought I was pregnant. I hadn't either until I realized I hadn't had my period for a month.

I had no idea how he would react and was too sick to care at the moment. I didn't even realize I'd fallen asleep still hugging the toilet.

Chapter Twelve

Marcel

When a man found out he was going to be a dad, a vortex to another world opens up and swallows him whole. I was joking, but it did change the scope of things for a man, and it changed his core as well. When I found out I was going to be a dad, it was when Sabrina was hunched over the toilet. I had come in after finishing a job for Leo. Usually, I try to disappear after every kill but now being committed to Sabrina, I had changed things slightly. Now I cleaned up at the warehouse as typical and tried to find some place to show my face at around town; then I'd go home or to her crib.

That was what I did after cleaning up at the warehouse. Once I made it to her crib and used the key she gave me, I looked around for her, only to find my future wife on the bathroom floor hugging a toilet. The first thing that came to mind was *oh shit*. I'd never seen her sick on this level before, but it was clear to identify, especially with the dry heaving sounds she was making. I took it upon myself to go into the take-care-of-her mode.

Sweeping her up from the bamboo floor and bringing the small trash can she kept in the bathroom, I walked her to her room, then lay her in bed. Feeling the bed sink with my weight once I sat next to her, I took a cold washcloth to the corner of her mouth to wipe her upchuck away and watched her stir.

"Hey, baby, you got the stomach flu? You don't look well," I asked, checking her forehead.

Sabrina lay back with her eyes half-mast, her face contorted at the same time her lips pressed together as if she was trying to hold back the next wave of vomit working in her stomach. I watched her shake her head, her lush hair forming a halo around her face as she tried to speak. That was when she worked her way toward telling me the truth. We had a rule now; no secrets, and she kept with that.

"You're back," she said with a groggy voice and a light, tired huff.

Chuckling, I nodded while rubbing her thigh. "Yeah, I am. Was looking for you and found you on the floor hugging your new man, Mr. Toilet. What did you eat that gave you a jacked stomach, baby? You don't have the shits too, do you? Not sure I can handle that yet."

"Shut up, Marcel." Sabrina gave me a feeble smile and weakly slapped my forearm. "I was good all night, but I suddenly became sick."

"Ah yeah? Damn, well, I know this bomb chicken and dumpling soup recipe that will help you out; just lie back," I said getting up.

"Baby, I don't think I can hold that down. It's not the flu," she said, sitting up.

"You sure? I'll get you something to drink then," I added while pulling off my tank and tossing it in her dirty hamper.

"I'm positive. This is the type of sick that only clears up after nine months," I heard her say while coming out of my closet with a new tank.

At first, I didn't catch it, but when I looked her way, she had a light smile on her face that had me pause. "Say what?"

"Ah, I'm pretty sure that I'm pregnant."

I heard myself chuckle while I stood there frozen with a raised eyebrow. It was like I felt the blood rush from my face at what she said. A baby? Fuck my life. How could we manage that? How could I be a dad, her man, *and* a killer? How?

From the expression on my face, I was sure she thought I was disappointed, but really, I wasn't. After being with her all this time, and after not having a family for so long now, creating a new life was actually dope for me. It had me thinking and reflecting on how we'd be with a kid running around both of our places. It also suddenly made me think about my family and the fact that they weren't here to share in this moment.

That's when I walked forward and sat down by her, then took her hand. "Wow. You sure?"

Moving her hand, she muttered, "Oh God," then quickly leaned over and emptied her guts again.

I sat there rubbing her back until she stopped, and I knew that she wasn't lying. I felt it in my spirit, and I chuckled again.

"I'm sure," she said once she was done. Her face looked so tragic and sad as she stared at me with a slight concern in her eyes. "Are you mad?"

Mad wasn't even in the equation, I thought to myself as I replied, "Naw. Why would I be? We both were fucking, and when you don't use protection, stuff like this goes down. I'm really good about it. Happy, actually, baby, and I'd kiss you, but you got too much going on in the mouth area right now, so a brotha needs to opt out of that and just do that forehead kiss thing."

I flashed a goofy smile at her as she laughed and tried to hit me. While I dodged her sick ass, my mind went to her pops. That nigga was still going around barking, trying to make Sabrina leave me. I really wasn't stressing none of it, but with this news of her being pregnant, I had a feeling his discontent was only going to worsen. It had me thinking about how fucked her father was and how good mine was.

That was when I decided since everything had changed now, since we both had created a new life, that I could give Sabrina the facts about who my family were and not some made-up bullshit that she heard through the grapevine.

Wrapping my arms around her, I let her lean against me while I kept her close to the trash can. "Listen, now that everything is getting better for us, I . . . Look, this has me thinking about some stuff that was said and that I just sat back and was quiet on. Remember when your dad went off and started talking about shit he don't know? Shit Leo fed him about my family?"

Sabrina shifted against me, tilting her head to look up at me with an anxious look like *what is this motherfucker about to say now* type of look. "Yes, what about it?"

"I guess this is a good time for you to hear about my family. Leo don't know shit about them but likes to think he does. My family wasn't hood, and I didn't grow up in the hood. They weren't rich or nothing, but we weren't in the dredges either. We all lived outside the hood. I could go a block over and be in the hood, but our neighborhood was cool. We were working middle class, one paycheck away from being poor. But yeah, I wasn't some hood kid until I decided by myself that I wanted to be just to kick it."

I felt tension in my spine, so I had to stop to get my racing thoughts in line before continuing, "My dad always told us, he kept us near the truth, that's why we never moved to a 100 percent good area. Shit, we really couldn't afford it anyway. My pops was a music teacher."

A warm smile, something I rarely had unless Sabrina triggered it, crept across my face. "Funny enough, my mom was a civil rights attorney. If she knew about what I did, she'd be pissed at me. But yeah, that shit your pops thought he knew ain't true. My parents worked hard to send me to GSU and to keep our single-family home put together. Shit, yeah, I ran the streets, but my family weren't thugs; just me," I explained, feeling all types of emotions as I spoke about my family. "They were good people, and our kid will have them in his or her blood."

My hands rubbed together while I stared down at them in thought. I was reliving their death, the news of it, and it had me on edge feeling like I needed to go out and kill. . . . Until I felt Sabrina touch my shoulder.

"I don't care how my daddy feels about where or how you grew up. I love you, and your family feels like they were good, caring people. My daddy can just keep on thinking you aren't someone. It's not his business; it's ours," she said resting her head on my shoulder. "Thank you for sharing this side of you with me and don't forget that our child will have your strength in his or her blood."

A smile played against the corner of my lips in a lop-sided grin. "You're welcome, and thank you, baby. I don't care what he thinks about me, but I wanted to tell you for our kid's sake because I have a legacy in a different way. Naw, it ain't money. I mean, I was given something from their insurance, but I've never touched it, and I won't. I just can't, baby. But I'll give it to our baby, that and this restaurant. That and giving our child nothing but love will be my legacy to our kid. I just wanted you to know. I'm feeling real good about this and us."

"That's all I wanted to know, baby, but now, I want you to keep telling me about your family so that you can remember them in love, and so our baby can know them," she gently coaxed.

I wasn't sure if I could, but I found out since being with Sabrina that whatever she wanted, I tried to give her in some small way, so for her, I'd do that as best as I could.

"Okay," I said while wrapping my arm around her, then resting my other arm against her stomach, "Just don't throw up on me. Oh, and keep your place and move in with me."

If I hadn't moved, I swear Sabrina would have head butted me. Baby girl jumped up and screamed so loud that it had me covering my ears.

"Really?" she asked in a shrilled voice.

"Yeah, really," I said, laughing. "Move in with me, baby. I have too much room, and it's safe, I promise."

"You sure?" she anxiously asked this time.

"Don't make me repeat myself," I said getting a little serious with it.

"Humph, then, yeah, okay! Okay!" She got ready to kiss me when she covered her mouth with both hands and sharply turned to empty her gut.

"Uh-huh, all that bouncing got you fucked up," I said feeling good as I rubbed her back.

Three months passed while our baby cooked. I had only her to share our good news, so the news ended up going to her mom and sisters. I knew that Sabrina's father would get wind of it through the grapevine and now that she had a little bump showing, but neither of us gave a fuck. With the reality that we were going to be parents, building up the restaurant became my priority while my continued work as a hit man slowed down due to a lack of requests.

I stayed on as a hit man because I felt like the extra money would help our child in the future. Naw, I'm lying. I continued being a professional killer because I enjoyed it, and as I already admitted, it helped me cap the memories of my family. Which brings to me to when the major shift of me being my own man and handling my own contracts as a professional killer came to be. I remember standing outside in my overalls with workman gloves digging in the dirt, turning the deli into a real bistro. My work crew was cleaning up the outside and building up the front patio for people to sit and eat, and I was helping with that.

In my new restaurant, I knew that I was going to continue the tradition of Italian food but do a fusion of old classics being updated with the times in a modern, organic twist. The goal was to draw in these multicultural hipsters around the area to line my pocket. It already was creating a buzz, and I had a lot of food restaurant magazines coming in to talk to me about the place and me hiring young minority talent who were known for their innovative style. Straight up, I was excited. I didn't think that I could pull it off, and if it weren't for Sabrina helping me do my homework on what people want in the area and looking into what's hot in the restaurant world, shit, I'd still be looking at an empty building.

But yeah, as I was digging in the dirt, planting trees for shading, I heard a sharp whistle, then my name being called out.

"Damn, Marcel, you changed everything," I heard, which had me turning toward the familiar voice.

Keeping my expression calm, I gave a shrug, pulled off my gloves, then shook the outstretched hand that was suddenly in front of me. "It's my place, so why wouldn't I? What do you want, Leo?"

Leo gripped my hand hard, then dropped it back as he continued to look over the place. "Business. I'm in need of your help on something."

"Oh yeah? What can I do for you, boss, since I'm your aide? Need me to read more emails and general mail? I mean, I could do that but might be a problem with me here and all," I said sarcastically.

Boisterous laughter erupted from Leo. He clapped an arm over my shoulder, and it took everything in me not to growl.

"No, my man. You know that you've moved beyond that. You're no junior aide, but no. What I came to speak to you about is that upgrade of yours. I need to know how you've been handling being my director. Any problems lately?" he asked walking with me into the restaurant. "Because I'm hearing that you've been ruffling the wrong feathers, mainly one feather. Still hearing the repercussion of that, and it's been what, eight or so months now. It's been bothering me."

Sawing and hammering clamored around us. The scent of fresh paint had my nostrils twitching as I listened to this dude all up in my ear. There was no questioning what he was talking about because when he mentioned the time about ruffling feathers, I knew that meant only one thing. Sabrina's father was still being a bitch, especially more so now that she was pregnant.

On our way to my office, I grabbed some wine with glasses in tow, then found a seat. "Damn, that's really disappointing that you're going through that, Leo. I mean, shit. If I knew that there was a specific problem dealing with me that was leaking over to you, I would have effectively cleaned that up with no problem. Considering that it's my problem."

As I poured Leo a glass, I watched how his body language tensed at my words. Yeah, he knew what the fuck I was meaning. It's the same thing that would happen to him if he pressed me wrong.

Quickly throwing my hands up, I gave a light nervous laugh while inside I wasn't giving a damn about his feelings. "I'd never jeopardize my work with you, fam, not at all. I appreciate everything that has come my way and want to keep it smooth."

Some of that was true. I continued to work with Leo for his father's sake since my contract was with the elder and not the junior. Leo could order me around as much as he wanted, but he knew I always had my own will in doing things because it was my gun being used for his purpose.

"I want to be clear here. I'm keeping my distance, but I still am on an honor code with our mutual friend. I said nothing about the threat you made to him. I mean, he should know better. I extended you out on good faith that he'd respect your place there in front of him; however, you know how fathers can be." Leo smirked, then shook his head. "My bad, you don't. But let me make it clear since you've backed away from working with him. . . . Don't mess up my work, Marcel."

Listening to him, I wanted to be like, *nigga, please,* but I kept it cool. In the political world as an aide, this was just how it worked. Every aide started at the bottom and earned their due to rise up to one day sit where Leo was. For me, I was using it differently as Senior Giulio taught me. As I rose to be a director for Leo, it was my main goal to make connects so that I could continue in cleaning up the politicians' dirty lives, or, occasionally, kill for them. By doing so in the process, I would make some good dimes and garner protection if anything ever popped off.

No politician wanted their dirty secrets out, and I was known for collecting a lot of those.

Now, Leo was sitting across from me, lecturing me, because I wouldn't kiss Sabrina's father's ass or fondle his nuts sac? And because he was on some ego shit trying to exert his power over me? Nigga, fuck outta here. He had no power over me; only his father did in the sense that I felt like I owed the old fart. That's it.

That's why I sat watching this fool flap his mouth with a concerned look on my face when I really couldn't give a damn. Sabrina was with me, and we were building a family. It was no longer her pappy's business—or Leo's.

"Not sure what you want me to do about it considering this is my private life, and it's off-limits," I said without a flicker of emotion in my voice.

I just sat there calmly with my fingers pressed to my mouth acting as if I cared about what Leo said. See, let me be clear. I don't hate this nigga; I just hate the fact that he thinks that I cared about anything he had to say. I didn't. He was cool for the occasional laughs, but once he got on his entitlement shit, I always felt since day one that he could kick rocks, and that's what I needed him to do as he spoke.

His old man was better to me. The old man was honest in his ways, all of them, but his son was a leech who didn't know shit about being a true criminal mastermind. Oh well, not my problem. I had no desire to be a criminal in that sense, so I never worried myself about it.

Leo gave another sharp laugh, then downed his wine. "Give an olive branch and show the old ass some respect. You owe me."

"Naw, I don't. But yeah, I did, and he showed me his saggy balls and rancid ass. I'm good on that. It's his bad if he fucks up the network. Period. Besides, I'm pretty sure one day he'll need my services, and when he calls me and realizes who the fuck he's calling, all that mouth of his will simmer down." I slowly stood as I said that, then recorked the wine. "This is yours as a gift as you leave. Enjoy it. It came from Naples."

I watched Leo as he smoothed a hand down the front of his shirt as he stood.

"If my pops snapped his fingers and told you to jump, you'd jump," he said with a hint of saltiness in his tone.

"Yeah, I would, but that's between us and not you. No disrespect, friend," I added, not even phased by his sudden spoiled tone.

I could tell that Leo hated me saying no to him, but fuck it. It was a new day and a new life for me. I was free contract now, and he didn't pull my reins anymore. Nigga will have to accept it, no matter how much he wanted me to feel his wrath. He knew that I still was working as his aide and bumping him up, so he needed to be grateful for that.

He reached for the bottle and whispered low, "We have a situation that will need your touch. It's been awhile, right?"

Nodding, I headed to the door and opened it, waiting for him to pass through. "Have a good day, Leo. I'll be calling the old man soon for an invite to the grand reopening."

This nigga always insisted on talking about my work as a professional killer. I didn't know what his fucking disconnect was, but if he didn't chill, I'd have to go reach down and rip his flapping tongue out. I'd be gentle, though. Make him suffer only a little out of respect toward his father. As he passed me, I gave a smile and followed him out.

I meant what I said. No criminal work was going to happen here, and Leo needed to respect that. After he left, and an hour later, I left my restaurant and finally received a call the *right* way. This kill was going to take some time to orchestrate right, but I planned on handling it; however, at that moment, I had to meet up with Sabrina and take care of this doctor's appointment. We had our child to check on, and I was pretty much excited about it as always.

Everything with the doctor was smooth and together. Sabrina and I were chilling, having lunch together, going back and forth about whether I saw a penis on the ultrasound even though it was too soon. Our food was being served while we laughed about it.

"I'm telling you, we are having a girl. That was her waving at you, no little ding-dong, okay, baby?" Sabrina said flashing her teeth while she laughed.

Her words had me smirking and shaking my head. "Naw, was a strong arm just like his pops. We're having a boy, baby, accept it. I'm getting the matching kicks and shirts already, just watch."

"Giulio Aide Director Marcel Raymond, what a joy to always see you, young man," I heard loud and clear behind me.

I slide back in my chair to stand and take the hand of our current district attorney. "Mr. Jackson, what a nice surprise to see you in here as well. What brings you in for lunch?"

"This is one of my favorite spots with my wife. We enjoy the seared Ahi Tuna. We were on our way out when I noticed you with company. This beautiful gem must be your fiancée?" I watched Kevon Jackson saunter his old ass next to Sabrina.

On some real shit, this old head was nosy, and I knew he was trying to fish out my relationship with Sabrina because it was known in the circuit that I was single and a good aide. The fact that he called her fiancée had me choking up because that was a bold title to make when meeting a woman for the first time. However, I knew that this was just how some old people were. Quick to play matchmaker.

Anyway, this old geezer was a big deal around ATL. Sharp when it came to the law, and he was known for his eccentric personality, nosy ways, and uncouth mentality. In other words, he didn't give a shit about manners. He just did him, and he was unapologetic about it. Chilling at a healthy 60 years old, Kevon was a former linebacker-turned-lawyer who worked in the streets of Atlanta cleaning it up and aiming to bring safe communities to the black population here, then eventually to other minority populations. He was a popular DA due to his philanthropy and no-care views on what's right and what's wrong. He was also a damn good connect, one I hoped to have on my side.

But, outside of that, he had me tripping because he was a touchy-feely type of dude when it came to attractive women.

Like right now, he was drooling over my girl as he pawed at her hand. It annoyed the shit out of me as I plastered a smile on my face. "Ah, well . . ."

"Hello, it's a pleasure to meet you too," Sabrina smoothly interrupted.

I guess she realized that I was stumbling over the fact that he had called her my fiancée. It was my bad, and I knew that I'd have to make it up to her.

Acting like the pro she was, Sabrina pushed back from the table to get a more comfortable position as she shook the old man's hand. "I'm Sabrina Lanfair. I've seen your face everywhere, sir. I'm honored."

"Lanfair . . . Lanfair," Kevon mouthed aloud as if trying to piece together some puzzle.

Mentally shaking my head, I frowned at this old dude as he was standing there trying to determine if she was related to the only damn Lanfair around. Thank God for his crazy-ass brain. We didn't need the questions.

Signaling to Sabrina that I was going to usher him on, I immediately rested a hand on the old man's shoulder and chuckled. "Sir, what can I help you with today?"

Walking with him, he glanced back at Sabrina, then moved closer to me. DA Jackson and I had met each other through the many multiple campaign parties and soirées that had been going on. My connection with him was new, but from how close he was to me, and the rumors that had been going around about issues he was having with his son, Naveen, I could sense that he had some business that he wanted to do with me.

"Is it true that you have networks that help with 'delicate' situations in the matter of cleaning?" he whispered low.

As soon as we rounded a corner, I moved out of his hold and clasped his hand. "Mr. Jackson, it is a pleasant honor to have run into you here. Thank you for the invitation to dinner. My fiancée and I will RSVP as soon as possible. If any changes occur, you have my contact information. Have a wonderful day, sir."

DA Kevon watched in surprise. I leaned forward, gave him a respectable hug, and muttered, "All I know is you call—set your request there, and never speak to me in public about something you were referred to me about. Nod if you understand."

For now, he had one pass from me to do this in public. It was clear that my name was reaching the right connects. I just had to make sure always to spin it in a way to keep myself clear of bullshit. Which is why I enjoyed politics. You learn so much from the real deal criminals in our government.

Stepping back from our hug, the old man made a grand show. He nodded, laughed, and squeezed my shoulder. "Dinner, don't miss it, please. My wife makes the best short ribs around Atlanta. Keep up the good work, son. Soon, I may be casting my vote your way."

Chuckling with him, I shook his hand again, then walked back to the table where Sabrina sat. I gave her face that let her know that I had handled it and sat down.

"Sorry, baby, just an old man looking for an escape clause," I said, reaching for my glass.

I saw that Sabrina was mean mugging me but not saying a thing. I figured that it had to be because I hadn't addressed her appropriately when the DA asked if she was my fiancée or not and because she had to introduce herself. I wasn't sure how to smooth it out, but I figured that I'd try.

"Baby," I started.

"You didn't have to *not* introduce me. That was disrespectful of you, especially when he called me your fiancée. I get that we aren't a clear couple but . . ." she started, then pointed to her stomach.

On some real shit, the nigga in me wanted to act up and ask her why she was tripping, but I kept that in close check. Since being pregnant, I learned that when Sabrina was pissed off, she could cut a nigga's throat cleanly with her words without even lifting her voice, and right now, that was what was happening as I sat there with a bored expression.

"And how are you just going to sit there and look at me like that, huh? I don't mean anything to you, for real? I get it," she said.

Scratching my head, I leaned forward and spoke low. "Pick up that glass to the right of you, baby. Do me that one solid."

"Why? What glass? Really, Marcel," she said reaching over to grab her full water glass.

Under it was a circular card. "Lift the card."

I watched her flip it carelessly with an attitude, then gasp.

"*That's* why I did what I did. He was busting me out before I could even ask you, baby. I'm sorry and please forgive me," I said enjoying the shock on her face.

"You're not joking right now, are you?" Sabrina asked while she waved her hands.

"Nope." Reaching over, I picked up the radiant cut sparkling diamond ring I had custom made for her, and as she sat in her chair shocked, I simply asked, "So, will you?"

Chapter Thirteen

Sabrina

I took a deep breath as I stood outside my father's door. I hadn't seen him since before Christmas. He knew I was pregnant; I was sure of that. Marcel had confirmed it for me. And now that I was getting married, I wanted to see if I could extend an olive branch to him. Marcel didn't care one way or the other. He wasn't in the business of "kissing ass," as he called it. His words stung a bit because I didn't see it as me trying to kiss my father's ass.

I simply wanted him and the man I loved to come to terms. I had no doubt Daddy loved me. The night I told him I was in love with Marcel, I'd like to chalk it up to the fact he had been drinking and hadn't been thinking clearly. Marcel thought otherwise. He told me that my father disrespecting him was one thing, but to put his hands on me and disrespect me was another. I'd come to find out over the time he and I had been together that often when Marcel said something, he meant it, my hurt feelings be damned.

Don't get me wrong; he cared about my feelings. But he was a man of honor and pride. He would never tolerate me being disrespected by anyone. Still, I wanted to see my father. I had hoped that he had missed me just as much as I had missed him. We'd had a good relationship before our falling out. I missed the way I used to be able to laugh and talk with him. In my dreams, I imagined the man I married would get along with my father, and they both would protect me with their lives.

I had no doubts that Marcel would battle the devil for me, but I did doubt my father would as long as Marcel was in my life.

"If you feel like this is what you need to do, Brina, then go on. But stop asking me to go with you. I'm not going. Othello doesn't care about anyone's feelings but his own. Your old man wants to talk to me . . . He knows where to find me," Marcel told me as he got dressed to head out to the bistro.

He was dressed in dark gray dress slacks, black dress shoes that had been spit shined to perfection, and a slim fit dress shirt that complemented his aesthetics. Marcel always looked damn good no matter what he wore. I couldn't seem to keep my eyes or my hands off of him. As he took the time to place the Movado watch on his arm, I watched him.

"Baby, please. I just want . . . I just want you two to try to talk again. Daddy had been drinking—"

"Fuck your father, to be honest," he said as he stared at me, a cold gaze in his eyes that told me there might have been more to his dislike of my father at this point.

Marcel didn't blink as he said those words to me. His eyes never left mine. At that point, I knew it was useless to keep trying to convince him to come with me. I threw the covers back and got up. The roundness of my stomach could be seen through the big tee shirt I had on. I always wore one of Marcel's tee shirts to bed. I tried not to show my displeasure with the fact he wasn't willing to try to work on the relationship between him and my father. But I knew he could tell I was pissed.

He stood in the doorway of the bathroom while I brushed my teeth, arms folded making the muscles in his chest and arms more defined.

"If you're going to be mad at me, be mad about some shit that I've done to you personally. Don't give me shit because I don't want to do what you feel I should. Your attitude is baffling, especially since it's your father you should be giving the cold shoulder. But I digress," he said.

Marcel walked behind me, placed his hands on my hips, then kissed the place on the back of my neck that he always did. I knew he did that on purpose. Anytime I was mad, and he touched or kissed me, my whole mood softened. He stood there and watched me through the mirror for a few more seconds. We always played the stare down game. Not sure if it was a way for us to air out our grievances without using words or another form of foreplay for us. Either way, I knew if he didn't remove his hands or leave soon, I'd be trying to figure out how I went from being mad at him to having him deep inside of me. He knew it too, which was probably why he gave a slick smirk before he turned to leave.

Once he was gone, I got dressed quickly. Pulled on a pair of comfortable dress slacks and a red blouse that had a little flare over the belly area. I slid my feet into a pair of four-inch black pumps, grabbed a sweater, and headed out. Didn't take me long to get to Daddy's house in the Brookhavens Estates in Atlanta. Daddy had it custom built, so it was nestled onto a quiet, private street. Outside the home reminded me of all the white plantation-style homes that were often seen throughout the South during slavery days with a slated roof and big white columns in front of it. The landscaping was impeccable as Daddy always had a thing about image.

I parked the car and nodded at Danny when he let me in. There was a coldness in his eyes. One that told me Daddy had probably said something else to him about the fact I was dating. I always knew Danny had a crush on me, but I often ignored it. There was just no way I would

date a man who had so much loyalty to my father that he
would do anything he told him to do without question.

The foyer was black-and-white with a high ceiling. I
looked up the stairs to see my father slowly stalking
down. He had on a teal smoke jacket, blue slacks, and
black square toe dress shoes. There was a stern look on
his face. He looked at my stomach and then the ring
on my finger. He grunted but didn't greet me . . . at least
not the way that he used to.

He walked past me, then said, "I'm in my study if you
want to meet me there."

Any slight chance of hope I may have had started to
dwindle. I made my way behind him as Danny walked
behind me. I found I wasn't as comfortable with him
at my back as I once was. It was as if I could feel the
daggers from his eyes stabbing me from behind. I got to
Daddy's office just as he was pouring himself a glass of
whatever the amber-colored liquor was in his decanter.
He took a seat behind the big cherry oakwood desk. He
was treating this as if it was a business meeting and not a
father-daughter talk. I wouldn't let him rattle me, though.

I took a seat and smiled. "Hey, Daddy, good to see you.
It's been awhile," I started.

He took a sip of his drink watching me over the rim
of his tumbler. "You're really going to marry him, huh?
Guess you have no choice since you done let him knock
you up."

I dropped my eyes to my lap briefly, then back up at
my father. "Daddy, I don't understand what it is about
Marcel that bothers you so much."

"He's no more than a thug masquerading as a man."

"He's good to me. He takes care of me, and he loves me,
Daddy. What more of a man could you want for me? Look
at what he's done with the bistro."

"Humph. Took some of your money to do it too, didn't
he?"

"Because we're trying to make a life for our child."

"Your mama told me you were investing before even knowing you were pregnant."

"That's what you do when you're trying to make something as a couple."

Daddy didn't say anything for a long while. He kept his drink in his hand and swiveled his desk chair around to look out the big window behind him. His backyard was indeed something nice to look at. Lush flower gardens boasting of different flowers. A stone walkway that led down to an oversized pool. Hedges trimmed to perfection. The back lawn lush and green.

"He has no family, Sabrina. If something happened to him, who's going to take care of you and that baby he done put in you?" Daddy asked without turning to look at me.

"We have money saved up."

"More to life than money. Who's gonna want a woman with a bastard child and a tarnished image? If he left home today and never returned"—Daddy stated, then turned around to look me square in the eyes—"who's going to look out for you?"

I had to catch myself before responding. His words hit me like a ton of bricks. I felt there was a threat in there somewhere. I couldn't be certain, but I got a bad feeling in the pit of my stomach.

Daddy kept going. "That's the kind of man he is, right? Because he has no father, no mother, that's why he doesn't care if you lose your father. He wants you to be out here alone just like he is. The boy don't know what a family is because he ain't got one, so how is he going to provide a stable home for you and a baby? He ain't fit."

"I think you're being unfair, Daddy. You came from a single-mother home yourself. You left Mama when I was 16. Let's not talk about all the fights between you and

Mama or the fact you divorced her and married your side bitch."

Daddy slammed his glass on the desk. A bit of the liquor sloshed around and splashed on the surface.

"You better watch your damn mouth when speaking to me, Sabrina. I'm still your father."

I could feel my anger rising. I should have listened to Marcel. It was a bad idea to come here.

"Then why don't you act like it? If you love me like you claim, then my happiness should be all that matters," I said.

"I should be happy? For you? For what? That you're throwing your life away on this piece of gutter trash?" Daddy bellowed out, then stood, slamming his fist on the desk.

It was time for me to leave. I tried. God knew I did. I would have loved more than anything to have my father walk me down the aisle and give me away at my wedding, but it just wasn't meant to be. For the life of me, I couldn't understand how Daddy could be so critical of Marcel when he ran with a whole criminal enterprise himself.

With tears in my eyes, I stood. "I think it's time for me to leave. I came because I wanted to try to mend our relationship. I'd give anything to have you walk me down the aisle and give me away," I said. "It's something I've dreamed about my whole life, but you're too fucking selfish to see past your own bullshit to be happy for me!"

"You marry him, and I swear to you, Sabrina Ophelia Lanfair, you're going to regret it! I'll write you out of my will—"

"Screw your will. I don't want or need your money, Daddy."

"You would choose him over me?"

I wiped the tears falling down my face. "You gave me no choice."

Those were the last words I spoke to my father before leaving his home. I walked away with my head held high and shoulders squared. I didn't know what possessed me to think I could talk to and find some common ground with him. His pride and his ego had always been bigger than the state of Texas. As I drove to the bistro, I cried all the tears I could cry. My baby would never know either of her grandfathers and that hurt. She wouldn't know one because he was already dead and the other because he was an asshole who couldn't put pride aside for the sake of our relationship.

It had been a year since Marcel had walked back into my life. We'd fallen in love, gotten pregnant, and were getting married, all in a matter of months. Yes, we moved fast, but we didn't feel that way. We were just happy and in love. As soon as I parked in the back parking lot, Marcel opened the door and walked out. He didn't say a word. Just opened his arms. I had to swallow my pride and walk into them. He had been right. There would be no fixing the relationship with my father. He stood there and held me that way until my tears subsided. It was him and me against the world.

And it would remain that way for the next three years.

Three years later . . .

As time went on, life was good for Marcel and me. We got married two weeks after he proposed. We'd gotten married quickly. I didn't want all of the hoopla; especially, since I couldn't get my father to say a nice word to me. Mama, my sisters, and a priest were all in attendance as Marcel and I pledged our love for each other. Afterward, we celebrated with a feast at the bistro. Marcel didn't want Leo to be there, and I didn't question him on it. Anytime Leo was around, I got a strange sense of impending doom. Senior Giulio couldn't make it but did send a nice check to make up for his absence. We took a brief trip to St. Croix for the honeymoon but had to hurry back as Marcel wanted to have the bistro opened by September that year.

Yes, he still disappeared in the middle of the night and sometimes came back days later, but that was the nature of the business he was in. It just became a part of the routine of our lives. Any time he went away, I said a prayer to the Most High that he returned safely. Wasn't that crazy? I said a prayer for my husband to come home safely after he'd been out there making sure someone else's husband, brother, father, etc., wouldn't return home? God was listening, though. Marcel always walked back into our home in one piece.

"Daddy," I heard our daughter, Lyric, yell when the locks on the door turned.

I smiled. She was born two months early on the third of November 2012. That was one of the scariest and happiest times of our lives. Lyric came out kicking and screaming, and the only person who could calm her was her father. Once he took her into his arms, her screams and cries ceased. He'd been wrapped around her little finger ever since.

On the political side of things, Daddy was chairman of the Fulton County Board of Commissioners. Leo Giulio was mayor. After the Feds couldn't find anything tricky or illegal on him, his campaign for mayor kicked into high gear. He sold himself under the guise that he would fight for the little people while my father was a staunch women's rights activist. How ironic? Atlanta had elected two of the biggest crooks around as mayor and chairman. Many more of their henchmen were set to take seats in the government as well.

Marcel fell backward when Lyric jumped on him. It was their thing and made her laugh so hard that it was contagious. She got a kick out of taking her daddy down. She was the perfect blend of him and me with two big curly Afro puffs on the side of her head. She was taller and smarter than the average 3-year-old. She already knew how to fight and use pepper spray. She had her father to thank for that.

"How you doing, munchkin? You're almost stronger than I am, knocking me down like that," he told her.

"I told Mommy I had more muscles now, Daddy," she bragged, then stood so she could flex her muscles.

"Yeah, you do. I can feel them."

"Yeah," she squealed and jumped up and down. "I can-I can-I can do twenty push-ups too, Daddy. Wanna see? You have to see, Daddy."

I laughed because she was on a hundred as she always was whenever he came back after being gone for a few days. That was our life. We had fallen into an easy routine. The bistro was the talk of the town. Leo had even held a few dinners and parties there. I had my own private financial advising business. Marcel had been teaching me lots of things. It started when I was pregnant. From learning how to properly use a gun to teaching me simple moves to defend myself. Five months into my pregnancy, and there I was learning how to roll over my head without harming myself or the baby. He was patient and gentle. Some shit, for the life of me, I just couldn't get. But there was no yelling on his end. A bit of frustration but not condescendingly so. That love and patience rolled over to our daughter. She started walking at 9 months. Being born prematurely hadn't slowed her down one bit. Our daughter had a jab that sometimes made me cringe when she swung at her father.

When he wasn't teaching me how to shoot or her how to fight or at the bistro, he was nestled between my thighs. For some reason, our bodies wouldn't be denied when one wanted the other. Still no permanent cell phone for him, but a cell and home phone for me. Anytime he left to do his work, he left a number for me to call that wouldn't work after he returned home. Of course, I could call him at the diner anytime I wanted. Life had been so well for us that it had fooled me into thinking I had married a normal man.

But trouble was lurking nearby. We should have known. It had been too easy for far too long.

"Let me get out of my work clothes, baby, and then you can show me. I need to see if you can beat me at doing push-ups," he said to Lyric.

She started jumping up and down before running to me. "Um . . . May I have a cookie after I beat Daddy at push-ups, Mommy?" she asked.

"Yes, you can, but you have to beat Daddy first," I said.

"Okay," she said.

She ran to the middle of the front room and started mimicking the stretching techniques she often saw me and Marcel do. He walked over, cupped my face in his hands, then kissed me. Slow at first, then more intense and heated. His hands moved from my face to slide down to my ass. He gripped my cheeks, then brought me closer to him.

He pulled back, cast a heated gaze down at me. "Missed you," he told me.

I smiled, then licked my lips, my arms around his waist. "Missed you more."

I was happy to see my then husband. It had been three days, but there was a look in his eyes that told me something was wrong. I searched his eyes asking him to tell me without actually asking him. I knew he wouldn't.

Not in front of Lyric. So I decided to wait until we were alone. After Marcel and Lyric had done push-ups until he feigned fatigue so she could win, we had dinner. Spent family time together, and then Marcel headed out to check on things at the bistro. I assured him that things were fine, but that place was his pride and joy besides Lyric and me. He had to see for himself.

Once Lyric was asleep, I decided to sit on the couch and wait for him. Before I knew it, my eyes closed. I woke up to movement in my home. I knew it wasn't my husband because the front door was wide open, and he wouldn't have done that. I jumped from the sofa upon seeing a masked man leaning down over me. At least, I tried to jump up. A punch to the face knocked me back down.

I yelped out, then brought my hands up to my face. I kicked my feet out and caught him in the nuts. I needed to get to my baby. The man in front of me fell to his knees. I picked up a vase and broke it over his head. I didn't see the other man coming from the kitchen. He caught me by my ponytail, then threw me into the wall. It hurt, but I didn't have time to focus on the pain. I reached underneath the chair and pulled out the mini-bat I kept there. Lesson number one from my husband was always to have weapons laying around.

When the man grabbed my ankle, I turned over to kick him with the other one. He grabbed that one too, which meant his hands were occupied. I sat up, swung the bat, and connected to his face. He fell back. I got to my feet, then stood over him. I beat him in the face with so much intensity in the four hits that my arms began to hurt. I dropped the bat, then headed toward the hall. A gun to my head slowed me down. My head started to hurt when I looked down and saw the man had Lyric. A gloved hand covered her mouth, and her eyes were wide. Her nose was bleeding, and her hair was wild. The purple Doc McStuffins pjs she had on had splatters of blood on the front. That motherfucker had hit my child was all I could think about.

"What do you want?" I asked him. "We have money."

He chuckled. "Money? If only it were as simple as money. Stop looking at the trees and see the forest, Sabrina."

I swallowed hard. He knew my name. That meant this was personal.

I yelled, "So what do you want?"

"We're just going to wait for the man of the house to get home, and then we can talk," he said nonchalantly.

He was arrogant because he knew he had the upper hand.

"Okay, fine. Just let my daughter come to me," I pleaded.

"Now why would I do that?"

"She's scared you, you piece of shit. Your beef is with her parents. Let her go."

He pointed the barrel of the gun upward to tap his temple. "Let me think about it. Hmm. Nope. Have a seat on the couch," he said.

I would have, but all I could think about was the look of terror on my baby's face. I rushed for the man only to have him whack me in the face with the butt of the gun. I went down hard, blood flying from my nose, dripping down my lips like a faucet.

"Mommy," I heard Lyric scream before the man covered her mouth again.

"Now, we can do this the easy way, or we can do it the hard way. Choice is yours, bitch. Get on the fucking couch," the man yelled, this time with much more bass in his voice.

I was dizzy; my world was spinning as I pulled myself up from the floor. One of the men I'd injured earlier had come to his senses. He snatched me from the floor, then threw me on the couch. I closed my eyes so the room would stop spinning, but it didn't help. I could hear the other man on the floor coming to as well. I was outnumbered again.

"Mommy, you're bleeding. I want my mommy," Lyric yelled again.

"Shut up," the man spat.

"You shut up," she shot back.

He slapped a hand back over her mouth. Next thing I heard was the man grunting in pain. She had bitten him. Wouldn't stop biting him. He finally yanked his hand from her mouth and shoved her into the wall. She hit her head and started crying.

"You son of a bitch," I yelled out.

Tried to get up, but got a gun pointed in my face for the effort. I looked down at the floor to see Lyric stirring. She crawled through the man's legs and ran for me. Before they could catch her, she was on the couch with me. The man closest to me tried to take her, but I wasn't having it. They'd have to kill me to get her away from me. I swung out wildly. Sometimes my feet connected. Sometimes my hands did, but either way, I fought. Gun or no gun, they weren't getting her from my arms.

"That's enough," the man, who I assumed was the leader, yelled. "Leave the child with the bitch. We still have them, and that's all that matters."

The other man stopped, then punched me in the stomach for the hell of it. I groaned out, then lurched forward and emptied my stomach.

"Stop it," Lyric cried, then threw her little frame over my body as if she could protect me. "I want my daddy."

I wanted him too. I was scared, frightened to the point I was shaking. My chest was heavy and eyes burned. Every time I inhaled and exhaled, my chest felt as if it was caving in, but I wouldn't let my daughter go.

"It's okay, baby," I whispered to her. "He'll be here soon."

"And he's going to beat their asses when he gets here," she added.

That was her daddy speaking through her. He had taught her certain words and phrases by default. I'd often told him to watch what he said around her, but to no avail. I'd stopped fighting against it after a while.

"Yes," was how I responded.

"I want my doll, Mommy," Lyric said after a while.

We had been sitting and waiting for at least thirty minutes, and the longer we waited, the more worried I became. Marcel should have been back by now.

"I want my doll, Mommy. I need my doll," Lyric said.

"Shhh, be quiet now. We can't get your doll."

She bucked and threw a tantrum like never before. "I want my doll," she cried loudly. "Give me my dollllll!"

"Shut that little bitch up, or I'm going to cap her," the leader shouted.

I snapped my head in his direction. "Fuck you. She wants her doll. She's a kid, and she's scared. Can't you see that?"

He jumped up and rushed over. I couldn't see his face, but behind his mask, I could see his eyes and mouth. His eyes had turned to slits. Mouth balled and turned into a snarl. "Quiet her or I shoot her."

"I want my dolllll!" Lyric kept at it, and I knew I couldn't make her stop until she got her doll.

"Please, just let her get her doll," I begged.

I didn't know why she wanted that damn doll at that moment, but I would give her anything to ease the fear I knew she felt.

The leader jerked his head toward the other man. "Go get the damn doll."

"I want the one in my chair by the window," she demanded.

"Fucking brat," he spat out.

The other guy disappeared down the hall, then came back with a black doll. The doll was almost Lyric's size and height with Afro puffs to match the style she often wore on her head. It was a doll her father had brought back from one of his work trips before.

Lyric took the doll, then nestled herself against my chest. She kept moving every so often. I thought it was because she was agitated, but then she placed something cool and steel-like in my hand when the men weren't looking. When I realized what it was, I gawked down at my baby.

She whispered, "Daddy says if you're always ready, Mommy, you never have to get re-pre-um-prepared. And in case of a mer-gen-cee, break the glass," she finished, pointing at the chandelier lights above us.

In my hand was a small gun. Had to be a Glock 19 Gen 4 as it fit into my hands perfectly. Marcel had taught me about the smaller handguns women sometimes use when their hands were as small as mine. The fact that my daughter had this gun stored in one of her dolls angered me and made me thank God for a man as crazy as Marcel all at once.

"Break the glass, Mommy, and cover your eyes," she kept whispering.

Lord, have mercy, what had Marcel been teaching our child? I clicked off the safety on the gun. I could tell the men were watching us now. Lyric had been whispering to me for a long while now.

"Yo, stop all that whispering and shit," the leader yelled.

"Fuck you," I spat back. I pulled the gun and shot the other man in the leg.

When the leader and the second man rushed for me, I shot into the chandelier.

"Cover your eyes, Mommy," Lyric yelled.

I did so just as lightninglike flashes went off in the house. I heard popping and cackling. The chandelier rattled and fell to the floor. I put Lyric around my waist, got up, and made a beeline for my bedroom. While the men screamed and yelled behind me, I rushed into the closet, grabbed the black duffle bag on the floor, then pushed a panel on the wall. It slid open quickly, then slammed shut behind us. I rushed down the stairs and pushed the door open that led to the garage. I didn't mean to, but I tossed Lyric haphazardly into the backseat, then climbed in front. She fell to the floor; hit her head on something.

The Charger was a push start, and since the proximity key was in the bag I grabbed, it took me no time to crank the car. I didn't bother opening the garage door. I crashed the car right through the garage door and sped out.

Chapter Fourteen

Marcel

I'd like to acknowledge that my wife was right. I was crazy. My thought process on the protection of my family had me on levels that just weren't attainable by the normal human being.

The choice I made in teaching my 3-year-old Lyric how to defend herself was not something easy for me to rationalize. My wife may not have known that. I agonized over it because I wasn't raised like this. I had a normal-ass childhood. I grew up hearing Jazz, Blues, Classical, hip-hop. I grew up listening to my mom debate with my pops about political shit and law. At 3, I was playing with my building blocks and reading in Spanish because my mother integrated early childhood education in our home.

At 3 years old, I was watching my pops teach me how to play his trombone, the piano, and later taking me to capoeira classes taught by an ex-Black Panther/war vet. The perks of living in a diverse and culture-rich DC. So, teaching my precious and intelligent baby girl what she knew bothered me. I didn't want to groom a child soldier, but I didn't want my baby girl assed out in protecting herself as a child.

Therefore, I made a hard choice. Love me or hate me for it. There were toddlers all over the world who grow up learning skills that American kids learn how to do at 12 years old or not at all. Especially in a tribal mentality, so I made that choice. At 3, I knew how to protect myself somewhat if I ever got lost, and I wanted the same for my baby girl. So, yeah, I did it; hid a Glock specifically made for my wife in our baby girl's stuffed doll, left the knowledge of throwing up a signal for me with my baby girl by having her tell her mother to shoot in certain places, and it saved my wife and daughter's life.

I was stuck in traffic when my Galaxy note tablet was dinging with alerts. At first, I didn't think anything of it. Thought that Brina had tripped the security by accident as she sometimes did when in a rush to leave the house. Nothing in my 27, almost 28 years of life would have had me speculating that Lyric's and her lives were in jeopardy. Nothing.

After marrying Brina, I had taken the steps in my life to continue to learn my craft and keep it separate from family. That meant from my mentorship with other professional killers and military soldiers, I learned to move all my business out of the state I lived in. Any offers that came my way continued to be from a secure line, and I made sure to keep my identity hidden. If I could not keep my identity hidden, I made sure to alter it in some way. As a professional killer, my name was Iago, a dig at my wife's father, or Mr. Charles Usher, a twist on my name.

Nothing more, nothing less.

When people reached out to me, it happened in multiple ways; the main one was when a potential client uttered that they wished something could be handled. This always and only happened in my close circles I worked in around the political officials. It was then I stalked them and studied them. If I felt that they needed real help, they would receive a business card with my untraceable number. They call. I go over the rules, and then we hang up. Afterward, they email or leave me a message of coordinates, and then the rest is on me. Whatever they needed fixed would be fixed.

Often though, word of mouth spread my expert work. I explain all of this because I'm making a point. Yes, I probably had enemies. They usually were people who wanted me dead due to my associations or because of some political shit. If anyone else was after me, it was personal and on some vendetta, and since no one knew me personally in my killing game anymore, except for a select few, then those select few were always watched by me.

Yeah, so, the fact that my crib kept going off had me curious. Reaching into the seat next to me, I tilted my tablet to take a look while my ride moved through the snail traffic. Everything appeared okay, but when another trigger was hit, I knew the alerts weren't accidental. Dropping it, I glanced up and saw an exit ahead. Motherfuckers were blocking me, so I took to the side medium, then hit the exit going down. Whipping around, I took an alternate route until I made it home.

My home was a big, beautiful house sitting back on some land for security purposes and so that my daughter could have room to play outside. I point that out because, before riding up on it, I sat parked, hidden by some massive trees scoping my home. If the threat was worse than some burglars, I needed to know. Every camera in my home was being shut off; wires snipped to keep me from being alerted. Whoever these motherfuckers were, were smart.

However, they weren't too smart; they underestimated my 3-year-old. As soon as I was hit with the chandelier alert, my cameras that were positioned in the trees ticked on and zoomed throughout the house flipping to night scope. At that same time, the sound of my smoke grenades and sensor grenades popped off.

A deep scowl formed on my face while watching my tablet. I scoped my home counting the threat. There appeared to be four men, each one shouting, covering their mouths, and looking around. I did not see my wife or Lyric, and that bothered me deeply until the familiar sound of our Charger blasting through our land out of the gates past me drew my attention. Turning in my seat, I saw it was Sabrina with a frightened but serious look in her eyes.

Pride had me nodding at my wife in respect but had me worried. From my angle, I could not make out if Lyric was with her, and I couldn't call the burner that was in the Charger because I wanted Sabrina to get as far away as possible. All I could do at that point was get out of my car, switch out of my clothes, grab my weapons, and hope. Staying in the lines of our trees, I kept the gas mask I had on secured around my face and goggles.

Motherfuckers wanted to try me? Come for my family? Clearly, they didn't know who they were coming for. However, I was more than happy to give them my introduction. Taking my time, I wrapped around to the front of my house to gauge if there were more men, and there weren't. Guess it was time to act a fool.

Walking to the front, I pushed open the front door and walked in, looking around. I heard nonstop coughing and shouts while I moved through the smoke. In the middle of our home was a huge foyer. Unstrapping some guns, I placed them on a table, then moved on with my shotgun.

"I can't see! I can't find that bitch either!" I heard shouted.

How strong that voice barked allowed me to gather that dude was in a room over, the living room. Shards of glass were everywhere, and I smiled. Glancing up at the celling, I saw the shattered chandelier. I continued moving, dropping low to grab a piece of glass and walk up on to the one that shouted.

Springing up, I hooked my arm around the masked goon's face. These were some amateurs, and I was curious to see who they were, but I had business to take care of. The familiar struggle of a dude such as him fighting against my hold sent me into my void. I squeezed tightly and ripped off the mask.

"Inhale, motherfucker, inhale," is all I said watching my target's eyes struggle.

Because of how I held him, he couldn't move to get behind my hold. All it did was cause me to squeeze tighter and wait it out. After a few, I carefully dragged him by his neck toward the door of our patio. Swinging it open, I pulled him out, felt him reach out fighting for life, fighting by gripping the doorway to stop me from dragging him.

I gave a deep chuckle as I squeezed. "That's all right. I didn't want any blood on the carpet."

That is all I said as I jabbed the shard of glass into my target. The first puncture was difficult because of how he fought me, but once that glass slide through his flesh, then everything came together. In and out, I stabbed, listening to him shout as his blood sprayed everywhere. His arms flailed around in a whirling manner. I slammed my elbow down into his face to stop him from screaming, then slid the glass across his neck cutting deep.

Dropping him, I stepped over him and looked down while pulling off my mask. "Since it wasn't clear who you were dealing with, let me introduce myself. They call me Marcel Raymond. Your life has just been terminated."

Tapping him with my foot, I smirked at the dead fish-eye stare of my target. I noticed that I didn't know him. He was a short, stocky, white guy with bug eyes. No identifying tattoo was on his neck or face, so I shrugged and walked back into the living room.

I noticed while walking back inside that it was silent, which meant that my cover had been blown. I guess that it was time to ante up my game. Heading through the corridor of my kitchen, I kept to the wall and took quiet steps while scoping my area.

No one in the kitchen, so I wrapped around back to the front, stopping near the foyer. Shifting my shotgun, I gave a displeased sigh and looked around as I walked in, more like strolled in. "Why must you motherfuckers make my ass act the fuck up? Not only in my own home but in front of my neighbors? I know they hear this shit, but damn, you really want to meet my special breed of beast, huh?" Releasing the shell, I continued walking. "So be it."

Rounding the corner, I stared upstairs and around. They were somewhere, and I was going to find them.

"You wanted me? I know you did, so don't be pussy, as in the cat. Come at me. Daddy's home, bitches!" I yelled, taking two stairs at a time.

Making sure to glance behind me, I saw a masked man appear in the middle of the foyer. I turned and then let off a round of my shotgun. Buckshot slammed into my target's legs as his bullet grazed my shoulder. Hopping over the banister of the stairway, I rolled, then grabbed the guns I had on the table. Letting off a round, I used my shotgun to stand, then ran after the masked man.

"Where you going? Don't you want me? I'm right here, nigga," I shouted following.

This was a distraction, which is why I stopped running and turned to walk. "Where's the leader? I counted four of you. There's now three; well, two and half, so what up?"

The whizzing of a bullet grazing my thigh had me keeping near the walls again. I glanced outside and chuckled. One was outside, bet.

"Marcel, we've been waiting. Glad that you're here, nigga!" I heard shouted from outside.

A smirk lined my face as I took my time moving through the house. "No doubt. Glad to grace you all with my presence, so what up?"

"You know the deal," the guy said shouting.

The harsh crunch of boots on glass drew my attention. From where I was in the back of the house, I knew several men were coming my way. There was no way to go after them. The only thing I could do was wait. As I did, I saw shadows flicker by, and I knew what to do. Dropping low, I ran. Bullets rang out, showering around me, but I was quicker than one of the gunmen. I landed a fist in one man's face as he stuck his head around the corner to see if he'd shot me. I took my shotgun and slammed it into the face of the second man, then got up.

Breathing hard, I blocked a fist coming for me. Turning, I shot off my Glock and watched the bullet connect with the man's face. His friend rushed me and slammed me to the floor. Several punches slammed into my rib cage causing nothing but blinding pain. I twisted, tried to turn, and gasped when a fist hit my chest.

Inwardly, I cursed as I worked myself away with my legs locking around my attacker's waist, then slamming my fist up against his face. Blood was everywhere running down my face and dripping into my mouth. It caused this fight to become difficult, but it wasn't stressful for me, because I was having a good time. Reaching out, both my assailant and I tried to grab our guns, but it was the window of opportunity where his weight shifted that allowed me to slam my knee up and push him off me.

Shifting in my position, I was on top now, and with me came my fists that slammed into his face. I clamped my hand over his nose and mouth, used my fingers to squeeze his trachea, then grinned when I snapped it and let go.

Dude gasped for air, and I watched. "So, again, you were after me? Damn, they could have sent professionals."

Carefully standing, I walked away, grabbed my shotgun, then shot into the chest of my attacker. The sink was in front of me, which meant we had fought our way back into the kitchen. Thankful for that, I turned on the water, washed my face, then tied off the seeping blood running from my thigh and arm. So I had miscounted. I had one more to go after, and that bitch was outside.

I knew that if I wanted information that he needed to turn into my special "art piece," so that was my aim when I walked down the hall from the kitchen, made a sharp turn, and opened the door to my studio. Moving to stand in front of a large art deco-styled painting of Harlem in the twenties, I hit the corner and watched it slide. Another panel shifted when I pressed my hand against it. After that, a row of weapons popped up. Grabbing an AK-47 and twin katanas, I headed out of the room and outside.

"Bring on who else you got," I shouted, waiting.

"There's only me and you, Marcel," I heard which had me turning.

Staring, I glanced at a tall brotha with scars on his face. He climbed out of the car and gave a smile. As he opened his mouth, I swung my hands forward, and two small marbles rolled underneath the Escalade. The brotha put two and two together and made a run toward the front of the house. A few seconds later, the truck exploded. Fire lit up the darkening sky. I smiled at the fireworks, then heard a gun go off.

Running, I stepped back into the house and watched the brotha with the scar say, "Damn, they didn't tell us what type of killer you were. You're on some high-tech ninja shit, huh?"

A deep chuckle came from me, and I fired back, "Yeah, man, on my Bruce Leroy, but check it, who the fuck sent you?" More gunfire popped off. I kept dodging until I came face-to-face with that nigga again. "And who gave you the right to come in my house and put hands on my wife and child?"

"Now you know I can't answer that," I watched the leader of all this say.

A menacing smile spread across my face, and I nodded. "I was counting on that."

Throwing my blade, I watched it soar forward. What I did was pretty much a distraction, and it worked well. It allowed me to shift my AK and let off some rounds until they hit dude. Shock lit up his eyes, but that went away fast as he shot off rounds at me. I hit the ground to dodge the bullets.

As I moved forward, I didn't give a damn. All I wanted was to bleed this nigga out, for my wife and daughter. Rushing him, I tackled him to the ground, then struck him. Bone cracked under each punch until I got tired of that and reached for my blade to skewer his palm.

His shouts sounded, and I smirked. "I live far enough from others where you can scream all day long. Ain't no one coming. I mean that explosion might draw attention, but we'll see. I know people, and I can keep them away. So, tell me your name."

Twisting the blade with my hand, my foot knocked on that dude's face, and I waited. No reply came, and that annoyed me. He must have blacked out, which wasn't good for me. I wanted to dig into him. But, shit, now I couldn't. I had gotten too zealous in my attack. Glancing around, I removed my blade and picked dude up to carry him inside. Kicking open the door to my basement, I walked on, until I stood in front of a storage shelf. Shifting the shelf, a hall opened, and I walked through,

turning, and then coming to another wall. Tripping it so
it could open, I stood in an unused room, with a metal
bed on it. Dropping dude on it, I strapped him to it, and
then left him, going back upstairs.

It was time for me to clean up, and as I did so, I noticed
that dude I had shot in the chest was still breathing.
Happiness filled me. I picked him up as well and took
him to that room, strapping him to another table I pulled
out. Once done, I patted the face of the leader and waited.

"You ready to talk?" I asked, stepping back.

Nigga said nothing, and I shrugged.

As he watched me, I put on gloves and pulled out my
burner. Several calls to my inside people in the police
kept them at bay long enough for me to do what I had to
do. After that, I called Sabrina.

Several rings hit, and I got nothing. I called again, then
finally heard her beautiful voice. "Oh God, Marcel, I've
been calling you. Where are you?"

"Baby, baby, listen to me. It's all good," I calmly said
with a warm smile. "I'm handling it right now. What I
need to know is if you and Lyric are okay."

"You're handling it? How did you know? Where were
you?" she screamed out as if her internal dam had broken.

The fear and anger in her voice worried me, and I
vowed that I was going to move us to a safer place so this
would not happen again. "I was in traffic when I got the
alert. I came straight home and handled it. Our baby girl
okay? Are you okay?"

"No, we're not okay. They tried to kill us! Lyric hurt her
head. She's okay but has a scratch on her forehead. Are
you okay?" she asked, her voice wavering.

"I'm home and finishing some things. Keep that cell
near you. I'll be coming for you, a'ight?" I started.

"But—"

"Keep it near you. I love you, baby. I'll call you back,"
I said.

Tossing the phone, I looked between both of my prey. "So, let's get the party started."

Stepping between them both, I began my game of "Who." I needed to know who sent them after me. Taking them both apart starting with their fingernails, then toenails, eyelids, and more, the information I got was enough to set me off. Washing my hands, I pulled on my gloves, then zipped the body bags closed. Apparently, Othello had finally reached his breaking point with me after all this time and sent these goons to come for my family. However, after learning about his character after all these years, it was unlikely that he was the one to do this.

Othello might put his hands on his daughter, but he would not put them in harm's way; besides, he had no idea I was a professional killer. I recalled the nigga with the scars speaking about how surprised he was that I was this good. That little thread tipped me off and led me to another idea of who it was.

Leo.

That little motherfucker must have finally lost his fucking mind and wanted to wipe me out. I chuckled low, then made another phone call.

Listening to the rings, I heard it answer, and I asked one question, "È *tempo?*"

Basically, I asked, "Is it time?" then waited.

"*Sì, è il momento. Come ho sempre detto, guardare le spalle. Avete il mio permesso. Contattatemi quando si è fatto,*" the familiar, usually warm but now sad voice replied.

The reply was, "Yes, it is time. As I always told you, watch your back. You have my permission. Contact me when you are done."

I stared at the bodies before me, then hung up. Since coming into Senior Giulio's family, I knew Leo didn't like me. Nigga always put on airs, always tried to make his father turn his back on me and treat me like shit, but for whatever reason, Senior Giulio never would listen to his son. It was later that I learned that I reminded him too much of his other son. Sometimes, I thought maybe that's why Leo hated me so much behind his façade.

Senior Giulio caught it, and it was later after I had Lyric that he called me to Italy and had me train with him one last time, as well as told me some truths. That truth was this: Leo had killed his older brother for power, power of Atlanta, and power of the family name. The years I spent under Senior Giulio's tutelage was meant for a bigger gain—to kill Leo—so that the legacy could be given to me. I was shocked at it.

Orphans understand the true meaning behind family, and that is honor, loyalty, and love. He was once an orphan and fell in love with his future wife in the same manner I did with Sabrina. He'd told me it was what let him know that I understood the true strength in love, and that was family. Leo didn't care about any of that. He only cared about himself and what his father's name and legacy could do for him. Because of that, I now had the approval to shift everything in motion.

Kill those who bring harm to what's mine.

Chapter Fifteen

Sabrina

The safest place to be was in the basement of the bistro. There was actually another small bunker underneath the basement. Marcel had always told me to come here and lie low if ever things got crazy. And it was safe to say, shit had just gotten crazy.

"Mommy, my head hurts," Lyric whined.

I ran a hand through my hair as I paced the cool, concrete floor. I'd left the house with no shoes, only the clothes on my back. My whole body ached. My head was throbbing. I sat next to Lyric on the small bed I had lain her on. There was a small gash on her head, but she would be okay. I took the white washcloth from the bowl of ice water and put it back on her head.

"I know, baby. Lie back for me," I urged her.

She was still holding on to that doll. On the one hand, I was pissed that Marcel would put a gun in such close proximity to our child. On the other, I could kiss the man while cussing and kicking his ass. Our baby knew more than I did in the heat of the moment. That made me ashamed in a sense. I mean, I knew all he had taught me, and I knew it well. Still, the fact that my daughter knew how to effectively throw a tantrum, handle a gun well enough to put it in my hand, and how to trip whatever was in the chandelier that had been hanging above us made me feel inadequate.

"I'm so proud of you, Lyric. You know that?" I told her
as I covered her head.

She smiled wide and nodded her head. "I did good,
Mommy," she bragged.

"Yes, you did, baby."

"Is Daddy coming now? Will he be here with us?"

I rubbed a hand in her hair. "He's coming, baby. I'm
sure of it."

The only thing I wasn't sure of was what this meant for
our family. Once I made sure Lyric was okay, I took the
black duffle bag I'd grabbed as I ran through the closet.
Inside were extra copies of all our personal papers.

*"Always keep extra copies of everything, including the
marriage certificate," Marcel had said to me a few weeks
before Lyric was born. "When the baby is born, always,
always, no matter what you do, keep more than one
copy of the birth record, birth certificate, Social Security
cards, and always keep cash on hand," he added.*

"Why do we always need extra copies?" I asked.

*"We may have to run one day, Brina, and I want you
and the baby always to be safe. I need you always to
have what you need . . . just in case. Just like the packed
bags in the car in the parking garage. We must always
be ready to move at a moment's notice," he said while
moving around our bedroom.*

*What he'd said made a flock of butterflies flutter
around in my stomach. Run? Where? Why? Was he
trying to tell me something without actually saying it?
He must have picked up on the look on my face.*

*"In my life, it would be crazy of me to think that one
day, my demons won't come back to haunt me, Sabrina,"
he said.*

*He walked over to the bed, taking my hand. I stood,
then looked up at him. I knew what he was talking
about. I knew he had done some ruthless things. I think*

what made me love him more was that he didn't try to
find a way to make excuses for it.

"Does that mean one day, we'll have to leave this life
behind?" I asked.

Marcel cupped my face in his hands, then kissed my
lips. "Yes, one day that may become our reality, but
know as long as I'm breathing, no harm will come to
you that I won't rectify. I wasn't playing when I said I'd
kill anyone who caused you harm. I do mean anyone."

I closed my eyes at the feel of his lips on my forehead.
Anytime he said those words, my mind always went
back to the night my father hit me. There was no doubt
in my mind that if it wasn't for the fact that killing my
father would hurt me, Marcel would have made good on
his promise that night.

That had been three years ago. I'd forgotten those
words until tonight. I made sure all the bank cards and
cash were accounted for. Guns, IDs, passports, keys
to different cars in different locations, burner phones,
Lyric's extra inhalers, and few other essentials were
all there. I looked over and realized Lyric was asleep. I
wasn't sure if I should have allowed her to sleep since
that thug had thrown her headfirst into the wall, but I
couldn't bring myself to wake her. I'd check on her every
hour to make sure she was okay.

I stood too fast and almost fell back over. My head
still didn't feel right. I managed to stand anyway. Pulled
my shirt over my head and looked at the cuts, scrapes,
and bruises. I'd come a long way from that scared, timid
woman Marcel had first encountered. I wasn't some
badass, kick-ass, gunslinging woman, but I was no longer
afraid of my own shadow. The feeling of inadequateness
subsided as my nerves started to settle. Maybe I wasn't
as inept as I thought tonight. Quiet as kept, I was proud
of myself.

I stepped out of the shorts and underwear I had on, then walked over to the small shower stall sitting off in the back corner of the bunker. When Marcel was having the bunker built, I thought he was a bit extreme in his defense mechanisms, but I would gladly eat my words now. I felt safe as no one knew it was here. The man who had built it came up missing soon after it was finished. The water and soap stung, but it felt good to get cleaned. I grabbed a pair of sweats from the trunk of clothes we had there. They smelled a bit stale, but a hint of Tide still lingered on them.

I waited around for another hour before Marcel showed up. When I heard movements upstairs, I jumped up and grabbed a gun. I knew no one would find us unless that person was really looking but being that someone had just attacked us to get to my husband made me feel anything was possible. I stayed hidden in the shadows when the latch opened. Didn't move until I knew for sure it was Marcel. He stepped down into the light, black book bag thrown over his shoulder.

He told me he had handled the situation, so I instinctively looked him over trying to assess injuries.

"Remember when I told you one day we may have to leave this life behind?"

I nodded. "What's going on?" I asked.

Marcel dropped the bag on his shoulder, then sat on the small bed beside Lyric. He pulled the covers back and looked her over, no doubt checking for more injuries.

"That day may come sooner rather than later," he said looking up at me. "Somebody put a hit out on me. Had to be someone with explicit knowledge of the double life I lead."

I placed the gun back in the safe-lockbox, then asked, "How-how do you know?"

"One of the motherfuckers I had to kill informed me of it. Said your pops was behind it."

My eyes widened, and the bottom fell out of my stomach. "Daddy may be an asshole, but I can't see him going this far, and why now? This doesn't—"

"Make sense?" he added, finishing my sentence. "I know, which is why I knew it was a lie."

He stood, then pulled his shirt over his head. He had patched up a wound on his abdomen. The square-shaped, thick, white gauze was red with his blood.

I grabbed the first aid kit and walked over to him. "Let me look at you," I said.

He moved my hands away. "I'm fine."

He tried to move around me, but I grabbed his arm. "Marcel." He stopped, took a deep breath, the looked at me. "Let me help you."

He frowned a bit. In his eyes, I could see a million things going on in his mind. But he took a seat on the other bed in the small space.

"Lie back," I urged gently.

He did, reluctantly so. I pulled on the latex gloves from the kit, then removed the gauze. I gasped at the extent of the wound.

"It's just a cut, Brina," he said. "Nothing major has been hit."

"Oh-okay. Still, let me clean it and redress it properly."

I was still a bit nervous. My husband had been sliced open, and my daughter was sporting a gash to her head. I didn't know if I wanted to cry or lash out in anger at the audacity of the men who had attacked us. I cleaned Marcel's wounds, then stitched him up. Anytime he winced or hissed, I felt as if it was me who had his injury. Once done, I redressed the wound, then walked over to the sink to take the gloves off and wash my hands. I turned back around to find him sitting up, head down, hands clasped together between his thighs. His forehead was furrowed like he was in deep thought.

"Who's trying to kill you, baby?" I wanted to know.

His eyes slowly met mine. "Leo."

I shook my head, then started pacing the floor again. While I didn't believe my father would have anything to do with trying to have my husband killed, I could believe Leo would. Over the years, Marcel's and Leo's faux friendship had become increasingly hostile. I walked in once on Leo telling Marcel that he had gotten beside himself and forgot his role in life. I hadn't paid much attention then as Marcel didn't like when I got into his business on that side of things. I didn't mention that I'd overheard that conversation either.

Still, something seemed all too obvious behind the whole thing.

"Wouldn't Leo be the obvious, baby?" I asked him. "I mean, first, they told you my father was behind it and assumed you would believe it. But you say Leo is behind it which would also be obvious. I mean, would he be that stupid to send men after you, then have them tell you my father did it only so you could figure out that it was really him? Doesn't that strike you as odd and desperate, even for Leo? I mean, he has done some cruel and desperate things to win that mayoral seat, but he's a smart man, no? He's cunning and crafty. He wouldn't come at you so haphazardly."

I watched the way Marcel's shoulders expanded as he breathed slowly. "Been thinking about that too. It's all too convenient. I do know that this is about more than me as well. I knew us marrying would ruffle some feathers. I'm surprised it took this long for someone to try to come after me, and I'm sure you will be who they target next. But, as always when it comes to black families, they tried to take me out first to make it easier to get to you."

"Me?" I asked, eyes widened. "Why me?"

"Baby, four years ago you sat at a table in the bistro with six of the crime world's most notorious lords. They handed you confidential files on the financials of their operations so you could help make it look legitimate. I've done work for those men, and while they would never disclose my identity to the world, us being married presents a problem for them. Between us, we have enough information to take whole enterprises down."

I let out the breath I had been holding. A whole new type of fear crept up my spine, and I looked over at our daughter resting peacefully.

"Oh dear God," I muttered.

A mixture of hot and cool sensations made me shiver at the thought. My breaths became shallow. I had been so worried about him being killed that the thought of them coming after *me* never crossed my mind. I felt so stupid that I hadn't thought of what Marcel had told me.

"Yeah," he replied, then stood. "This is about more than me. This is about us and how we could crumble an entire criminal enterprise. We have too much power, and because of that, we have targets on our backs."

Tears burned my eyelids at the thought of Lyric being here all alone if we got ourselves killed. A weight pressed on my chest as my stomach knotted in fear. I couldn't leave my baby here alone. Panic resided in me, but I didn't want to alarm Marcel or worry him with it. Clearly by the way he moved like a heavy anchor had been attached to him, he had enough on his plate.

For as long as we had been together, it had never crossed my mind that my work for the crime bosses would come back to haunt me. It had been years, and I'd never opened my mouth. Had never said a word about what I knew. Some of their financials were hooked to some pretty heavy political players in the U.S. government. I'd gone in and made it all legitimate on paper. I had to go in and structure bank deposits, so they didn't look suspicious. And since each man sitting at that table did indeed own legitimate business, I had to make sure the deposits made sense. During the weekdays, there was no way one Laundromat should be depositing over ten thousand dollars a day.

Then I had to look into financial institutions elsewhere, like in Panama and the Bahamas as they were very accommodating to criminals looking to legitimize their cash. They were unrestricted with regards to banking laws and anti-laundering procedures. I decided against the Cayman Islands since they were the typical go-to for criminals. Also, China and Pakistan had a history of well-established underground banks that helped in that as well.

I also made the shell companies seem more profitable than they were. There were also the legitimate companies like the bars and strip clubs, the casinos and all other avenues of legitimate cash I had a hand in stabilizing. More often than not, it wasn't the drug dealing or extortion that got these kinds of criminals caught. It was their attempt to hide all the money. And I knew where all their money was. Common sense should have told me they would come after me sooner or later. I never once thought about how my dealings would affect our daughter, and for that, I wanted to bang my head against a wall.

I didn't want to, but I couldn't help it. Anxiety hit me like a head-on collision.

"The next forty-eight hours are critical, mama. We have to decide whether we stay and fight or do we leave the life we know behind and start anew somewhere else," Marcel said.

I knew he was serious by the tone in his voice.

"And those are the only options we have?" I asked just to be certain.

He cast a gaze at our daughter. "If it were just us, I'd say we stick around, but she makes all the difference in this. It's no longer about us. We have to do what's best for her; everything else is moot."

"So, once we leave, if we decide to leave, then what? What about my mom and my sisters?"

Marcel ran a hand over the waves in his head. He reached into his pocket and held a phone out to me.

"I suggest you call them now and say your goodbyes."

My heart fell to my stomach. Tears clouded my eyes. "What does that mean?"

I knew what it meant. I just didn't want to accept it.

"Sabrina, I need you not to be emotional right now, okay? I'm not being an asshole. I'm just telling you this is not the time. I need you to get it together because this is important. You have to know, without a doubt, that you're willing to go to the end of the world and back with me. We can't make moves to disappear if we have to unless you're 100 percent with me. I know you don't want to your leave mother and sisters behind, but if we have to move, then we have to move soon."

I covered my mouth as my tears fell. Mama loved Lyric so much. It was going to kill her for us to disappear like we never existed. My sisters would be up in arms about it. But most of all, it was going to hurt for a long time knowing that this phone call could be the last I'd have with them. I moved closer to Marcel's outstretched hand and took the phone.

A few minutes later, after my emotional response to our reality had subsided, I woke Lyric. It took her a minute to get her bearings about her. She rubbed her eyes and yawned. As soon as her eyes found Marcel, she made a beeline to him, jumped around his waist, and wrapped her arms around his neck.

"I-I-I did everything you said, Daddy," she told him.

He gave a lopsided smile. "I know you did, baby. You did well too. Very good."

I sat on the bed and dialed my mother's number, praying she was awake at this hour. She answered on the fourth ring.

"Hello?" her voice was groggy, and it was clear the ringing phone had awakened her.

"Hey, Mama. How are you?" I asked.

"Sabrina? Girl, what are you calling me for this time of night? Everything okay?" she wanted to know.

I could hear covers rustling in her background. I assumed she was sitting up in bed, probably grabbing her glasses so she could see better. Sometimes Mama felt as if she couldn't speak well without her glasses on. I had no idea how one correlated with the other, but that was just the way her mind worked.

"Um, yeah. I mean . . . I just wanted to talk to you. Lyric wanted to as well. We were up. She's, ah . . . not feeling very well," I said, speaking as truthfully as I could.

I knew Mama was smiling when she said, "Well, let me speak to my grandbaby. See what Nana can do to help her feel better."

I handed Lyric the phone. "Hello, Nana," she beamed.

"Hello, baby. You don't sound sick," Mama said.

"I hit my head."

"Oh no. How'd that happen?"

Lyric looked at her father, and he shook his head. "Was running and hit it on the wall, Nana."

Marcel and Lyric had a relationship that even she and I didn't have. They communicated without words sometimes. I was sure his shake of the head was to tell her not to tell Mama the truth. She was a tough cookie, and it was all thanks to the man holding her in his arms. As I listened to my daughter speak with my mother, knowing it could be the last time I'd hear her voice in a long time, quite possibly for the rest of my life, was a humbling experience. Marcel and I had lived the good life, a modest one, but a good one. We weren't flashy although the bistro did very well, and each of our side jobs was lucrative. We were both smart enough to know that living a flashy kind of life wasn't the way to go.

Once Lyric was done, she handed me the phone again.

"She's going to be just fine. Little thang smart as a whip. You and Marcel are doing a good job with her," Mama complimented.

"Thank you," I said. "Mama?"

"Yeah, baby. You sure you're okay? You don't sound so well yourself."

I didn't want her to know I was crying. My head fell back, and I looked up at the ceiling.

"I'm okay. Just tired and sleepy. Was worried about Lyric."

"Oh, okay, then. I gotta get up here in a few hours and head to work. Let me get all the sleep I can. Dealing with old-ass Mrs. Drescher gets my nerves to jumping. Old-ass, rich, Jewish woman called me 'colored' yesterday," she said, then laughed. "I have to be well rested dealing with her. I love you, baby, but call me tomorrow, okay?"

I knew that wouldn't be possible. I wanted to keep her on the phone for as long as I could. I couldn't and as bad as I wanted to find something, *anything* to talk about, I knew it was best I didn't prolong the inevitable.

"I love you too, Mama."

"Okay, baby. Now good night."

"Wait, Mama."

"Yeah?"

I just needed to remember her voice. "Have a good day tomorrow and always remember, no matter what, we love you. My family . . . We love you."

I could hear her smiling. "I know you do. Rest well, Sabrina. Give my love to Marcel."

I laid the phone next to me. I wanted to call my sisters but couldn't bring myself to go through the whole thing again. Wondered if I should have called my father but thought better of it. Hadn't spoken to that man in three years. I'd seen him plenty over the last three years, in passing and in social settings, but he wouldn't spare me a second glance. Maybe starting over somewhere else wasn't all bad.

Chapter Sixteen

Marcel

Having my family cooped up in my hidden bunker wasn't the big aspiration I had in my goals of life for them. It honestly only added to how pissed I was about the situation. I had broken down to Sabrina the choices we had to survive right now. There were only two. Either we go, or we stay and fight. Giving Sabrina that ultimatum was more so about her finally understanding the life she committed herself to in marrying me. Was it fair? Nah, but it was unavoidable.

I lay, holding my baby girl at night, rocking her as was our thing. As we all slept, my other arm was also wrapped around Sabrina. Every morning around three or four—it always changed—I'd low-key leave to set things in order for us. That routine continued off and on for at least a week until I, ultimately, moved Sabrina and Lyric out of the bunker.

Every move I made was purposeful in regards to us possibly being watched and made damn sure that when I moved that my actions were always undetectable.

"Dad-dee," I heard my daughter say as she sat in the backseat in her car seat swinging her little legs.

Sabrina was beside me watching me and surveying our surroundings as I asked her to do. She and I wore hats and leather jacket hoodies, while little momma wore a hoodie as well.

"What is it, baby girl?"

Switching lanes, my attention was on her but also on everyone around us while my gloved hands gripped the steering wheel.

I watched Lyric casually play with her doll. I had switched out the gun because I was with her and had a chip phone hidden in a soft clip in her doll's puffs. The gun was hidden against Sabrina's inner thigh.

"Can we see Grandma?"

That simple question had me thinking as I checked the van ahead of us that turned on to another ramp. That was our decoy just in case we were being followed. I had some friends working that one as we rode out of Atlanta.

"I'm thinking about it because Daddy is going to have to do some extra work." I felt Sabrina's eyes lock on me.

I was contradicting what I had told her earlier, but this was our daughter. I wasn't ready to fully tell her that we might have to leave her only home.

"But Daddy has a question," I said softening my voice into a playful banter.

"Yes! What is it?" Lyric spat out in happiness.

"How would you like to go visit some dolphins? Or ride the back of a tall giraffe? Remember those pictures I showed you?" I asked, watching her.

I moved into a new lane, then made a sharp turn up a ramp. Watching my surroundings, I then turned and headed toward Roswell.

"Yes, sir," she said sharply, joyously laughing as she made her doll dance. "I want to ride the giraffes. I think we can hide better with the giraffes."

Shocked, I chuckled to myself, then glanced at Sabrina.

"Then maybe Grandma can come visit us, and aunties, yeah?" she added sitting up to make me stare her in her eyes in my rearview mirror.

Yet again, she was in my mind, as she always was since an infant. It made me smile. Made me adamant about protecting her and her mother. A major part of me was sick with the idea of leaving what I had built, but shit, I knew me. I could easily rebuild later, and if my daughter wanted to play with the giraffes, then that's what we were going to do.

"I think that's a damn good idea, baby girl. I promise that I'll try my best to make that happen," I said with warmth in my voice.

"Okay," she said relaxing back. "It's okay if you don't. I'll still love you, Daddy."

Grinning wide, I relaxed and sped on. "I know you will, baby, and that and your mom's love is all I need."

Whipping our ride, I drove us through an underpass, then turned until we made it to a gated condominium complex.

"*Wow,* baby," I heard Sabrina say.

"Daddy, where are we?" Lyric asked while I punched in codes.

"Your new home for now. We live way up there with the balcony," I said pointing toward the massive high-rise.

Disappearing in a parking zone, I glanced at Sabrina and then leaned forward to open my glove compartment and pulled out a set of spare keys. "These are to a safe deposit box in BB&T Bank. If anything ever happens to me, if I 'disappear' for any reason, go empty that box. Then you and Lyric leave right from the bank to the airport. Make no stops. Do you understand me?"

Sabrina's eyes held wild panic, but she nodded. I needed her to understand what I wasn't saying, and it comforted me when I reached up to rest my hand against her neck that she stared at me all in like the very first day I saw her.

"You'll be protected here, on my word. I have trusted eyes that will be watching you."

"Whatever you do, we'll follow," Sabrina said, and it made me kiss her with loving passion.

Tongues dancing, I let my teeth nip her lower lip, then leaned back with the sound of her soft moan. "Just keep chill, and we'll be a'ight for now. I can't promise 100 percent safety, but you will be protected. So for anybody to get to you, they'll have to go through hell first."

After that, we found our way upstairs and in our new home. Lyric jetted inside as if she had lived in the large four-bedroom condo before. All I saw were her little Skechers flashing their lights, and it had both of us following until we found her in her room in her huge canopy bed.

"Damn, she just said fuck the rest and called dibs. She must have known what the deal was," I said laughing while dropping my hoodie back.

Sabrina's arms wrapped around me as we stood and watched Lyric rest. "You have her name on the wall and Doc McStuffins everywhere. Duh, she knew this was her room, and she's like you. She sleeps on her own terms."

Feeling embarrassed as I chuckled, I turned to get my arms around my wife. "True enough. Let me give you the rundown, though. As before, see that mermaid? There's artillery there and under her bed, as well as in the closet. The chandelier in the entryway is rigged the same. The kitchen has three switches . . . one by the coffee machine, one under the ledge of the island, one by the refrigerator. They all trigger an alert and shift the kitchen into a safe zone with weapons."

"Marcel—" Sabrina started.

"One second because I'm not done. Our bedroom and bathroom are decked out the same way with alert triggers. We have videos, and my additional eyes can be here under one second if something goes down. No one, and I mean *no one,* knows of this place. Don't bring anyone here. I need to clear everything up first. If we decide to stay, then we'll speak to the front desk and add names, okay?" I asked, explaining to make sure that she understood all of this. "There're three exits as well, with three rides waiting for you. The Charger, a truck, and the ride we rode in. I need to go back out now, baby."

Sabrina gave me nods, then abruptly stood back with a tilt of her head. "Really? You just dropped us in this gorgeous place, and you're leaving?"

"Baby," walking her backward, we found ourselves against a wall, and I planted my hands on each side of Sabrina's head as I spoke to her. "All I want to do is stay under you and inside of you. Slip deep into you and bless our home right, but I can't. Leo is who I have to deal with and is why I'm leaving. Keep chill and think about if we are going or staying. If you got any ideas about doing business with the mob or anything else, I'm listening. Otherwise, write it down."

Sabrina's gaze stared up at me. Our closeness was making it uncomfortable for me, had my manhood eager, but I knew that I needed to focus on this family. Even as my wife's small hands slid up my chest, then her arms wrapped around me, I tried to check myself. Until she said, "Leo has an off-shore account. The money goes directly to a Ginny Briton and an L. J. Briton. I'm pretty sure that L. J. stands for Leo Jr., and I'm pretty sure that this Ginny is his mistress. And, baby? I'm pretty sure that this is one secret that he doesn't want known. Maybe . . . Maybe you can use it as leverage."

Everything she said had my mind churning. Leo had secrets that I knew could get him ousted from his state seat. However, something like what she was saying could do so much more.

He hurt my family; then I figured that I would only play well with the scales if I did the same to both of his families.

"Where is this account based?" I gently asked.

The flicker of anxiousness flashed across Sabrina's beautiful face. I found myself kissing her temple and keeping our connection strong and reassuring.

Exhaling and looking away while shaking her head as if she was making a mistake, she whispered, "Anguilla."

Grinning, I picked Sabrina up and took her to our room where I decided to push back an hour of my time and spend it making my wife's walls quake and line them with my DNA. She was on my side, even though it was hard, and I wanted to honor her and show her how much I appreciated it. I also wanted her to know that she never has to sacrifice a piece of her morality ever again. I got that covered for the both us.

After putting her to sleep, I dressed in my best, shaved, slipped on my geek glasses, and then drove to the offices of Leo Giulio.

"Excuse me, sir?" was sharply said my way fifteen minutes later.

Checking out the short blonde with the cocoa-brown skin, I gave a respectable smile and stepped back from the oak double doors that led to Leo's office.

"I'm sorry, I'm on the list," I said flashing my aide badge.

"And you are?" she said swiveling in her chair to get a better look at me.

Better look meant my dick print as that was where her eyes were zoomed in.

Mama was sizing me up good, her eyes stripping me, and it had me coming closer.

"Director Aide to Mr. Giulio," I said slowly, resting a palm against the side of her desk. "And he would most definitely want to speak with me."

"Oh, I was under the impression that that position was vacant," she said still studying me.

"No, ma'am, as you see, I'm here in the flesh," I said back.

Whenever I was out of town, my position would go vacant until I got back. The rest of the aides handled all my "business." Clearly, this woman wasn't clued in on that, or she knew some shit that I didn't, such as, technically if Leo was gunning for me, I should be dead. Which would make sense why the position was vacant.

"True, and very sexy flesh at that," she muttered the last part as if I wouldn't hear her. "Well, Mr. Giulio is busy right now."

"That's fine; he'll still see me, cutie," I said with a slick smile.

Before she could distract me anymore, I walked off and pushed through the door. Leo was *definitely* busy. Busy between the thighs of one of his female aides. I stood there watching as a pretty peanut-butter brown sista arched and fondled her melon-sized breasts. Her fingers slipped over her cocoa areolas to pinch and tug at her nipples while her face was frozen in a mask of ecstasy.

A lot of smacking and slurping was going down while I took a seat and pressed a finger against my temple to watch the show. If it weren't for Leo leaning back to strum his lover between her thighs, this nigga wouldn't have even known I was there. Had I been trigger-happy as well, he wouldn't have even been aware to plead for life because both he and his aide would have been dead by the gun that rested on my lap.

So I sat there and waited as the X-rated show went on . . . until he stopped and noticed my presence.

"Holy shit! Marcel," he said, stumbling backward.

"Don't mind me; go ahead and do your friend," I said with a bored tone. "Don't get me wrong, though, I see she was enjoying how you ate her, man, but you might want to flip her around and bust that nut. I'm just saying. Would make things more interesting. Don't you think, cutie?"

The woman I addressed was embarrassedly gripping the front of her shirt as she watched. She quickly stood, but the slick smile that flashed on her face let me know she was the type that enjoyed being watched, but for all intents and purposes, she had to pretend as if she wasn't. Which is why she tugged at her skirt and rushed out of the room. I was pretty sure she was so flustered that she didn't even notice that I was carrying heat.

As she went by, I simply leaned to the side and watched her in approval. "I think you moved up in the game since your last one. Baby girl got a nice phatty."

From the corner of my eye, I saw Leo adjusting himself and pulling up his clothes. He haphazardly pulled his shirt closed, then took a seat. "What are you doing here? What the *hell* do you want?"

I watched him curiously. Nothing in how he addressed me said that he was a man who had put a hit out on me. Now, he could have been playing me, but I knew that he wasn't from years of studying him and others I've come across in my work. So, it was really bothering me to conclude that something was up, and I had no clear clue what that was.

Tapping my fingers across my gun, I sat and watched him, not saying a thing, still accessing him, still trying to put the pieces of this all together.

"Marcel, what do you . . . wait . . . wait . . . What's with the gun?" he said finally getting the picture. "What do you want?"

"I thought it was to see you dead, but I might be wrong about that right now. I'm still deciding," I calmly said.

"Dead? Dead? Why? Have I been nothing but like family to you? Loved you like a brother?"

Fear made people talk the most bullshit ever known. That's why I enjoyed taking my time with my kills occasionally. Shit could be a riot. A straight comedy show if you got the right mark. It all was determined on the grade level a person's so-called moral compass ran. The Leo I knew was operating on a Level H of having a moral compass. That meant that he was the worst of worst, but when pressed with a stressful situation, then the motherfucker suddenly remembered his Hail Marys full of grace. Such as the case scenario going on now.

"Now you feel that way? My man, now you feel that way?" I gave a sharp, sarcastic laugh, then stood up.

"I'd never do something like that to you, especially with how close you are to Father, and how much he loves you, bro," Leo quickly expressed.

Slowly strolling around the room, I stopped in front of his office door, then locked it. "Nigga, I've known you for a while now, and in the whole time I was given the chance of being a part of your family, you've only seen me as a rival. So don't play me."

Turning his way, I walked slowly toward his desk with my hands behind my back, gun included. "You might want to tell your secretary to go to lunch or let her off for the day. Me and you need to have a long conversation about you trying to kill my family and me. Mainly my wife."

Feigned shocked lit up Leo's dusky features. I knew from how he worked his mouth that he was about to stumble over some lies, but I didn't have time for that shit at all.

"Do what I said, or I'll shoot you right now, and we both know I don't want to do that . . . just yet," I calmly stated.

It was then that I continued my pacing, admiring the artwork that Leo had on display. A mint condition Jackie Robinson baseball was on his mantel. Because I wanted it, I took it off its holder. Moving on, I checked out a unique, colorful painting over the mantel of his fireplace while listening to Leo dismiss his secretary.

"There," he said slamming the phone down.

Once I felt he was done with his dramatic tone, I turned to see him raising a Glock at me. I mean, I wasn't shocked by it, and it truly made my day; however, it also annoyed me because that meant I'd have to put bullets in him earlier than I wanted.

"Leo," I said, quickly squeezing the trigger.

A slight thud noise sounded, indicating it hit Leo in his calf where I aimed. The additional sound of him scream-ing had me walking toward him from an alternative angle to move out of the way of his gun.

"You shot me! You *really* shot me," he yelled, cradling his calf.

"No shit and you held my wife and daughter hostage and tried to kill them and me, or nah?" I said leaning against his desk. Tossing the ball in the air, I grabbed my briefcase, popped it open, and placed it inside. "Let's be candid while you clean yourself up."

"I didn't come for you, Marcel," he hissed our between his teeth. "Why would I do something so dumb when you are nothing but an asset to me?"

"Exactly for that reason. Let's not be dumb here. No one knows what I do. No one. Tell me how killers could come to my home and specifically look for me, then spit your name out." As I spoke, I adjusted my gloves. "Either you did it, or you told my business to a common enemy, something you know never to do, my man. So what's the deal?"

Leo screamed, then stopped. When I looked his way, he was lunging at me, trying to slice me with a knife. The power that came with that attack caught me off guard. I wasn't expecting that because it had been a long time since I saw him fight with his hands. He was always a gunman and nothing more. Therefore, his quick swipes had me leaning back and sliding off his desk as he came for me baring his teeth.

A swift kick to his shin could take him down, but how he was twisting his body to avoid my fist had me keeping on guard from being sliced by his blade. The slam of his fist to my face, split my glasses down the middle, shattering them and causing me to stumble backward. I shook my head trying to clear my vision and then crossed my arms to block his punches, then swipe away his knife as he yelled.

"You shot me, nigga! I didn't come for you. Too many people want you dead for the favors you've done for shifty motherfuckers like me. Why would I risk losing your talent by killing you?" he shouted through each swing.

The side of a table hitting me knocked my gun from my hand. Our ruckus caused all types of shit to fall in our battle royal. Of course, this was some bullshit, but it was a fun one for me. I jabbed forward and landed a blow to Leo's throat, causing him to gag.

"Because since day one, you wanted me dead, nigga. Called me your pop's nigga pet," I spat out slamming my elbow into his collarbone. "You're greedy and can't accept that I don't want shit from y'all but my right to live my life on my own terms. Essentially, my freedom."

That move left me open for him to hit me hard in my ribs and allowed him to stumble back shaking his head before thickly saying, "Even if what you're saying was true, you're still here, nigga. What you do leaves you with an X on your back! Dumb-ass nigga. If it's not me, then it's someone else!"

Fire had my lungs blazing while I caught my breath. Both Leo and I stared hard at each other while we stood our ground.

"It wasn't me," he said panting and resting his hand against the oak paneling of his wall. "I still need your gun, and my pops demands you live always," Leo breathily said, then looked down at his leg in disbelief. "You shot me."

Wiping sweat from my eyes and blood from my mouth, I limped forward, grabbed my gun, then walked around him. There was no trust here with him and me, but there was loyalty on my end. It was clear again that some shit was off base, and his word wasn't going to be enough.

Body aching, suit fucked all the way up, I did my best to keep chill. I was knocking on that void and wanted to cross that threshold badly, but I was schooled better than that.

Pausing, I stared Leo in his swollen eye, then sent him slamming to the floor with one punch. "Yeah, and you get to live . . . for now."

I walked out of his office, disheveled and in my thoughts as he yelled obscenities behind me.

Nigga could have been playing me, but for now, I planned to let him live. I had to. Though I had clearance to end him, I knew his death would be too much for his pops. I also needed him alive to watch him. It wasn't that I didn't believe him; it was because what he said I had already thought out. It could have been anyone who wanted me dead. I needed more info to figure out who, though. I needed them to know that I was alive just to test to see what was to come next. Because something in the air said my life was on borrowed time, and I needed to find out the truth, for the sake of my family.

Chapter Seventeen

Sabrina

No secrets. That was what my husband had said to me when we first got together. We had to be completely honest with each other. That was his thing. And yet, after him revealing that spare key to a safe deposit box, I realized there would always be parts to him or parts of his story I'll never fully know. I paced the cool, wooden floor of the new condo he had us holed in. It was top of the line, I had to give him that. I had so many questions for my husband that he needed to answer. But I was guessing he already knew that since he made sure to slip deep inside of me before he left. He knew when it came to him and the sexual intimacy we shared, I couldn't think right to save my life.

To be honest, what he had shown me scared me. It scared me because that meant I didn't really know my husband as well as I thought. What he had shown me told me there were deeper levels to the shit he had going on. I stopped walking when I heard the locks on the door turn. I was still jumpy and antsy. Although Marcel had told me we were safe, I grabbed a gun that was strapped underneath an end table next to the couch.

I stood with it aimed at the door.

"Put the damn gun down," Marcel said as he walked in.

He was holding his ribs, which mean he'd been in a fight again. I lowered the gun and ran a hand through my hair.

"What happened?" I asked.

It took him awhile before he answered. He snatched off the leather jacket and gloves he had on. I watched as he laid guns and knives he had strategically placed on him on the bar. He stripped his shirt off, then sat on the stool. The stitches I'd given him had come undone. He cut his eyes at me, then pointed to the decanter filled with amber-brown liquid above the fireplace. I grabbed it, then popped the glass stopper. I poured him a healthy helping into a tumbler, then passed it to him.

He took the liquid to the head, then slammed the glass down on the bar behind him.

"I don't think it was Leo," he said. "I'm not saying this for certain, but I'm saying he didn't respond the way a man who assumed my death was in the books should have."

"I mean, although he would have been the obvious person, that doesn't mean he didn't do it. Leo is a manipulator," I said.

"I know this, Sabrina, but given how long I've known the man, I'm going to say there is a 90-percent chance he didn't do it, which leaves your father—"

"And the mob," I quickly added so he wouldn't turn his attention solely on my daddy.

Marcel's eyes leveled on mine as he spoke. "It leaves your father who's left to visit."

I frowned, then swallowed quickly. I rolled my shoulders. "Pay . . . Pay him a visit? For what, Marcel?"

He tilted his head and looked at me as if I were dense. "Until I find out who tried to kill us, *everybody* is a suspect."

My spine stiffened. "I want to leave."

"We can do that, but I'm not leaving until I know who wants me and my family dead. Makes no sense to run if we don't even know who's after us."

"You're the one who said we had to leave," I snapped.

I felt myself getting angrier at the notion that if Marcel went to see my father, and he was the one behind the botched hit, Marcel would kill him, no questions asked. It wouldn't even matter that I would be hurt behind my father's death. Marcel had no filter like that. And, no, my father and I hadn't spoken in years, but I still loved him. I wished he wasn't so damned stubborn so Lyric could know the man he was when he wasn't an angry asshole. Regardless of the mistakes my father had made, when he was in my life, it was good, for the most part.

Yes, Daddy had anger issues, and there was no doubt in my mind if he and Marcel were in the same room and Marcel accused him of trying to kill us, things would go left pretty damn quickly. Daddy was a proud man, and so was my husband.

Marcel stood, took the decanter from my hand, and poured himself another drink.

"No, I did not say we had to leave. I said we had to choose on if we were going to stay and fight or leave. I emphasized the leaving part because that would be better for Lyric. Until we leave, I'm checking under every rock to see who is trying to kill my goddamned family and me," he yelled, then caught himself.

When he glanced down the hall, I knew he was check-ing his tone because Lyric was in the back room.

Tears burned my eyelids as I watched my husband down another shot of liquor. He was in pain. That was obvious by the way he kept his arm around his abdomen.

"Don't kill him, Marcel."

"Sabrina."

"Don't kill him. Promise me!"

He shook his head. "If he sent men into my home, he's dead."

I licked my lips, then moved closer to him. He stepped back.

"Baby, can't you just talk to him like you did with Leo."

"I shot Leo."

My eyes widened. "What? You said you talked to him."

"Yeah, we talked. I didn't like what he had to say, so I shot him," he said through clenched teeth.

Marcel moved down the hall. I moved quickly behind him. "Let me talk to him, baby. Let me . . . I know him . . ."

He turned to me. The look on his face said his patience was wearing thin. "Sabrina, stop. Don't do this. Don't spazz out on me right now because this is your father. Somebody tried to kill us, and if he had anything to do with that, he's a dead man."

I balled my fists and slammed them against his chest, not in anger, but in resignation. I already knew the man I married, and I knew when he said something, he meant it. I believed him the first time he told me if my father put his hands on me again, he would kill him. I could tell by looking up at him now, compassion for the fact that Othello Lanfair was my father meant little to him.

I lay my forehead on his chest and softly cried because I knew no matter how hard I tried to talk him out of it, it was no use. He stood there with me a few moments, one hand on the small of my back, allowing me to let my emotions get the better of me.

"I have to go back out, Sabrina," he said.

There was no malice in his voice, but a sternness that told me he meant business. I slowly gazed up at him through blurry vision.

"If you have to kill him, don't make him suffer," I said, then stepped back.

Marcel wiped my eyes, then cradled my face in his hands as he kissed me. His tongue was thick and velvety against my lips. I felt the heat I always felt when he kissed me.

He pulled back and looked down at me while my face was still in his hands. "I'll never make you those kinds of promises."

I closed my eyes and inhaled deeply when he left me standing in the hall. Thirty minutes later, after he had wrapped his waist thoroughly, put on a clean shirt, and grabbed a black duffle bag, he left again. For the next few hours, I paced my front room. Lyric woke up, so I fixed her something to eat. The fridge was already stocked, which was a good thing, but my daughter was a picky eater. She had this strange thing where she liked her peanut butter and jelly sandwich toasted. I always had to make it like it was a grilled cheese sandwich. She wouldn't eat it otherwise.

As the hours passed, night came and went, and Marcel still hadn't come home yet. When he hadn't come home by noon the next day, I turned the TV on, paying close attention to the news, looking for anything that would tell me if Marcel had killed my daddy or not.

"Mommy?" Lyric called.

"Yes, baby?"

"Is Daddy gone for b . . . ba . . . um . . . What's that word, Mommy?" she asked while holding her doll close.

"Business?" I said for her.

"Yes, busy-nuss," she said.

I smiled. "Yes, baby. He'll be back soon."

As soon as the words left my mouth, the locks turned, and Marcel walked in. Lyric ran to her father first. I stood, anxiously wringing my hands as I watched. I looked on in silence while Lyric talked a mile a minute. I didn't say a word until he looked over at me.

He put our daughter down and then asked her to go
to her room. She disappeared down the hall with no
questions asked.

"This is the first time in my life that I haven't done what
I set out to do, Sabrina. I didn't go see your old man, and
somewhere in the back of my mind, I feel that shit is
going to come back to haunt me."

I was so elated that he hadn't gone to kill my father
that I didn't see the way his face was set in stone. I tried
to rush in to hug him, but he held his hands out to keep
me back.

"Marcel," I called out, confused.

"No, back up off me. You don't get to do this to me,
Sabrina. You don't get to use my love for you against me,"
he said. I stared a bit confused by his words. "You don't
get to interfere with my work, because then, you become
a liability," he said. "This is the first—and last—time you
ever step between me and my work, you got that?"

"But—"

"No buts," he snapped, cutting me off. He shook his
head. "No buts. Don't do it again. Somebody tried to kill
us. They injured our daughter, could have killed you and
her. And you don't want me to see about a nigga because
he's your father."

"You said you didn't believe them when they said it was
him anyway."

"Yeah, but that doesn't mean I need to leave any stones
unturned. Don't fucking step between me and my work
again. Don't do that shit."

I was quiet for a while, then I said, "I'm sorry."

"The hell you say," he snapped. "You're not sorry about
shit. You're sorry because you don't want me talking to
you like I am right now. Don't"—he said harshly as I tried
to walk up on him again—"don't you fucking touch me."

I stopped because I knew that he knew what I was
doing. Just like he used his touch to calm me down, I

was attempting to do the same thing to him. I knew if I touched him, he wouldn't yell or curse or look at me like he wanted to strangle me. He was angry now, but if I touched him in any way, his anger would subside. If I kissed him, he would stop the hostility. Yes, it was some very manipulative shit to do on the surface, but in reality, I only wanted him to calm down enough to not be so pissed off at me.

I hated when he was mad at me. He knew that. So even though he was adamant that I didn't touch him, I tried to anyway. He gently pushed me away from him, then stormed down the hall to our daughter's bedroom, slamming the door shut behind him. He didn't come out for the rest of the day. When he was hungry, he sent Lyric to the front room to ask me for food.

I decided to let things be as they were. There was no use in beating a dead horse. If he wanted to stay mad, then so be it. In the meantime, I decided to do something about my part in the fucked-up situation we were in. I walked into the hall and grabbed my "business" laptop. I had Wi-Fi access. The only thing I was worried about was what my husband had shown me earlier. He was connected to a whole other subset of people, and if they got wind of what I was about to do, I could go down and take all the people I was about to contact down with me.

But if any of the mob bosses I'd worked for thought for a second that coming after my family and me was okay, they were dead wrong. I logged onto the laptop, then went to the website for one of the many strip clubs the Giulios owned in Vegas. The one thing that set this website apart from the others was that it was a secret. There was a black hole through this website that only certain people had access to. I was one of those people.

Once I logged on, I saw that several of the men were online as this was where most of them communicated when they didn't want their messages to be intercepted. I logged into the chat room. I didn't want to make this long and drawn out. I typed a simple message:

Someone is trying to kill my family and me. If anything happens to me or any member of my family, there is a file that will be anonymously emailed to every federal agency in the United States. This is not a threat. This is my insurance policy. Don't call my bluff.

I logged off immediately, not wanting to see the responses or have them possibly trace my whereabouts. I wasn't stupid enough to believe that anywhere was 100 percent safe. The men I worked for were resourceful and had extremely skilled individuals working for them who could probably hack into the Pentagon if they so wanted. I unplugged the laptop, then took the battery out before putting it back in the closet.

I looked at the time. Marcel didn't plan to come out of Lyric's room anytime soon, so I grabbed a blanket and a pillow and made my bed the sofa for the evening. I'd finally gone to sleep after tossing and turning for the better part of the night when a slap across my ass woke me up. The smack was so hard that I jerked awake to find my husband staring down at me.

I turned over on my back and barked out, "Why did you hit me?"

"Get up," was all he said.

He had a cell phone in his hand, one I didn't even know he had. He dropped it on the table in the middle of the floor, then said, "Talk."

"About what?" I asked, kind of pissed there was stinging on my ass cheeks from his big-ass hands.

I sat up.

"Not you. Leo, talk," he said again.

I was confused. "I thought you killed him," I whispered.

Marcel cut his eyes at me. "I said I *shot* him, *not* killed him."

Leo's voice cut in. "If you two are done forcing me to listen to your foreplay, I'd like to get to the heart of the matter."

"Say what you have to say, bruh," Marcel said, the annoyance in his tone matched what was in Leo's voice.

"Sabrina, what made you think it was okay to threaten The Family with federal exposure?" Leo asked.

Marcel tilted his head as he looked at me, then quirked a brow.

I spoke up, no fear or hesitation in my voice. "If one of you assholes thinks it's okay to come after me and mine and think I was just going to lie down and take it, you have another think coming. Someone came into our home, Leo. My child was injured, smacked around like she was a damn dog. I had a gun put to my head. I was fucking kicked and punched because someone thinks me and my husband are liabilities. That is *not* okay. We have never betrayed any of The Family's trust."

"And why the fuck would you two automatically think it's us?" Leo snapped.

"Who else would come after us so damn hard like this? Who would have the fucking audacity to break into our home?" I asked.

"Like I told the nigga you're married to, it wasn't me. Which meant it wasn't anybody in The Family."

If only Leo's constituents knew how gutter he could sometimes be with his language, they'd never vote for him again. He put on a good front for the public, but behind closed doors, when pushed, he could be the most hood of men.

"And how do you know?" I barked at the phone.

"Because for any hit to be approved, it has to go through my father, and I can assure you, he doesn't want any fucking thing to happen to his precious son . . . Marcel."

There was so much venom in Leo's voice when he spat that last part out that I could taste it.

"Marcel isn't his real son."

Leo chuckled. "What's your point?"

"The point is, anything is possible."

The fact that Leo kept chuckling annoyed me. "Sabrina, Sabrina, beautiful, sexy, little Sabrina."

"Lay off my wife, Leo," Marcel said coolly.

As if Leo had ignored him, he continued, "Stop looking at the trees and see the forest, Sabrina. I know my *pseudo* little brother is still there in the room with you as he keeps guard over you like a hawk."

"Don't insult my wife, asshole," Marcel said. "Are you done?" he asked.

"Your wife just opened up a can of worms that I may not be able to put the lid back on. If The Family didn't have a hit out on you before, they most likely do now."

Marcel said, "Looks like you better let those niggas know that this isn't what they want."

Leo sighed. I could hear him drinking something as when he swallowed it was loud. Then he hissed.

"Little brother, whether or not you know it, I've always looked out for you. Yeah, there is a bit of jealousy between you and me—"

Marcel cut Leo off. "Nah, nigga, that's *you* with the jealousy issue."

"True. True, but regardless, Pops loves your black ass and over the years, I've come to as well. I mean, hey, in my own little way. Know what I mean? So, listen to me when I tell you this. . . . Get Sabrina and Lyric out of the States until I see what I can do to calm shit down with The Family, a'ight? Your wife has some big balls. To threaten the whole family with no regard to their power takes brass balls, bruh."

I thought Marcel would be pissed at me since he was earlier anyway. I'd gone behind his back and did something he had no idea of.

So it came as a surprise when he simply told Leo, "She did what she felt she had to do to protect her family. I do the same. Not gon' be mad at her for that."

Leo grunted. "Maybe one day I'll marry a woman who can hold her own like Sabrina over there."

"You can't keep your dick to yourself, Leo," I said, remembering a conversation I'd had with his wife a year or so ago.

He laughed. The fact that his dick didn't control my husband made me appreciate him more. I'd never worried about him dicking down other chicks and bringing drama home. It was quite possible that if Marcel cheated on me, I'd kill him. He knew this. I'd made it known plenty of times.

"Yeah, yeah, so I've heard," Leo finally said. "Sabrina, your father would like to see you."

That got my attention. I smiled a bit. "Really?" I asked.

"Yes. Especially since he received a phone call that threatened his life because he's your father. And because you threatened members of the mob."

My heart deflated. For a minute, I got happy thinking that Daddy had finally come around. Thought maybe he finally missed me to the point of wanting to see me. That wasn't the case. He only wanted to see me because I'd placed him in a bad situation.

"I'd suggest doing it tonight so you guys can get out of here by morning," Leo added.

After that, he hung up. I looked at Marcel. I was about to say something, but then something Leo had said dawned on me. I thought back to the words one of the men who had attacked me said as well—and then it hit me. It finally hit me.

"I need to see my father."

Chapter Eighteen

Sabrina

Getting Marcel to let me see my father alone was like pulling a lion's teeth while he was in the middle of a feast. He cursed and yelled, but I was adamant about going to Daddy's alone. I needed to get something off my chest. There was no doubt in my mind that my family and I had to leave the States now. We could no longer stick around. I knew that sending that message would ruffle some feathers, but what did they expect?

I couldn't think about that now, though. I drove up to the front of my father's home, got out, and walked up to the door. Danny stopped me. I hadn't seen him in three years. He looked much the same, just manlier. Muscles were more defined. His baby face was still there, just with more handsome features. I smiled at him.

"What do you want, Sabrina?" he asked me.

The tone in his voice startled me a bit.

"I need to see Daddy," I said.

"He isn't here."

"You're lying. If Daddy wasn't here, you wouldn't be here."

He grunted, hands still clasped in front of him, standing as the proverbial bodyguard would. Earpiece in his ear. Gun visible on his hip.

"Yeah, well, lots of shit has changed since the last time you were here. Mr. Lanfair isn't here."

Just as I got ready to go on a profanity-laced tirade, Kat opened the door.

"It's okay, Danny. Let her in," she told him.

Danny gave me a look that unsettled me. I'd never been anything but kind to the man, so I didn't understand his attitude toward me now. But he moved aside and allowed me entrance. Kat was still as beautiful as ever. Still had the page boy haircut that was now dyed red and styled in a way that framed her face. Her makeup was done to perfection, and she had on a tight-fitting pencil skirt that showed she was still in good shape. She had on black heels that displayed her toes and heels with straps around her ankles. The blouse she had on also showed she had a new set of perky breasts.

"Please excuse Daniel. He's been a bit overzealous as of late. Othello has been on the warpath, and Daniel just happened to say the wrong thing at the wrong time and caught hell from your father," she explained with a plastered-on smile. "Anyway, what brings you by?" she asked, taking a sip from the wineglass she had in her hand.

I followed her from the expansive black-and-white Italian, marble-tiled foyer into the sitting area near the kitchen.

"I came to see Daddy," I told her.

She chuckled. "Wow, it's been three years, girl. Took you three years? Beautiful family you have, by the way. Lyric looks just like you and Marcel."

I cast a blank look in her direction. "Thank you. Took me three years because Daddy practically banished me from his life."

She waved a hand, and her eye awkwardly twitched. I had to wonder if Daddy had hit it too many times.

"You know how Othello can be," she said.

I nodded once, taking off my leather jacket and gloves. I smiled. "I do."

She watched me closely, then moved over to the small wooden desk in the room. She set the wineglass on top, then said, "Well, he's not here right now—"

"I know. That's okay. It's you I really wanted to see anyway."

"Oh?" was all she said.

We stood there for a long time watching each other. The muscles in my jaw twitched, and I felt each pressure point I owned heat up. She pursed her lips together, then ran her tongue inside of her cheek.

"How did you figure it out?" she finally asked.

"Something one of the men who attacked me said finally resonated with me. Leo repeated the words to me tonight, and it triggered a memory. After Daddy hit you in the back of the limo the day the South African diplomat was killed, you came home with me. We were discussing the death of Mayor Kasim, and you asked me if I really thought he'd died of a heart attack. I foolishly said yes, and you told me, '*stop looking at the trees and see the forest, Sabrina.*'"

I tilted my head as Kat helped me to finish the last part of the sentence.

She shook her head as she swallowed slowly. I moved closer to the desk.

"I finally see the forest," I said coolly.

The faux smile left her face, and her eyes turned cold. "I wanted you to know it was me. I told him to say those words to you before he killed you. Wanted it to trigger a memory just before you died. They were supposed to kill Lyric too," she began. "It was supposed to look like a hit on Marcel, and you just got caught in the crossfire of your husband's affairs. To the outside world, it would look like a robbery gone wrong. To those of us close to The Family, it would look like a hit on a man close to the Giulios. And you just had to fucking ruin it. I'm so sick of you Lanfair bitches ruining everything," she snarled through clenched teeth.

"What have I ever done to you, Kat? I've always gone out of my way to be nice to you, even when Mama and my sisters hated me for it," I said with a frown.

"Bitch, I don't need you to be nice to me. That's *your* problem," she yelled, face turning red. "You think too much of yourself. You think every fucking thing is about you. I had a child beaten out of me by your father. Do you know what happened after you walked out of here and chose a goddamned cook over your father? Huh? Do you know?"

Kat was yelling so loud and hard, I could see every muscle in her face working. I felt like shit, actually. There I was thinking it was because of Marcel's work that we had been targeted. Shit, I thought there was a possibility that it was because of my work with the mob as well. When, in the end, it was all because of shit neither one of us had any control over. The fact that I was the reason my family had been targeted for something so trivial ate away at me.

I shook my head. "No, Kat. What happened?" I asked just because.

"I had to take your ass whippings for you. It got worse, progressively so, after you walked out of your father's life. Before then, the beatings were sparse, and then every time we crossed paths with you or drove past your stupid little bistro, Othello would take his anger and resentment out on me."

"How is any of that *my* fault?" I wanted to know.

"Oh my God. You still don't fucking get it! You're one spoiled little bitch. I tried to fuck your husband once. Did he tell you that?"

My spine stiffened, and all emotions left my mind. "*Excuse* me?"

"I tried to fuck your husband once. Men are dispensable. I thought he was like all the rest of them; thought he was like Leo. Thought maybe he was led by his dick too. But nooooo. Sabrina had gone and found her the perfect little husband. He smacked me because I tried to kiss him; then he tossed me out of the bistro like I was trash in front of the whole damn staff. Like I was nothing but a piece of shit! All in the name of Sabrina Lanfair." Kat started pacing behind the desk like a caged animal. "Another man putting his hands on me because of *you*."

At that moment, I felt sorry for Kat. For as angry as I was at her for what she had done, my father had damaged her. From the moment she started to have an affair with him behind my mother's back, he had been no good for her.

"I'm sorry you—"

"Bitch, I don't need your apologies. I needed you to die. Why couldn't you just die? Why couldn't Marcel come home like he was supposed to? They were supposed to shoot him before he got into the house. Stupid fucking amateurs. Ugh! But, I should have known, perfect little Sabrina and her perfect cook husband would have an escape clause. It's not fair that you get to have a child, and I don't. The first time it was your mother's fault your father beat a child out of me. The second time it was your fault because your selfish ass couldn't let the goddamn cook go. When you walked out of here that day, the day you told your daddy you were pregnant and marrying Marcel, he . . . He beat *another* child out of me, Sabrina."

I frowned and shook my head. Daddy was wrong, so wrong for what he had done to her. And as bad as I wanted to feel for her, I couldn't. She turned to the bookcase behind her and placed her head against the shelves. Her hands were in front of her. She was crying. Shoulders shook as sobs racked her body.

"I can't have any more babies. The last miscarriage, because of the severity of the beating, ruined any more chances for me," Kat continued. "So I wanted to hurt Othello like he had hurt me. I wanted to take away his favorite child. Wanted him to know what it was to lose a child violently. Took me a whole year to plan your death, and those stupid idiots messed it up," she shouted, then spun around quickly.

When she did, she held a gun in her hand. She fired so quickly that I almost didn't dodge it fast enough. I jumped behind the couch in the room as bullets chased me. Shots rang out back-to-back in a cacophony of noise. Kat kept firing until I heard her heels running across the floor. I moved from behind the couch just as she ran. I football tackled her to the ground. The gun went sliding to the doorway. For as bad as I felt for what she'd had to endure, she sent men to harm my family and me. I'd never get over the look of fear and blood running from Lyric's nose.

As we wrestled on the floor, I grabbed Kat's throat. There were grunts, claws out, and teeth bared as we fought. Kat was stronger than she looked. I could hear her skirt rip, and she managed to get on top of me. Straddling my hips, she socked me in the face. Because of the hit from the gun I'd received from the previous attack, Kat's punch rattled my brains, and the pain made me grit my teeth. I yelled out at the second punch to my mouth. I felt my upper lip split.

I bucked my hips, threw an elbow to Kat's face, and knocked her off of me. I'd been wrestling with Marcel for years. Through all the training, I could probably get a full-grown man off me if push came to shove. If Kat wanted to fight, then she had to bring it. When she fell over, she tried to crawl away. I hopped on her back, grabbed the back of her shirt, then slammed her head to the marble floor. I tried to crack that bitch's frontal lobe.

She screamed out as her blood painted the floor. I stood, then pulled her up with me.

"Get up, bitch," I snarled.

I wrapped an arm around her neck and applied pressure, just the way my husband had taught me.

The fact that I could hear her struggling to breathe pleased me. "Arrgggh . . . give me . . . let me . . . fight . . . back. Give me a . . . fair fight," she croaked out.

I thought about it. My husband told me never to play with a kill, but I wanted to do more than kill this bitch. I wanted to *hurt* her. I let her go, then shoved her forward. She stumbled, then turned to me. One of her heels had already come off. She kicked the other one off. I didn't have that problem. I came dressed for a fight. Black leggings and a black spaghetti strapped tee shirt. Combat boots were on my feet.

I took a fighter's stance. I remembered Marcel's words as I did so. I knew how to street fight but didn't have the technicality that came with the nature of fighting smart. He always stressed boxing stances and foot placement. He said they determined the effectiveness of your offense, defense, and footwork. My back foot heel was slightly lifted from the ground. He told me to keep it simple. A basic toe-heel line would be all I needed in many cases. This was one of those cases.

Kat ran in for me. I chased her down with hooks from both hands. Right. Left. Left. Right. Her head snapped back with each hit. I had solid balance without sacrificing my mobility, which was a good thing. Each time that bitch tried to come for me, my hits and body shots pushed her back. The more blood rained from her face, the more satisfied the demon in me became. I smiled at the fact I was kicking her ass. Got too happy that I was hurting her like those men had hurt my daughter. Then she caught me with a foot to the pussy that took me down to my knees. Several knees to my face placed me on my back.

I didn't have time to wither in pain, though. That bitch jumped on top of me, one hand around my neck as she pummeled my face with her other closed fist. I tried to reach for her neck, face—anything. I clawed and slapped trying to get her off me.

"Stupid"—punch to my face—"fucking"—another punch to my face—"spoiled little bitch," she spat as she hit me.

Her face twisted in anger and rage. I didn't recognize the woman on top of me. Her blouse had been practically ripped from her body. Her perfectly paid for breasts gave a slight jiggle each time she hit me. As she tried to beat me to death, I reached down, brought my leg up, and reached into the side of my boot. I grabbed for the hunting knife I had placed there. As soon as she got ready to bring her fist down again, I shoved the jagged blade into her rib cage. Her fist stopped midstrike. Face frozen, eyes wide with her mouth opened in shock. I yanked the knife out and jammed it back in again. Snatched it out, then stuck it into her neck. Blood spewed into my face when I pulled the knife out. She fell over on her back, life fading from her eyes. I slowly sat up, thankful that the hitting had stopped and even more thankful I was able to breathe again.

I stood, then looked down at her, blood dripping from the knife. "*Nobody* comes after my family," I said.

Tears fell from my eyes. I'd never killed anybody, and it hurt that I had to kill Kat. But I couldn't risk anybody hurting my child or my husband again. I took a deep breath, and each time I did, it felt as if my lungs were on fire. I jerked my head up as I heard Danny round the corner. I wondered what took him so long as I knew he heard the gunshots. I held the knife out at him simply because my fight-or-flight instincts were still in high gear.

"Are you o—"

He stopped his question abruptly when he saw me standing over Kat's body with the knife aimed at him. He looked from me to Kat, then back at me. For a moment, I thought he was concerned about me; then his worry turned into a scowl.

"I told her she should have sent me," he said coolly.

I ran a tongue over my dry lips, eyes furrowed, as I watched Danny as his words gave notion to the fact he was in on Kat's team.

I shook my head. "No, nope. Not you too, Danny." My head started to hurt at the obscenity of it all.

"You knew I liked you," he started.

I couldn't believe what I was hearing. "Wha-What?" I yelled in disbelief. "You have to be kidding me right now."

He stalked closer to me. I backed away. "At first, I thought it was because you thought you were better than me. I mean, because I was just a bodyguard for your father, but then . . . Then you *married* him. A *cook*," he said like he couldn't believe it.

"If one of you assholes calls my husband a cook one more time . . ." I yelled.

"You'll *what?*" Danny asked.

I swallowed the bile and disgust I felt at the whole situation.

"Why, Danny?"

"You never noticed me, Sabrina. All I wanted was a chance," he said.

I didn't even have it in me to explain to the delusional man that I just wasn't into him. I couldn't get over the fact he was so blindly loyal to my father. He would do anything my father asked of him. Not to mention, there was something weird going on between him and my father.

Danny rushed me, hands angrily around my throat. I stabbed the knife into his left arm over and over. That didn't stop him. I felt myself getting light-headed as the knife slipped from my hand. My arms weren't long enough to do much else. As I felt myself going limp in Danny's hold, I couldn't help but wonder where my father was in all of this.

Chapter Nineteen

Marcel

I did my best to keep her from going. Tried to use her Achilles' heel, our daughter, to make her listen to reason, but she went on her way, and there was no stopping her. Which was why, after waiting an hour, then dressing our daughter and packing up our car for our move, Lyric and I headed out on an adventure in watching Mommy's back.

"Shit! I knew she was up to no good," I cursed under my breath while gripping the steering wheel of my car, staring at the parked car that belonged to Sabrina in front of her father's home.

"Oooh, Da-dee!" Lyric cooed giggling behind it.

A deep line formed across my face, and I sat back in my seat letting go of the wheel and glancing at my little girl, the light of my world.

"I'm sorry, baby girl. Sometimes Daddy says things that could be said better. You understand?" I asked, noticing my daughter's adorable big cocoa eyes and big cheeky smile.

She shook her twin puffs and said, "No," then went back to sucking on her twist cup.

"Good, just don't repeat what I said; now, you under-stand that, correct?" I asked reaching out in the backseat to tweak my daughter's nose.

Her legs started kicking due to her excitement and energy, and she nodded. "Yes, sir!"

I dropped my head back and said, "Good. Now, let's get your mom on the same level so she understands not to do as she sees me do."

My frown returned to my face as I sat back watching the house I had trailed Sabrina to, her father's crib. This day had gone on too long for a nigga. My body was still in pain from handling Leo, and now I was busy protecting my wife's back when I should have been handling her pops. Thinking of him, after sitting out in my blacked-out, armor-protected Escalade for a while, I was about to check on Mr. Lanfair's whereabouts since he wasn't at his crib when I heard a gunshot. Several gunshots, actually.

Rubbing my temple, I sighed and glanced at my daughter. It was times like this when I wished her grandmother was here because I was about to put my daughter's life in danger just to save her mother who was only acting to protect her family. Funny thing about it, though. I didn't understand why gunshots had to ring out for that to happen, but I was sure that I was about to find out.

Taking my ride up the driveway, I parked and then got out. Quickly moving to the back to take my baby girl out of her car seat, I spoke softly to her. "Now, you're about to see Daddy handle some people, okay? I need you to remember what I said. When you see Daddy hit a man or shout, you what?"

"Hide and if Daddy is in trouble, throw him the bear," she said tilting her head quizzically when, in reality, it wasn't a question but a statement for reassurance.

Kissing her forehead, I settled her on my hip. "Yes, my little ninja. No matter what you see, stay hidden, okay?"

"Okay, Daddy, I will!" Lyric threw her arms around me, hugging me, and I walked us to the door.

Reaching out, I turned the handle and pushed. There was no need for knocking, not when I heard gunshots.

Stepping into the huge foyer, I glanced around at the place and quietly moved through the house. I could hear fighting, could hear Sabrina's sharp hisses, then shouts. My baby was scrapping, and from what I could tell just by passing the room she was in, Danny was nowhere around.

Quickly, I took Lyric to the kitchen and then opened the cabinets. I found her favorite, peanut butter. Since I knew she only ate it grilled, I grabbed her some crackers, a bowl, and a cup of water. Setting it in front of her, I put the peanut butter in a bowl, laid the crackers out, and then kneeled to sit Lyric down.

Dropping her hoodie back, I kissed the tip of her nose and looked into her eyes. "Now, baby girl, Daddy needs you to be my partner. Stay here and eat your snacks. If you hear or see anyone that is not Daddy or Mommy, hide."

Lyric leaned back to look up at me, then hopped down with her bear in her hand. She moved her chair back and crawled under the table. "I'll hide here."

A huge smile lit up my face, and I quickly handed her the snacks, then put the chair back. "My smart little mama. I'll be back. I love you."

"I love you too, Da-dee," I heard Lyric say.

Taking one more look at where she was, I felt a slight comfort because she would not be seen. As I disappeared down the hall, I stopped when I noticed Danny. He had rushed downstairs at the sound of the fight. I watched him say something, then storm in the room. Nigga didn't know I was even there, which made my day. Adjusting my black gloves and grabbing the small gun that lay in the middle of the door frame, I crept to the room and saw this bastard choking Sabrina.

Her legs were kicking, and she was clawing; water lined her squinting eyes. From what I could tell by the way she bared her teeth and her face contorted because of the pressure from Danny's grip, Sabrina was seconds from blacking out.

Fury had me grinding my teeth as I heard this nigga talk some stupid-ass shit.

"I loved you, but you had to let that wack-ass cook in between your legs. He was never worthy," Danny shouted, shaking Sabrina in the process. "I am—"

For a second there, I almost stood by to compute what the hell he was saying, but how my temper worked, that wasn't an option. Rage had me ready to go off, especially when he began to work with his belt and mumbled some shit that she about to find out that he was "worthy." Something like red washed over my eyes. My breathing became short, and I swear we were back when she was 19, and that nigga had her tied to the bed.

Was no fucking way that I was about to stand there and let this bold as shit go down again. Not after what Sabrina went through the first time. Stepping forward, I paused when she bared her teeth, then pressed her hands together as if in prayer. I watched her swiftly move them in the middle of Danny's arms, then pulled them apart to grab his face. She aggressively shoved her thumbs into his eyes, digging deep until he started shouting in pain.

Tucking her leg up, she planted her foot against his solar plexus and pushed. "Get the hell off me!"

Smirking, I moved in as Danny went stumbling backward, and as he fell, I squeezed the trigger of the gun I held and watched the bullet go clean into his skull, his blood mingling with Kat's. From the blank expression on her face, the blood that spilled from her side, along with the knife by her side, I knew that chick was long gone.

"Baby, how bad are you hurt?" I asked, staring up at her with pride.

While I spoke, I was moving like the professional I was. I dropped to one knee, stopping to grab the knife, wiping her handprints off and placed it in Danny's hand.

Turning, I took the gun, wiped it off, gripped Kat's hand, moved her some to shoot off a round, and laid her back where she fell. I didn't do the kill here, but the art in making sure a room looked right after a murder was something I enjoyed. After glancing around and making sure everything looked somewhat correct, not perfect but normal, I moved to Sabrina, noticing where she had slid against the wall while rubbing her neck and trying to get air.

Fear, love, and relief were in her eyes while she stared at me, her chest rising up and down erratically. She stared up at me confused at my presence. "How—"

"It's all good, baby. Was no way I was going to let you talk to your old man completely alone." Offering my hand, I leaned down to the help her up, then kissed her deeply. "Damn, I love you so much, Brina. You did this, baby. Damn, I'm proud."

Grinning, I pulled her close to me, needing to touch her to feel that she was okay, "Listen, we need to go. I don't have time to stage this shit anymore, but we need to go."

Giving me a nod, Sabrina held my hand tightly and allowed me to help her to the front door. Once I saw that she was good and not going to waver due to stress, I quickly jogged back to the kitchen to get our baby girl who was curled up under the table. Gently pulling her out, I hoisted her up to carry her on my back. We all quickly moved as we made it to the front of the place, then got in front our perspective cars.

Snapping Lyric in her car seat, I shouted to Sabrina, "Get in my ride. I'll have someone pick it up."

"I thought . . . I thought you didn't have the time," Sabrina asked in a raspy voice.

"I don't have the time to do it myself, but I do have the time to make a call. Get in, baby; it's time to go," I repeated myself at the end.

Ultimately, I was able to get us in the car, call up Diggy to bring in a cleaning crew right now to dispose of Sabrina's car and check anything that I wasn't able to look over. As we pulled out, I didn't notice that we were being followed, due to the need to get Sabrina away from two dead bodies. We made maybe a few blocks away before I saw that another blacked-out Escalade was trailing us.

"We're leaving Atlanta now right. Please say yes," Sabrina asked, her voice still choppy.

Distress had her shaking subtly. It added to my worry about my family, but still, I was a proud mother-fucker about how she handled herself without me.

The need to keep her calm had me reaching to take her hand, bring it up to my mouth to kiss as I nodded. "Yeah, it's about that time."

I hit the gas and tried to get us to the highway as quickly as possible, but it was too late. They had surrounded us. In my hurry to get Sabrina and Lyric away from the scene of the crime, I didn't do a good job of paying attention to my surroundings.

"Looks like the shit has come to roost. Take the gun in there. Our plane tickets are in there too. Go. Go. I want you two protected," I said watching behind me as several men in black climbed out of their cars.

A wild look in Sabrina's gaze had her looking rapidly from me, then behind me. "This is my fault," she said. "I can't leave you."

Unlocking the door and undoing my seat belt, I shook my head and opened the door. "Nah. I love you, baby, and I promised you since the day we decided to hook up that I would always protect you. So far, I've been keen to my vow to hold you down and our daughter. Besides, I'd rather take this on and know you both are alive and untouched than to play some *Fast and Furious* shit and leave you both in danger. One time was enough. I love you, baby. I love my princess, but I got to handle this."

"But . . ." she started to say while reaching out to cradle my face, but it was already too late.

The door flung open, and hands dragged me out of the car. Looking at both Sabrina and Lyric, I let what was going on be what it was. As soon as I was out of the car, two burly motherfuckers had me by the arms forcing me forward as they dragged me.

"Fellas, let's talk about this civilly, a'ight? I'm not some dude that can't walk toward a car on my own. Come on now," I said pulling. "Am I really that much of a danger?"

I kept talking in hopes that it would distract not only my attackers but Sabrina as well. Yeah, she had just taken down Kat, but these men looked to be as professional as I was. I prayed she didn't think she was enough of a killer to start shooting with our daughter in the car. Especially since we didn't know who else was with the men. They could have had shooters hidden somewhere. For Sabrina to go gung-ho would have put not only her in danger, but Lyric as well. I couldn't have that.

As I asked that, I pushed my body forward, contorted it to get free, then landed several blows against my kidnappers. Sabrina screamed for me to come back to the car, but I was too busy to do so. I stood sandwiched between two WWE-sized bastards, working out my jump kicks, punches, and upper cuts. Every time I moved, one would follow. It got to the point where, they landed blows on my back, my front, on top of my head, and then some.

Weariness from dealing with Leo and running around all day is the only reason why I ended up on the ground beaten to a bloody pulp. The sound of gravel crushing under the weight of another car had both Humpty and Dumpty stopping their stomping of me. Each man stepped back, and I breathed hard, trying to hold on to the rest of my energy. Blood seeped from the corner of my mouth, my lungs burned, and the bones in my face and ribs ached like a bitch.

Going after both men was just a tactic to see who I was dealing with. The real deal was coming my way, and when he said, "I told you to leave him for me," I knew exactly who it was.

I shifted on my side, but the numbing pain had me spitting blood. The aching pain on the right side of my rapidly swelling face had me hazily staring up as I felt a fist slam down on my face. Hissing at my discomfort, my teeth ground against each other, my jaw locked, and I gripped the gravel asphalt under me, trying not to show any weakness.

"You low-life motherfucker," someone shouted at me with every blow.

I did my best to shield it. Did my best to roll away, but wherever I moved, this lame asshole moved.

A large Italian shoe slammed in my stomach, then pulled back to stomp me on my back. "You came into my life, took my daughter, got her attacked, and now you kill my wife and son! You vile piece of shit!"

It was safe to assume the fact that he knew they were dead, which meant he had been home. Why and how that nigga assumed it was me who had done the deed was baffling. It had me wondering just how they were able to catch up with us as fast as they did. Had he been watching us the whole time?

But that wasn't the kicker. Danny was that nigga's *son?*

"Daddy, no," I heard Sabrina shout out.

I laughed as I let this nigga get his aggression out. So now, I killed his son? That nigga who called himself in love with Sabrina was his *son?* Man . . . If that wasn't some *Flowers in the Attic* bullshit that I've ever heard, and that's exactly what I slurred out to him.

Then I ended with, "You're one stupid motherfuck—"

Before I could finish, his fist slammed in my mouth. The force of it was so strong that it whipped my head to the side. Rolling my shoulders, I used that moment to roll forward and tackle Othello Lanfair to the ground. It was my turn to get some blows in. We scrapped. We went at it, one-on-one, like two mighty bucks, coming off the ground to ram each other against the hood of his car and the surrounding cars behind us.

When I squared up, I sent a strong upper cut against the old man and ducked down to ram my other fist in his side. The sound of his harsh grunt was my joy. But it was when he brought his fists down my head that I knew this old man wasn't half stepping. Using my training, I swiped my foot out to trip him up and make him stumble back onto the ground.

Dropping over him, I slammed my elbow into the old man's face, relishing at the spittle and blood that covered his face.

But see, when I felt myself in that zone, I heard, "Stop! Marcel, please . . ."

"Fuck, Sabrina," I shouted back and pushed up off of her father. "I told you not to step in my business again."

Pissed off, I almost whipped my head around to go off on her, for yet again, letting her father get the better of us, for being okay with this nigga putting his hands on me now and trying to kill me. But I chose to focus on kicking his ass instead.

Quickly, pushing up, I stomped him and hazily looked around at his goons who watched silently with their hands folded in front of them.

"Did you not hear him, huh? Danny was your *brother*, Brina, and this fuck boy must not have given a fuck about him lusting after you."

Slamming my foot down on his neck, I watched this dude try to push my foot off him as I spoke. "See, Mr. Lanfair, before I put that bullet in his skull, that nigga had the nerve to have Sabrina choked up and seconds away from snapping her throat. All . . . for . . . loving . . . me."

Spitting blood, I went to punch this idiot again, but someone quickly pulled me off of him, and I struggled. "Come the fuck on . . . This is how you fight? Dirty? No fairness in this shit, huh?"

Othello leaned on his arm and worked to push himself up. He pulled off his jacket, tossed it to one of his men, rolled up the sleeves of his white button-down and worked his tie loose.

"There's no honor amongst thieves, boy. If you don't know that shit, then you're not really from the street, know what I mean, son?" Othello gave a quick swipe of his nose, then smirked, hitting me with his Staten Island accent.

His condescending manner had me laughing my ass off. I was waiting for him to hit me, straight expecting it. But when he pulled out a blade and motioned for his goons to hold my hand out, I stopped my laughing and watched him with intent.

The span of my hand was spread out. I tried to yank it back, but it was no point. Mr. Lanfair had it in his hand, and he twirled the blade between his fingers with seething satisfaction.

"I'm going to take you apart, boy, bit by bit, and show your gutter trash ass what street life is *really* about," he said with pride.

"Daddy," Sabrina shouted and ran toward us.

"Get the hell back, Sabrina Ophelia. I told you he was beneath you, but you never listened to me. You chose to dilute our family and breed a child just like him, and you expect me to be down for that? Fuck that shit. He almost got you killed, and then he killed my wife and Danny. I'm going to take him down, and it's beyond time," her father shouted, pointing his knife.

Mouth dropping into a frown, I dropped my head to scope a way to get loose. It was then that I glanced up at him and tilted my head. "But I'm *not* from the streets."

"And he didn't kill Kat. I did," Sabrina cried next to me.

"No," Othello said as if he hadn't heard his daughter. "You don't have it in you, and I saw him leaving my community just as I was driving in. I get to my house, see Kat and Danny dead. I know it was him," he growled low.

Sabrina shook her head. "No. As you can see, I was in the truck with him. Look at me! Look at the bruises, Daddy. It was me—"

It was then that she surprised me. From what I could see from my peripheral, Sabrina had pulled out her gun and pointed it directly at her father. His shock was satisfying.

He stood there with a gaze of confusion and hurt in his eyes, and when he looked down, I knew in my heart that Lyric was behind her watching him. I turned to see and saw her giving him a mean face while holding her doll. Everything was put in perspective for me, and I didn't want this.

"Baby . . . Take Lyric back to the car," I said softly. "Let me take my Karma and be done with it."

"I can't. You didn't do anything wrong. Kat . . . she . . . She attacked me, Daddy. She told me that she had sent those men to the house to kill me," she explained.

"Why are you lying to me like this? You're doing this for this bastard? I'm *over* it," he spat. "First off, daughter, Kat wouldn't plan something like that. She wasn't smart enough to do something so arrogantly stupid just to hurt me. She wasn't ruthless like that. Second, I can't believe that she had the resources to do anything like that. I won't believe it."

The edge of the knife was seconds from slicing my fingers, but it was the gun going off near Othello's foot that stopped it. Both of Othello's men shifted their hold on me, and this allowed me to push free, slam my elbow in one's neck, then take his gun. Popping off two rounds, Humpty fell to his knees, then fell forward dead from several bullets in his head and body.

I turned to point the gun at his other goon. I thought about letting him live, but nigga really annoyed the fuck outta of me, so I squeezed, and I watched him fall backward. It was then that I exhaled, quickly turned to check on Lyric, and was relieved that she had her ears covered and Sabrina held her hand over our daughter's eyes while still pointing the gun.

Limping back, I weakly kneeled down and picked up Lyric.

"Baby girl, I'm here," I whispered.

"Da-dee," she said holding me tightly.

I held her to my heart and looked over her head at her grandfather. "Tell him all, Sabrina, and make sure you fucking listen, old man."

She glanced at me, then slowly approached, still pointing her gun. "I killed her, and then Marcel saved me from Danny."

Tilting her head to the side, she ran her hand over her neck to show him the bruises. Even through her beautiful dark skin, you could see swelling there. If her father had a heart for his daughter, the sight should have pissed him off, as it was pissing me off.

"He said he loved me, that I was supposed to be with him, but I couldn't. I couldn't be attracted to someone like him and now . . . Now finding out that he was my brother, I praise God that he didn't take it even further like he planned. I believe if Marcel hadn't shown up, Danny would have raped me." Sabrina licked her lips, then wiped at her eyes.

The reality that his world was tearing up around him was evident on Othello's face. He dropped his knife, shook his head, and began talking with his hands in a mixture of disbelief and irritation. "Danny . . . Danny was a good boy. He loved you like a sister, and he'd never do something so foul like that. He wanted nothing but to protect you. Marcel did that to you."

Sabrina shook her head and balled a fist at her side. "Marcel is *nothing* like you. He doesn't believe in treating the people he loves like animals or property, and Kat? You destroyed Kat so that she made it her mission to find whatever means possible to hurt who you loved like you hurt her. She wanted to kill me to hurt you.

"Don't you see how your anger has hurt everyone around us? You talk about no honor amongst thieves; well . . . I have to say the same on my end. I'd kill Kat all over again for trying to kill me and almost killing my daughter over you beating her and, in turn, killing her unborn babies too many times, Daddy," she shakenly said. "I'd let Marcel pump a thousand bullets into Danny if that meant keeping him off me. And . . . I love you so much and tried my best to see the good in you, but if anyone is going to protect my family from you . . . It has to be me."

Then like that, Sabrina pointed her gun at her stunned father, and I turned my back on them both to walk to the car, shielding Lyric from what might go down. See, I was a family man, and right now, this was family business between Sabrina and her father. If she chose not to kill him . . .

Her gun going off made Lyric jump in my hold, and I put my final thoughts to rest.

Epilogue

Marcel

Killing and mayhem were not what my wife was about. Already, what she fell into was affecting the safety of her world, so I had to do what I always promised her. Protect her, this time from herself. Taking the gun from her shaking hand, I turned to look her in her bloodshot eyes, then reached up to wipe her tears away. She understood what she needed to do, so she said nothing as she walked back to the car and climbed in, silently closing the door.

I stood there watching the crestfallen face of a man who knew that he had lost everything. The hole of a bullet next to his feet . . . Proof that Sabrina had come very close to killing him. I wasn't sure if the mental synaptic connections in his brain were finally telling him that it was all because of his rage and methods of pushing off his power on others, but I really didn't care. What I cared about was behind me, and keeping them safe was a high priority.

Therefore, I took several strides up to him. He threw up a hand to tell the rest of his men to keep back, and we stood face-to-face.

In a low, even tone, I rolled my shoulders and kept the gun at my side pointed downward as I spoke. "Two things can go down right now, Mr. Lanfair."

The proud and mighty Othello Lanfair slipped his knife in his pocket, then began rolling the sleeves of his shirt down while looking away from me.

"And what is that, boy?" he asked sarcastically. "Because, clearly, my daughter is lost. She tried to kill me, but she couldn't do it. So you're going to pull the trigger next? Huh?"

With the snap of my wrist, I pressed the end of my Glock against his bowed head and sighed. "I mean, shit, fuck, yeah. However, for the sake of my wife, and standing here a father myself, I'm going to let you know some shit about me that maybe you'll finally understand."

I moved that gun, stepped closer, and then snatched him by the face as I leaned in to speak against his ear. "At any time and any place, I can, and may, kill you. . . ." Mr. Lanfair tried to pull back, but the energy and strength in me were back, so I had the back of that nigga's neck on lock as I schooled him on some things. "Shhh . . . Don't get brass balls now, nigga. I need you to listen and understand this. See, the rumors you've heard about me in the shadows are deeper than what you computed me to be. I'm not some thug who has a knack for killing."

Patting his cheek, I chuckled low. "Nah, this shit runs deeper than that. See, your wife Kat slightly understood it, which is why she sent killers after my wife in hopes that they would kill me as well. But what you two didn't get, and I never intended for you to understand, is this . . . as sanctioned by the United Streets of America, Good ol'Merca, I have the authority to be kind and let you go, toy with you, and lock you up for some sick-ass shit . . . or take my time and kill you slowly."

"What?" Othello hissed out, trying to pull away.

He got ready to say something else, but I quickly intercepted. "This is no joke. You're about credentials, correct? Well, you got them, but you missed the final piece. I can kill you however I want and be *allowed* to, considering what you just tried to do to me here. I want you to know that."

Patting my hand on his back, I leaned back and gave a tight smile. "So as you sit alone, in your fucked-up mansion, realizing that you don't have that woman you loved to beat to death. Or that loyal son of yours who was lusting after his own sister because you couldn't be man enough to tell him the truth, also start thinking about me. Marcel."

Othello's eyes were already wild with pain from Sabrina's act of defiance, but now that nice little light of understanding was also settling within his mind, and it had me stepping back while speaking low. "Pops Lanfair, I thank you for the gift that is Sabrina. I really do. I will do for her what you couldn't and wouldn't. You never have to worry about me putting hands on her or verbally abusing her. My DNA doesn't make me that way. This simple, college-educated thug, chef, and killer will make sure she has the world. But you . . . You, sir, now have the chance to worry about other things. Such as wondering if that spoon of Grape Nuts or Shredded Wheat an old-ass dude like yourself enjoys eating, has a funny taste because the milk is sour and not because I poisoned it."

"Or . . ." I said as if we were on a game show, and I was the host, "think about the next time you're walking out of town hall, and you are suddenly surrounded by too many people, that when someone brushes you, it's not me, hitting you with a lethal dose of something to give you a stroke. Or the next time you hear a gun go off, it ain't me. These things, and more, could be yours—if the price is right! And you never forget who the fuck I am, and don't you ever come for Sabrina, my child, or me. Ever. Do you understand me now? You have officially been 'X'ed. Sorry for your losses, but they had it coming."

I watched that old man's mouth drop even more as he tried to formulate words that were not "Fuck you" or something else. I glanced around at the faces of his team and made a mental note.

"You and your people be blessed, Mr. Lanfair. This life ain't easy, but Karma has a way to deal with disloyal niggas like yourself. I'll be watching." Then I climbed in my car, and we rode off.

I got my family out of there and back to the apartment so we could clean up. Time was of the essence. We needed to get clearance and get out of the country as quickly as we could. Until things calmed down and until Leo handled The Family situation, I needed to make sure Lyric and Sabrina were safe, by any means necessary.

Going into hiding wasn't something I really wanted to do, but I knew that to keep my family safe and give them a sense of peace, it was something that I had to do. Sabrina had lost so much, and I wanted to do my best to rectify it as smoothly as possible. I mean, everything I did over the years of having her in my life was for her. Loving her off the bat wasn't something I expected to feel when I first saw her, but being the grown man I am now, I easily recognized that that's what happened.

Now we had a family, and it was time to focus on bring- ing stability to that foundation. This was the next chapter in our lives, and it could only get more interesting.

"Next flight Delta 215 DC to Victoria Falls . . ."

"Mr. Charles Raymond, we welcome you and your fam- ily to Delta Airlines. Considering your special class, you all may board early," a smiling attendant with box braids pulled up into a bun waved a hand toward the gates.

Senior Giulio had people everywhere. I'd always appre- ciated it, but even more so now.

Sliding my arm around Sabrina's waist, I felt her drop her head against my chest and sigh as we headed to the gate. "Thank you for loving me and staying true to your word. I love you so much, and I'm sorry for causing us to leave like this."

Kissing her temple, I let her go so that she could walk in front of me as I held Lyric on my side. "Like I said, it wasn't your fault. You did what you had to, to protect our family, and now it's my turn."

"Da-dee! Are we going to see the giraffes?" Lyric's bubbly voice said, interrupting me.

She played with the back of my collar and looked around with curious wonder.

"Yes, baby," I said with a smile in my voice and glancing at Sabrina.

We finally made it to our first-class seats. I did a quick check, then sat down next to Sabrina, who had been silent.

"Baby," I started but was stopped by her soft lips.

Tongues entwining, I took the power of that kiss and turned it back on her with a nibble on her bottom lip.

"No more lies," she said, pulling back.

Studying her gaze, I gave her a reassuring nod. "No more lies, baby. You know it all, and no more you stepping in the line of danger."

"I can't promise that," she said with a chuckle. "I'll do whatever to protect us."

Sabrina's pops said there is no honor amongst thieves, but I knew that was a lie. If everyone around you was untrustworthy, then whose fault was that? Yours. There was always honor if your family is based on loyalty and love.

It was also there if you kept your head in the game and were smart about shit. Because all those snakes trying to harm you would be killed by you and your family once they slithered into your garden. That was what protection is, and that was what true solidarity was. I learned it the hard way, and so did my wife. However, because of us, those lessons would go on with our daughter, and I was proud to know already that she would be okay in this life if she ever truly understood our story.

The End